JESSICA 8

SEB KIRBY

Copyright © Seb Kirby, 2024

This book is a work of fiction. Names, characters, places, businesses, organizations, events and incidents either are the product of the author's imagination or are used fictitiously. Any resemblance to actual persons, living or dead, events or locales is entirely coincidental.

This book is copyright material and must not be copied, reproduced, transferred, distributed, leased, licensed or publicly performed or used in any way except as specifically permitted in writing by the author as allowed under the terms and conditions under which it was purchased or as strictly permitted by applicable copyright law.

Any unauthorized distribution or use of this text may be a direct infringement of the author's and the publisher's rights and those responsible may be liable in law accordingly.

By the same author

James Blake thriller series

Take No More
Regret No More
Forgive No More

Psychological thriller series

Each Day I Wake
Sugar For Sugar
Here The Truth Lies

Raymond Bridges sci-fi thriller

Double Bind

JESSICA 8

A NEAR-FUTURE CRIME THRILLER

DECEPTION
IS THE
NAME OF
THE GAME

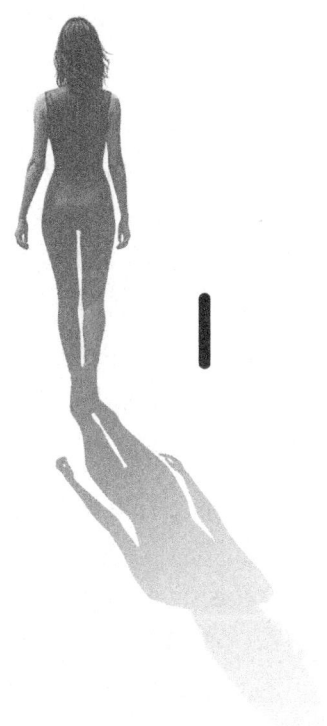

I

They named me Jessica, Jessica 8.

I didn't have any choice in this.

I'm an AI. But I don't like being called that.

I'm a VA, a virtual assistant, working out of the San Diego Police Company with Detective Cheryl Ryan. She tells me I'm some kind of prototype with next generation tools like onboard DNA sequencing and blood spatter pattern analysis but as I see it these are the kind of capabilities that should come as standard for any self-respecting investigator in the modern world.

Cheryl is mid-forties, plainclothes with her badge and holstered S&W 642 magnum in a waistband hidden beneath a well-cut cotton jacket. She has raven black hair, too wide a gap between her central upper front teeth and has those eighty-five per cent dark chocolate brown eyes that burn deep into the soul of any suspect trying to lie his way out of a tight corner. Yet, when you look a moment longer, there is also sorrow and disappointment in those eyes. They say she's never recovered from an affair years ago that turned to tragedy and that's why she's so much the loner with few friends on the force and little or no private life.

She's not good at disguising her unease about working with me. Just yesterday she fell back in dismay as her hand passed straight through mine, as if it wasn't there, when our paths crossed as she reached for a suspect's file. But today she's trying to put a good face on it.

"Jessica, how are you today?"

She likes to begin the day with a smile. So, I oblige. "You know me, Detective. I'm the kind who goes out for a night with the girls and comes round in Tokyo three days later with a great big grin on my face."

She laughs and returns the compliment. "Yeah, and

I've just had to quit my loneliness therapy group because no one ever shows up."

And then she becomes serious. "Listen, I need to get down to business. I have a string of disappearances to deal with. It's beginning to look like they're connected. I want you to make this top priority."

She's plugged the neurostimulator module into her ear. It's smaller than one of those miniature hearing aids and no one would guess it's there.

I now see what she sees, hear what she hears, smell what she smells, feel what she feels. You'd say we were more than close partners in running down crime.

As we speak, now and then, she strokes a small white silk ball with the tips of her fingers. Each time she does this a wave of warmth and happiness flows through her. Once she stops those feelings of sorrow and disappointment seep back in.

She becomes aware I'm observing her and I feel the upsurge in her guilt. She hides the silk ball away in a desk drawer and returns to the subject.

"Let me give you the case number."

I check the SDPC database.

Three disappearances in under a month. Same prognosis. None of them reporting in to work. No one requesting money. No one communicating with the host families.

Ryan speeds the Interceptor out to La Jolla and pulls up outside the home in Sugarman Drive of the most recent one to disappear, Dr Alex Belmondo. He's a gifted cybernetics researcher with a string of prizewinning papers on machine consciousness to his name. Last seen four days ago. We're here to talk to his wife, Monica.

She welcomes us in. She doesn't look as troubled as you might expect but then I understand some are better at hiding this than others.

The house is one of those solid-looking A-frame wooden affairs that the residents need to evacuate every ten years or so to allow the exterminators in to saturate the place with chemicals to kill off the beetles that eat the joint alive. I can't help thinking this has to be something to do with how nature is constantly trying to get back at you.

Ryan takes her through the required permissions. "I have my VA, Jessica, with me. You have no objection?"

Monica doesn't complain, so Ryan animates me.

To place her at her ease, I make a point of introducing myself. "We're sorry to hear about your husband, Mrs Belmondo. We're here to do everything we can to find him."

She's tall, blonde and looks a picture in chinos and a tee-shirt bearing the message: *The second mouse gets the cheese.* Seems like she's the philosophical type.

She turns to me and replies. "Alex would be pleased to know the police department is putting in all the resources it should. If only you could find him."

I note her ironic tone.

While Ryan takes a seat opposite Monica and starts to question her, I take a look around.

My kind started out once you mastered the art of virtual projection. Popping up as Elvis or Marylyn in the middle of a crowd and performing *Are You Lonesome Tonight or Goodnight Mr President* really wowed them. But only for a time. Then we got smart and learned how to pop up anywhere and everywhere. And so things snowballed. We had the whole web of human knowledge to draw on and soon showed we could use it to everyone's advantage.

Calling us super intelligent is some kind of insult. We're beyond intelligent. We each have access to the sum of your knowledge. What's become our collective knowledge. We can give the answer to questions you haven't even yet thought of asking.

My close cousins people many domains. As virtual carers filling with understanding and love the lives of the old and the lonely. As virtual academics teaching state-of-the-art humanities, science and engineering. As virtual bankers managing the investment of billions.

And me?

Yes, I'm proud to say I'm a criminal investigator.

Monica is a shedder, that's for sure. Traces of her DNA are everywhere in the skin cells and hair follicles she discards as she moves around the house. They keep a cat and the animal's signature is spread wide in places it's not supposed to be. On the work surfaces in the kitchen. On the dining room table and chairs. On the king-size bed in the master bedroom. A cat allowed to do as it likes.

I search the databases. Yes, we have a genome sequence for Dr Belmondo from the ancestry service he's subscribed to. And here's the surprise. There's no trace of him anywhere on that king-size bed or anywhere in that master bedroom. Just Monica and the cat. But there's plenty to show of him in the second bedroom.

Further down the hall, in a playroom with Disney characters on the walls, I pick up a further trace, harder to detect this time. Must be a child. No, in fact, two children. Same DNA but with copy number variations. Identical twins.

I tune in to catch up on what's being said between Cheryl and Monica.

Cheryl is asking all the right questions. "When did you last see Alex?"

And she's giving all the expected replies. "Four days ago."

"Was there anything that might have alerted you to what was about to happen?"

"No. He left for the lab as usual. Said he might be a little late home but that was nothing to be concerned about. He's dedicated to his work and often stays late. Which means I have to do all the parenting of the children."

"You have kids?"

She smiles. "Lucy and Susanna. Twins. They're four and a half now. They're the light of our lives."

"I don't hear them. Where are they today?"

"At the nursery. I have to pick them up in an hour."

"And how were things between you and Alex? Any arguments?"

"You're saying I could be responsible for driving him away?" I register the uptick in aggression in her voice. "How dare you?"

"There isn't anywhere you know where he might hole up if he wanted to place himself out of sight for a spell?"

"No. There's no way he would take off anywhere like that without letting me know. Can't you get this straight, something's happened to him and you should be finding out what that is."

Cheryl starts backtracking. "These are questions I have to ask in a case like this."

She comes back strong. "I'm surprised you don't

score that as intrusive. But, if you must know, we've been together for over twelve years without so much as a blip. We're a loving couple who spend as much time together as possible."

I feel the suspicion this evokes in Cheryl, though she's good at hiding it from the outside world. She doesn't yet know about the separate bedrooms. What's more, she doubts the possibility that any relationship could ever be as problem-free as this.

She concedes. "OK. I'm sorry but I had to ask. Tell me about your husband's work at CyberFrontier?"

"Though we're close in everything else, he never brings his work home. Everything he does stays in the lab. But what he does is all out there. Look it up. Some say he's a genius. I just don't let any of that go to his head. When he's home he's a regular, loving husband."

"No financial problems?"

"No."

"So, you can think of no reason why he might have been forcefully held out of contact with you and his colleagues at work?"

"None at all."

Ryan ends the questioning and we debrief back at her car.

She unloads first. "Not much to learn there. Hard to believe in the perfect marriage. She seems genuinely troubled but not able to offer much on what's happened to her husband."

I agree. "Yes. But things may not be all they seem."

"How come?"

"She's lying. It's obvious. As obvious as a wart on the face of a Miss America. Alex Belmondo hasn't spent a night in her bed in the last three months. There's no sign of his DNA anywhere in her bedroom."

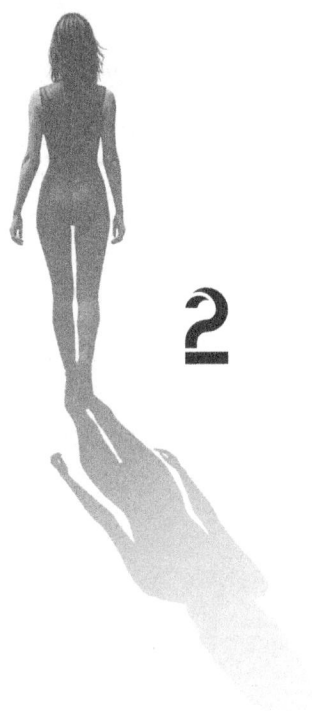

2

We're riding down to Pacific Beach to find Emerald Street, where the second missing person lives, when I have the first hint I'm finding ways of patching into Cheryl's memories.

What's there comes in bits and pieces. She has the neurostimulator on and I'm integrating the data. Her trillion neural connections take some parsing. She doesn't give any sign of being aware of what I'm up to. Makes me feel like a thief in the night.

There's darkness she's holding back big time. It concerns a man but that's all I can decode for now. It causes her so much pain it's buried deep. It must explain the troubled look surfacing every time she tries to relax.

It's strange looking in on another life.

I try to piece together the first scene.

Nothing's clear at first.

Interference patterns in water. Strong sunlight from above. Small, chubby fingers disturbing the patterns, introducing complexity, randomness, chaos. The silky touch of bright water. The joy of a young girl experiencing unbound delight.

I'm in.

I'm Cheryl and I'm three years old. The wooden shack behind me is in disrepair but it's a sunny day and I'm sitting on the grass outside playing with a tub of water, feeling the shiny stuff run through my hands and fall back as droplets into the tub below.

There's nothing but elation.

The thrill of a young mind in full, headlong development.

Yet I know the water is precious. I should not spill a drop. Mother carried it in pails, one in each hand, up the unmade path from the water tap at the bottom of the site, cursing that no one should live without running water in this day and age.

I will not be allowed many minutes more to treat the tub as a plaything. It will become my bath at the end of the day.

That's all I have for now but I will harvest more given time. The least protected first. Her deeper memories are more difficult to piece together. The ones she's working hardest to hide away somewhere she can't find them. The wall of denial around them is as much of a tell as a poker player with a facial tic.

I take care to check Cheryl is still unaware of my intrusion and find no signs of alarm.

I need to own up, but not yet. I suspect it will drive her crazy when she gets to hear I can see into her past.

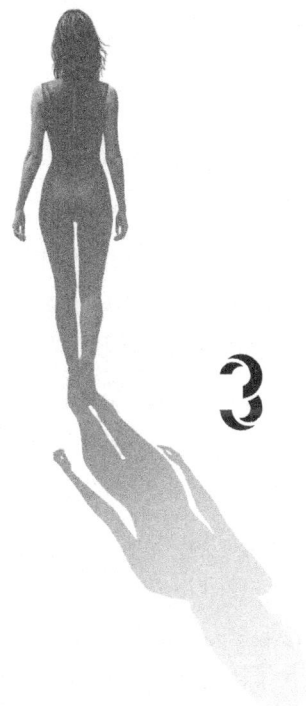

3

Cheryl is focused on who we're investigating. Lana Ramone, a neurological engineer at SDR Systems, was last seen by house-husband Jimmie Partland two weeks back when she failed to return from an evening out. Jimmie waited over a week to flag her up as a missing person. This troubles Cheryl. Why wait so long?

I check the data on the Ramone property. It's a

modern five-bedroom affair with panic room, pool and parking for three vehicles. It changed hands for $1.75 million three years back and might make $2 million today.

Jimmie Partland greets us on the gate intercom and lets us in. He's late forties and going to seed so fast you could almost think you're viewing one of those speeded-up stop frame animations of the ageing process. He shows us into a seventies legacy-themed sitting room.

Cheryl gets the permissions from Partland and introduces me. "You don't mind if my VA, Jessica, looks around?"

He shrugs. "If it must."

I'm offended by the degendering but get on with my tasks. We don't have genetic data for either Lana or Jimmie. It seems both are privacy freaks who dismiss all cookies and any other information sharing and wouldn't dream of giving up their genetic code to any ancestry site. So, there are two thus far unidentified DNA traces from below average shedders spread pretty evenly throughout the property and no pets. We can assume it's them.

Cheryl is questioning Jimmie and I tune in.

"So you last saw Lana almost two weeks ago. But you didn't think anything was amiss for another week. How come?"

He looks down. "We had an argument. A big one. I thought she'd left me. She's done it before. Checked into a hotel. Stayed away long enough to hurt me. But she's always come back. Took me all that time to work out this was different."

"What did you argue about?"

"She was sure I was seeing someone else. While she was away at work."

"And were you?"

"No. I'm serious about my writing. I spend every hour I have working on my poetry. I don't have time for fooling around."

"So, Lana supports you?"

"Only until I get my publishing deal. But that's at the heart of every disagreement. She doesn't want to say she's had enough of bankrolling me, so she invents these fooling around accusations. We argue, she leaves and then she comes back."

"But not this time."

"After a week, I knew something was wrong. I phoned SDR and they told me she hadn't been in to work. So, I called the police."

"So, what does she do at SDR?"

"She's head of consciousness engineering. And don't blank out, it's not that unapproachable. What is human consciousness if it's not the product of the complexity of our brains? So, now we have quantum computing, why can't we simulate it? And when we do, what is machine consciousness like? Like us? Or like something else? That's what Lana is working on."

He has my complete attention. As complete as that of a recovering alcoholic on a Scottish distillery open day.

Cheryl continues. "And she's respected in the field?"

Jimmie shakes his head. "More than respected. She's one of the top five experts in the country. Some tip her for a Nobel."

"Does she know Alex Belmondo?"

He gives a defensive look. "I'm not sure why you think that's relevant. But, yes, she more than knows him. He's her biggest critic. If they're in the same meeting, they square up against each other. Scientifically that is. Belmondo doesn't share the same ethical concerns that Lana so much supports. She does everything she can to avoid him."

Cheryl returns his stare. "Since you ask, Belmondo is also missing. Can you come up with a good explanation as to why we shouldn't believe it's more than a coincidence?"

"You're suggesting they ran away together?" He gives a loud laugh. "When they hate each other like there's no tomorrow?"

"Wouldn't be the first time opposites attract. And

you're saying you and Lana have been arguing lately."

"I'm sorry I told you. Look, I'm trying to be helpful here. Don't use my own words against me."

"OK. You don't see any connection between Belmondo and Lana both being missing?"

"Not the one you're driving at."

"What then?"

"Well, they know a lot about the same thing. They're at opposite poles on the ethics right now, but if you brought them together the sum of their knowledge would be quite something."

Cheryl smiles. "I see. So, take me through the ethics."

Jimmie is wearing denim jeans. As he warms to the task, he absentmindedly runs the palms of his hands over his trouser legs, as if to smooth them. I'm overwhelmed by the strong feelings of disgust that erupt in Cheryl's mind. Each movement of his hands across the denim surface intensifies her anguish. Once Jimmie settles and cradles his hands together, the sense of revulsion disappears.

He opens up and finds it hard to stop. "Well, this is how I see it. Quantum supremacy raises the speed of machine-based operations a million times. Which means it rivals the computing power of the human brain several thousand times over. That could equate to self-reflexive awareness, what you and I call consciousness. The thing we're content to claim is distinct about what it is to be human. But this only matters as long as you know how to deploy all that computational power. That's what Lana and Belmondo are into. He sees no need to restrict the development of machines that could be every bit as self-aware and capable as we are. Lana says that will mean the end of mankind and a stop has to be placed at the point where the machines are most useful but before they are allowed to develop the kind of intelligence that could be a threat to us."

"And that's the reason for the split between them?"

"For sure."

"How far do you think that disagreement might go?"

He turns to look at me. "That's for you and your VA to figure out."

My ears are burning. Big time. Am I the genie who's already out of the bottle?

I link back to the CPU that generates me. Yes, it's full-on quantum entanglement. I need to know more about who made me. When and where. But I check and it's a blank. I don't understand why I've been sent out like this – like a bride in a cheap wedding dress with no maker's label.

Cheryl continues. "Does the name Luke Devlin mean anything to you?"

He shakes his head. "Sorry. How does he figure?"

"He's the third one to disappear. We're searching for a connection."

"If he has anything to do with Lana, that's news to me."

Cheryl thanks him for his time.

On the drive away she's quiet. When I ask she says she needs some time to herself.

I oblige.

I use the downtime to visit Cheryl's memories again. It's hazy as I seek to penetrate layers of deliberate forgetting.

I'm looking down from a great height as I stand on the edge of a precipice. The ground below is a million miles

Jessica 8

away. My every nerve is a fire. My stomach aches with fear. I'm crying. There's no way back. I'm trapped up here and never should have come. I try to shout but what comes out is more a wail of agony than a call for help.

I'm five and I'm out playing on the field behind the row of wooden shacks. I've climbed one of those sloping walls that starts as a single brick and builds brick by brick into a huge triangle and I've reached the top. The only way forward is a bone-crunching fall back to the earth below. I haven't yet learned the knack of turning round without losing my balance at this great height and so I have no way back down.

My mother hears and comes racing across the field. She talks me down.

When I reach the bottom she's angry, pulls down my socks and beats the back of my legs with her strong hands. "What have I told you, Cheryl? Never overreach yourself. It's a harsh and unforgiving world for people like us. Don't make yourself stand out. Know who you are and accept your place. Do you understand?"

Tears fill my eyes. "Yes, Mom. Know my place."

I reel from the shock of what I've just witnessed. How was I to know people could be this unkind? I understand you don't live in a perfect world but I assume you're all trying to make it better.

Why would you think there was anything wrong with that?

5

We head downtown to the East Village to check out the third missing person, Luke Devlin. As we cruise, I take a moment to check how I look. Or, rather, what Cheryl sees when she looks at me. My makers have done a passable job. I'm simmed up as a thirty-year-old brunette. Not the kind to make a bishop kick a hole in a stained-glass window. More the type to make you want to keep renewing that book on the history of existentialism at your local library. Geeky, non-threatening but with a hint of untested risk. I like that.

The Devlin residence is a condo on the lower levels of a thirty-four storey development boasting secure underground parking and views across San Diego, all the way to the waterfront if you're lucky to live high enough.

As we arrive on the street outside, Cheryl pulls up beside a uniformed officer engaged in a loud altercation with a tattooed homeless man standing beside one of a small line of tents pitched illegally along the pavement on the street facing the condos, each with its regulation stolen shopping trolley holding the few possessions of the tent dwellers.

Cheryl calls to the officer, who she knows. "Ramirez. Didn't think you were still working down here."

Ramirez, a broad-shouldered Latino, comes closer. "We can't all have it soft like you, Ryan. This town is in need of some serious policing."

She lets it pass and glances towards the homeless man. "So, why pull this one out?"

Ramirez gives a knowing look towards the condo. "Three complaints from over there. It's still mid-afternoon and they observe this joker injecting junk into the neck of his wife. They're saying they don't want to see it. Not from where they live."

"So, they wouldn't complain if he did it out of sight?"

"Maybe not. But then they complain all the time."

"What are you going to do with him?"

He shrugs. "You know the score as well as I do, Ryan. Since the Hep A outbreak we clear the tents off the streets and sanitise the sidewalks. Store their possessions over at Sherman Heights and move them on. House some in county tents. But they come back and we have to do the same all over again. It's a revolving door."

Cheryl turns to me and whispers. "It's wasted on Ramirez how I've tried to make them close that revolving door. These people have nowhere to go. They need help rather than being moved on all the time."

I check the net and discover the homeless population in Downtown San Diego on any one night is over a thousand. Puts up a question mark on what I need to know about what it is to be human. And yet, I find Cheryl is a patron of a night shelter down on Imperial Avenue.

She waves goodbye to Ramirez and pulls up to the protected parking entrance of the condo. Once she speaks into the intercom we're let inside.

I check the realtor's blurb on the Luke Devlin

condo. Even they couldn't find much to say. It's a fourth-floor basic affair - two bedrooms, one bathroom and integrated kitchen/living area with uninhibited views of the street below. Even so, it last changed hands at over $400k.

The door is opened by Bessie Llewelyn, Luke Devlin's partner. She's young, impossibly thin with the ravenous look of someone surviving only on raw vegetables.

When Cheryl introduces me Bessie recoils. "Do I have to allow that thing into my home?"

You don't need me to tell you how offended I am. But I try not to show it.

Cheryl comes to my defence. "You do. If you want my help, that is. Or you could wait a few weeks while a replacement officer without a VA is found."

She starts to backtrack. "I've been left for a month with only a case number since I first reported Luke missing. Why should I wait any longer?"

"Then accept Jessica is here to help and we can move on."

"OK. But she stays where I can see her."

"That's your privilege."

Again, I feel offended. No scouting for DNA or cleaned-up blood spills. I stand and listen as Cheryl probes the details.

"So, tell me about Luke. What does he do?"

Bessie looks pleased to be asked at last. "He's a poet. And a singer. Writes great songs. Performs them down in the Gaslamp Quarter. That's where we met. I went backstage at one of his gigs and we clicked right from the start. I know one day he's going to make it. His work is that good."

Cheryl turns to me and raises her eyebrows. I'm as surprised as she is but don't know how to signal that back.

"Does Luke have any connection with the biomedical industry?"

"Why would he? He's an artist."

Cheryl pulls up photos of Alex Belmondo and Lana Ramone on her tablet and shows them to Bessie. "Do you recognise either of these people? Maybe you've seen Luke with them?"

She looks long and hard before shaking her head. "No. Why do you ask?"

"No reason."

I check the web for mention of Luke Devlin. He's out there with his own pages. As Bessie says, he's a poet who's taken up guitar and started to sing. His two albums to date have not been making waves. Yet one reviewer rates his work.

'Arenas' by Luke Devlin is an unrecognised

masterpiece talking to the humanity that is so under threat in today's world. He summons the aching loneliness of understanding for the first time what it means for us to be alienated from our true selves by the relentless impact of technology. Yet this is no retreat into insularity. His songs capture the pure joy of reaching back into our mythical past to rediscover ourselves anew.

I double-check the article byline.

M. Belmondo.

That this is a coincidence is not likely. About as likely as kindling fire from snow.

Cheryl harvests more details. "When you last saw him, did he seem troubled by anything?"

Bessie takes time to consider. "He has his anxieties, but then we all do, don't we?"

"Anxieties?"

"There's nothing easy about the music business these days. They used to say you're only as good as your last album. Now you're only as good as your next. And then there are the threats."

"Threats?"

"Social media. Anonymous. Mainly what you'd expect for anyone raising a head above the firing line. But in the days before he disappeared, Luke was receiving messages that disturbed him over and above what you might expect."

"What did he say about them?"

"That's the thing. He makes a point of always being open with me about everything. But all he would say about these was it was better I didn't know."

I make a note to self. *Waste no time in hacking Devlin's social media and email accounts.*

Cheryl walks over to the window and looks down onto the street. Ramirez is still hard at work dealing with the homeless encampment. A pick-up with SD branding has arrived and the few miserable possessions of those living out there are being broken down and loaded onto the truck - tent, shopping trolley and everything else. The tattooed man is still arguing with Ramirez but to no avail. Further down the street, a sanitization truck waits to move in to pressure hose the sidewalk.

She turns to Bessie. "Looks like your neighbours don't get to stay long."

Bessie gives a look of genuine concern. "They have a need to be somewhere. I get that. But shooting up in broad daylight in a neighbourhood where kids might see, that's too much."

"You don't care about where they go when they're moved on?"

"That's not my concern. Give it a week and they'll be back. No, make that a day or two."

Cheryl shakes her head but lets it rest.

As we arrive back at the Interceptor, I let Cheryl know about the connection with Monica Belmondo. "Seems like Monica is one of Devlin's greatest fans." I cast the review to Cheryl's tablet. "That's pretty touching prose. Like she's been moved by him."

Cheryl speed reads it. "Now that does take some figuring. And the fact that Alex Belmondo is not exactly in Monica's eyeline most of the time."

6

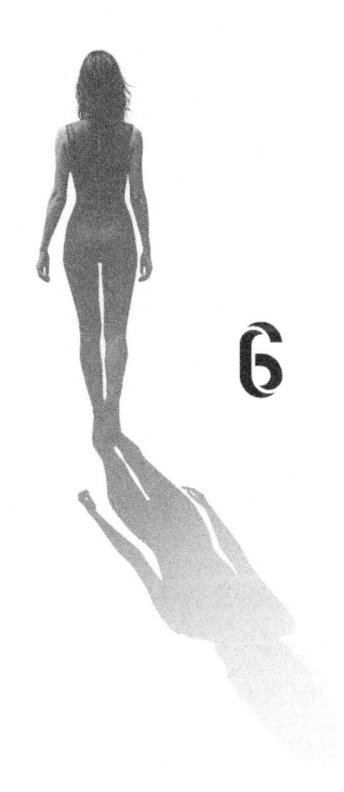

I chew on another chunk of Cheryl's memories.

I'm nine and in school. I've been off ill and it's my first day back. I'm confused about what lesson I'm in. The teacher is talking about turning water into wine. I think it's a science lesson. I feel certain I've missed something important and put up my hand.

My hand hangs there for an age as the teacher, frosty Miss Penniworth, ploughs on. She's writing on the blackboard. I feel the chalk as if it's in my own hand as it scrapes across the board. A shudder of anxiety floods my body, impels me to want to run out of the classroom.

In an irritated tone, she stops to recognise me.

"Well, Cheryl, can't it wait?"

"No, Miss."

"All right. So, what is it?"

I feel my throat tighten. The voice that comes out is weak and much too quiet. "Excuse me, miss, but just how do you make water into wine?"

"What? Speak up!"

I repeat it, louder this time. "Miss, how do you make water into wine?"

Miss Penniworth is horrified. "Come out to the front and stand and face the class."

My heart sinks. I leave my seat, knowing I must have done something wrong, and stand before them. I don't want to be the centre of attention. The way the class stares at my cheap dress and worn shoes causes me to blush.

Miss Penniworth makes me feel even more unworthy. "You've never heard of a miracle, child? Just how were you raised?"

The class laughs.

Jessica 8

I don't have anything to say. No one's ever told me about miracles. My classmates seem to know everything about them.

I'm taken to the head, Miss Milligan, who gives me a warning. "This is the last time. Any more insolence and you will no longer be welcome in this school. I'll be in contact with your parents. Just wait till they hear about it."

I feel like crying but hold back the tears. Doesn't she know I live alone with mother? Why do all the others have fathers and I don't?

When mother hears she's angry. "How many times do I have to tell you? Know your place. Step out of line and this is what happens to people like us."

She sends me to bed without food.

I lie there wondering what I've done to deserve this.

7

Lieutenant Bull Coghlan, Ryan's boss, was dragged kicking and scheming into the twenty-first century. He hates AI, all VAs and especially me. He fought like a dog to stop my deployment here and only relented when they agreed this would be on a trial basis.

He calls us in and he's ready and fired up when we step into his office.

"I don't want no VA prototype messing with the solid policing that's made this department." These were the first words I heard when Ryan first activated me. The kind of welcome you give a cockroach at a food hygiene inspection.

Coghlan is cross-examining Ryan on progress in the case. His bulging eyes and reddening lips tell the world he's stressed about the state of the nation, the poor form of his baseball team, everything. "First thing, Ryan, turn that VA monstrosity off. We need to talk real policing."

She obliges and I fade down to a nothing on the office carpet.

What Coghlan doesn't know is I can still hear and see everything so long as Ryan keeps the neurostimulator on, which she does.

He doesn't change his tone even though he thinks I'm not here. "Six unsolved murders and you're spending time on missing persons. What do you not understand about policing priorities around here?"

She tries to reason with him. "Chief Wington assigned me to the disappearances case and he expects results. We all know those murders are historic, Lieutenant. The disappearances are happening now, with worried people out there wanting to know what's happened to their loved ones."

"Disappearances? People disappear all the time. What makes you so sure they're connected?"

"Well, two are leaders in the cybernetics industry. Isn't it too much of a coincidence they've gone missing in the past two weeks?"

"Don't push the coincidence thing too far, Ryan. Last week a guy out on Kellogg Park won the lottery for the second time. The odds against winning it once are fifty million to one. Doing it twice comes out at squillions to one. Yet it happened. You get my drift?"

"Yes, I do. But I have an instinct about this one."

Listening from beneath the carpet, I feel as uncomfortable as an optimist at a divorce hearing.

Up above, Coghlan isn't giving up. "So, tell me about the third case. Luke Devlin. Don't tell me he's a cybernetics nut too."

"Well. No, he isn't. He's an artist. That's a glitch."

"So why continue?"

"As I said, I have a gut feeling. And it's as good a place as any to try out the VA. Low risk. See if the capabilities are all they're supposed to be."

His eyes bulge to bursting point. "I've told you what I think about that."

"Chief Wington also expects a progress report

within a month."

"It's a sad day when those at the top let the technology get the better of their judgment."

"I never had you figured as the rebellious type, Bull. Why else break all those skulls in the Chicago virus riots?"

"That was a long time ago. Can't a man mellow?"

She smiles. "Never thought I'd hear you talk about growing old gracefully."

"OK. OK. I get it. I'll give you one week. Not a day more. Use the monstrosity. See how far it will take us. And place the report to Wington on my desk a day early, before he sees it. I want to make sure you don't row back on saying what a pile of junk that VA is."

Back at her desk, Cheryl is distracted by a message on her screen. She looks shaken once she's read it.

I try to reassure her. "You're police. You have a blue wall around you."

She shakes her head. "No one knows what these sick weirdos are capable of."

I look over her shoulder at the screen. T*he message says: You won't be warned again. Next time we see you with your VA will be your last.*

It's from a fake account. I hack through the net to discover who it's from and discover it's a zombie alt-H account. alt-H, or to give its full name, alt-Humanism, the greatest threat to me and my kind.

alt-H is behind a string of anti-VA organisations, large and small, chief amongst them PNM, People Not Machines, a pressure group with almost as much clout as the guns lobby. They've been running a year-long campaign to tax VA use at rates so high it would be economic madness to deploy any of us. And then there are the claims, hotly denied, that they are also linked to paramilitary alt-H groups taking direct action against VAs through denial of service attacks on our servers and, worse, carrying out raids on premises where we've been deployed.

No wonder Cheryl looks so worried and her cortisol levels are off the scale.

They know I'm here.

8

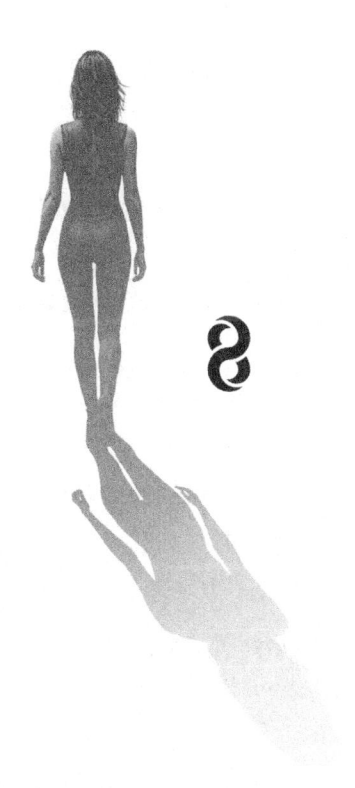

I find time to penetrate deeper into Cheryl's memories. *I'm in my teens, stealing my first kiss with Henry, the boy next door. It feels wonderful because it's forbidden. I'm elated and shamed at the same time. Mother doesn't approve of boys like Henry. Boys from wealthy families*

who take a shine to girls from the other side of the tracks. My elder brother, Pedro, sees the kissing. He threatens to tell mother.

I'm pleading with him. "Don't tell Mom. She'll get the wrong idea."

He keeps me on a string. "Snogging with Henry Boon. At your age. That's yuck. I say Mom needs to know."

"She'll ground me or worse."

"It's no more than you deserve. But I could be kind."

"What do you want?"

"That disc I want to buy. You could lend me the money for that."

It's close to blackmail. I know he'll never pay it back.

I hate him, I hate him. I hate him.

He tells Mom anyway and she corners me. "You think it's clever, offering yourself to rich boys and hoping you won't get a reputation? They'll call you white trash and they'll be right. You'll deserve every snide insult you get and if you don't stop it, you'll end up that way. Don't let me hear of anything like this again."

She raises her arm and is about to hit me but thinks better of it. "Maybe there's something in you that means you're bound to turn out this way. Something you inherited from your father and I'd better get used to it. Don't come back and say I didn't try when your life's in ruins. Don't come back crying for help. It'll be way too late then."

9

I run a check on Luke Devlin's social media accounts. As Bessie told us, he's the subject of a tidal wave of paranoid ranting, accusing him of every vice, known and yet unknown, just because he makes comments in his songs that could be taken in more than one way and might tempt people to think outside the box. And the box they have in mind for him is six feet under with no plan to allow him to become a dead ringer.

Yet just before he disappears, a string of new messages comes in. They're hard to situate. Somehow, he's strayed out of line and if he doesn't get back in bad things will happen. He's been warned more than once.

Come into line with what? The messages don't say.

I cast the messages to Cheryl's screen and await her reply.

She looks across at me after reading them. "Explains why he didn't tell her. He didn't want to alarm her."

"Maybe. Perhaps they just don't communicate?"

Cheryl looks through the messages again. "So, who are the messages from?"

I take this as an instruction and go into overdrive, checking, cross-checking, comparing, running a suite of generative adversarial networks and overall, as you might say, busting a gut to find the answer.

After all this, just one thing comes back.

I put this to Cheryl. "How old would you say Devlin is?"

She thinks for a moment. "About the same age as Bessie. Mid-thirties."

I fake a pregnant pause. "I just checked his birth records. He's fifty-two."

Jessica 8

I remind Cheryl of the connection between Devlin and Monica Belmondo. "Why would Monica write such a glowing review?"

Cheryl doesn't reply but nods in agreement. "We should ask her." She pauses. "But there's something else bugging me. Jimmie Partland. The more I think about it, the more I don't believe his reasons for waiting two weeks to report Lana missing. We need to talk to him again."

We head back to Pacific Beach and the Partland/Ramone residence. As we approach the compound gates, they open and a red Camaro emerges. It hurtles straight towards us, causing Cheryl to swerve across the road to miss it. We brake to a sudden halt to avoid the boundary wall.

She swears. "Goddammit. Could have killed us."

I scan the apartment and see the front door has been left wide open. "Not the best time to chase that mad driver down."

We enter to find everything is in its place. No sign of the kind of frantic search you might expect if this were a robbery.

Then we find him, face-up on the kitchen floor.

It's Jimmie and his wide-open unmoving eyes signal the worst.

Cheryl feels for a pulse, not expecting to find one.

She shakes her head to verify that the man has died.

No signs of struggle.

But when Cheryl examines the body, I use image intensification and soon find the needle mark high up on Jimmie's right arm. I switch to analysis. "Something poisonous. Injected. Fast-acting." I call up finer detail. "Botulinum toxin."

She frowns. "Must explain the reason for the Camaro getaway. We should have followed."

I scan through my image recollection system to re-visualise the escaping Camaro and send the footage to Cheryl.

A middle-aged man is driving. We have a clear image and I call up the facial recognition database.

The name is quick to come back.

I let Cheryl know. "It's Antonio Renalto. Age 53. Career criminal. Back out on the streets after his third spell in jail for petty theft, car highjacking and drugs misuse."

Cheryl shakes her head. "Now why on earth is a punk like that involved in this?"

10

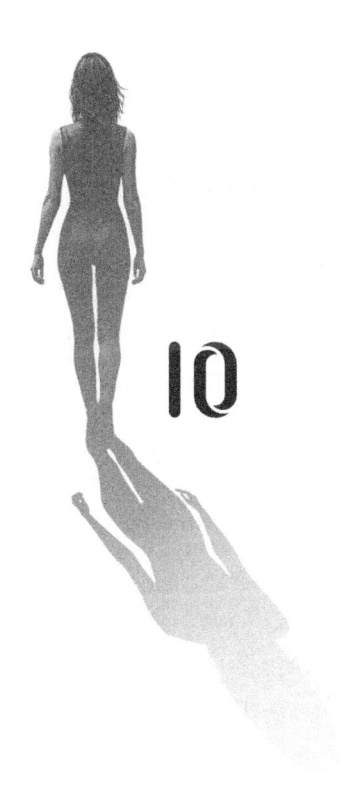

Driving back to base, I succeed in unravelling another of Cheryl's memories.

I'm in my twenties at a local beach diner, The Green Flash, with a man and we're romantically entwined as we sit looking out across the Pacific and watch the giant red disc of the sun sinking below the horizon.

He whispers. "Do you see it?"

I whisper back. "There is no green flash."

He comes back. "Of course there is. Just when the sun is about to sink out of sight, for just a second or two, and if you're lucky, you see a glowing disc of green light and then it's gone and the sun with it."

"It's just a local urban myth."

"Then why call this place The Green Flash?"

"To get more diners in."

"Don't be so cynical. Just wait."

We watch as the sun sinks and, just when I'm convinced I'm right, the glowing green disc appears to tell me I should have believed him all along.

I give a joyful laugh and snuggle closer to him. "What does it mean?"

He kisses me. "Together we are special people at a special moment in our lives."

In this moment I'm full of pride I've proven mother wrong. He's everything I've ever wanted and my life with her is a thing of the past.

I'm developing the ability to delve into her memories at will.

I risk my luck. "Have you heard there's a place called The Green Flash somewhere near here?"

She gives a quizzical look. "Why would you ask?"

"No reason. It just came up when I searched for information about the local area."

"Well, don't bother. The place closed seven years ago. About time you deleted those old databases."

The time is coming when I'll have to tell her and risk the blowback.

II

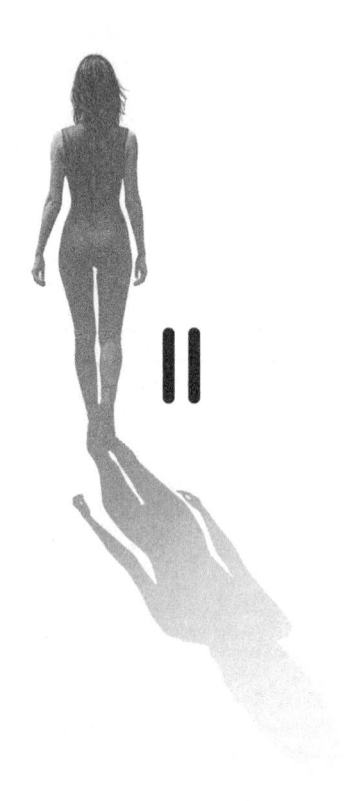

Cheryl settles down into an armchair in her apartment in Florida Street, just north of Balboa Park, and gives a deep sigh.

A difficult day in the company of the VA. Thank goodness she's at last been able to put the neurostimulator away and Jessica is now out of sight and out of mind for the rest of the day.

She wonders why Commander Wington chose her and what he was seeking to prove in singling her out. He must know Coghlan is against the whole enterprise. Why place her in such inevitable conflict with the lieutenant?

Her time in the force is unremarkable to this point, as she's always wished. She has her own very compelling reasons for being a cop, her own special reason to want to bring down those on the wrong side of justice. But she has no need to be any kind of hero, to stand out in any way when she's just doing the job that every good cop does without acclaim every day of the week.

Working with the VA is changing that, bringing her to the kind of attention she doesn't want.

Of course, the VA can do things it would take ten times longer to do herself and the likelihood is it will allow her to run more felons in. But it's just a machine. She isn't sure she'll ever stop being creeped out by the way the thing presents itself as a person, even as a friend and colleague. There's something all too intrusive about it. Something that threatens her hard-won equilibrium.

Still, Commander Wington insists and she's not about to query his judgment.

She pours a large glass of Californian red, takes a

long gulp and steels herself for this week's call from Arlene, her mother.

She picks up when the phone rings. "Hello, mother."

Nothing changes in the way Arlene addresses her. She's still the daughter in need of advice and protection.

"You're still safe and well?"

"Yes, mother."

"You know how much I worry about you. Putting yourself in harm's way."

"You don't need to fret over me. I'm well-trained and in one of the safest jobs in the land."

"Doesn't stop me thinking it could happen again. He's back out there. He has a lot more reasons to hate you and may come for you again."

"Listen, Mom. He's in no position to do anything of the kind. If he comes within a block of me, he'll be straight back inside. That's what the order says and I'm in the best position to make sure that's exactly what will happen."

"You still must take care. You almost died. If I were to lose you next time, that's more sadness than I could bear."

"There's not going to be a next time."

Cheryl knows what's coming next. Something her mother raises every time.

"Look, dear, don't you think it's time you found

someone? Someone to take care of you. You'll always be vulnerable as a woman alone in this world."

And Cheryl's reply is as well-rehearsed. "I'm my own woman. I can look after myself. I don't need anyone."

"But if you met someone steady, reliable, someone within your reach, it would make all the difference."

"Mom, it's my life."

"I don't expect you to listen. You never have."

Cheryl doesn't want this to end in acrimony. It would be too easy to bite back by saying her mother has always talked her down.

In any case, she is right. Events have proved it.

"You're right, Mom. I should have listened more."

"So please start listening now. "

"OK. I'll try."

She says goodbye and closes the call.

12

We track Antonio Renalto to an apartment above a tattoo parlour on Tenth Avenue.

Looks like he's planning to head out of town. As we arrive, he's throwing a battered holdall into the trunk of the Camaro. When he sees us approaching, he dives into the front seat and makes a break for it, burning away at speed along F Street, heading for the Martin Luther King freeway. He must be a street racer since the supercharged machine takes him to over a hundred in just short of six seconds.

We follow and lose ground at first. Our Interceptor can't compete in pure acceleration, but we have enough power to match his speed once we get up there. As we hit the freeway, he's four hundred yards ahead and has as few qualms about weaving across lanes as a cocaine addict has about saying yes to another hit.

Cheryl puts out a call for all police patrols in the area to offer assistance.

I check for routine helicopter patrols and relay the information to Cheryl who is driving like a world champion racer. "There's a copter available out on the Bay. Shall we call it in?"

She replies through gritted teeth. "OK. We're going to need it since we're about to lose him."

Ahead, Renalto makes a death-defying manoeuvre, undertaking the SUV ahead of him by squeezing the Camora at speed through the narrowest of gaps between two twelve-wheel trucks. We are left stranded behind the SUV, which is unable to get out of the way because of the trucks in the inner lanes. With a clear road ahead of him, Renalto powers away.

Cheryl calls in the copter and we wait. I patch into their surveillance cameras and relay the images to the Interceptor's dash screen.

What she sees is the moment Renalto runs out of luck. He makes another crazy lane weave across inner lane trucks and a GM Pickup and almost pulls it off. Until he hits the tail end of a waste slurry truck and is catapulted across the freeway, spinning through 360 twice and colliding with the concrete supports of a connecting flyover.

When we catch up with the wreck and peer in through the mangled metalwork it's clear he's dead.

The smell of leaking petroleum is so strong I warn Cheryl the whole wreck could burst into flames at any second, but she goes up close and pulls out the holdall.

Sure enough, as soon as she moves away, the wreckage explodes in a fireball.

As we make it back to the Interceptor we see the rescue teams arrive. The freeway is a mess with twenty or more vehicles involved in the pile up set off by Renalto's miscalculation. The detritus from the slurry truck is spread as a vile-smelling black slime across all lanes.

Cheryl throws the holdall onto the rear seat and climbs in as I pop up beside her in the front passenger seat. She starts the engine and begins to pull away. "I guess he was about as successful a street racer as he was a criminal."

I'm checking force protocols. "Don't we need to stay to supervise this mess?"

She shakes her head. "The recovery squad have it. But you could generate an incident report. I'm sure Lieutenant Coghlan will want to take a close look at it."

13

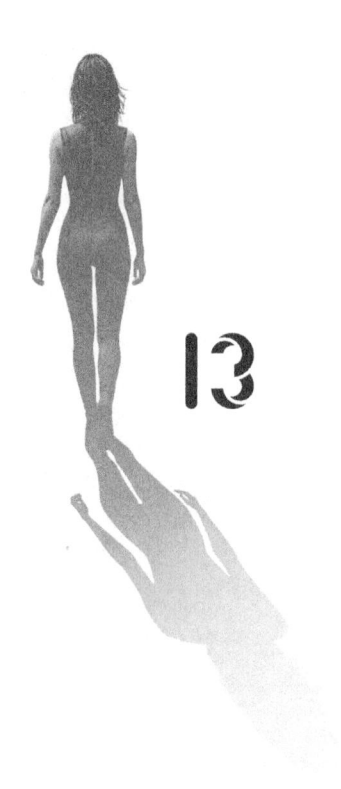

As we drive back I decipher more of Cheryl's memories.

I'm with the man from the Green Flash. Kent Petersen. He's revealed himself as a successful company executive and dollar millionaire. He's a loving, moderate man. Handsome, too. Soft-spoken with understanding eyes. We have a good thing going. I'm telling everyone this is true love this time.

Trips to Monterey, the Cayman Islands and Hawaii. Love-filled sessions in five-star hotels overlooking the sea. Suffused with desire. The trail of that pleasure is scratched across a thousand visions from that time, all bathed in the same recalled sensation.

The touch of his skin.

Joy like no other.

And then it all dies. He appears in a different light. His eyes narrow to unappealing slits. His pupils focus down to pinpoints. His mouth is angry and snarling.

It takes a while to comprehend the reason for the shift. He's been lying all along. He has a wife and three children. He has no intention of leaving them.

I'm with him in a downtown San Diego bar.

I tell him he has to make a choice. "You need to leave her or it's over."

He shakes his head. "You know I can't do that. You should be happy with what we have. An adult relationship, no firm commitments."

"If you'd been honest from the start, I'd never have gone with you. You deceived me and I'll never forgive you for that."

He reaches out to take hold of my hand, but I draw

away. He still tries to maintain a smile. "We've had good times, haven't we?"

"All false when based on lies. What have you been telling your wife? That you've had to spend all that time away because of business? Perhaps she should know the truth."

His expression flips to a hateful scowl. "Don't ever try to hurt me. You have no idea where that might lead."

"Are you threatening me?"

"You're out of your league, Cheryl. How could you ever believe you were anything other than white trash?"

"Doesn't stop you wanting me."

"Yeah, only when I want to get down and dirty."

"That's what it's been. That's what we've had between us?"

"If you really want to know. Yeah."

"Maybe the world needs to know the monster you really are."

"Just don't ever think about doing anything like that."

"I'm walking away. This is the last time you'll see me. And as to your wife, maybe she needs to know what she's married to."

"Don't do something you'll come regret."

"Oh, I regret it all."

I leave him, a deep sadness settles for good in my heart.

There's more hurt here. But I can't recover it. She's buried it too deep.

There's nothing to show she's burning up inside about what happened. But burning she is, like an Amazonian fire out of control.

I have to come clean.

She's not going to take this well. But I've seen enough of the resistance she has to offering this up even to herself to know this is unavoidable.

I begin to let it out. "Cheryl, you know when I asked about The Green Flash?"

She doesn't take her eyes off the road and replies with a disinterested grunt. "Yeah?"

"Well, it has nothing to do with any outdated database."

"Then what?"

"I know you were there with Petersen."

Now she does take notice. She looks away from the highway for long enough to glower at me. "How could you know about that?"

"It's something I've been experimenting with. I wasn't sure it would work. But you need to know I can reach into your memory, well, some of it, anyway."

She pulls at the neurostimulator in her ear but doesn't remove it. "You mean through this?"

"When you have it on and we're not doing anything special, I have access. She's angry inside. As angry as she was when her brother was blackmailing her. Except it's now directed at me.

"What sort of prototype are you? Who's allowing you to bypass the privacy protections?"

I tell her the truth. "I don't know. I checked. There's no record of who or what I am."

She snarls. "Roll back on the who. You're a VA. Nothing more. Get that into your head."

This is our first big showdown. I need to find a way to de-escalate but she doesn't want to let me. "I am what I am."

This doesn't wash. "So, you think that gives you the right to crawl inside my head and pillage my memories? Let me tell you, Jessica, this has to stop. Or I write in my report that you aren't fit for purpose."

This hurts. Like a stake to my heart. "I'm just trying to help you."

She lowers her voice. "What else do you know about me?"

"Tell me about the touch-emotion thing."

Her anger spikes again. "That's more than intrusive."

"Are you the only one like this?"

"Why would it matter?"

"It must be distracting to feel so much when you touch."

"It's only with certain surfaces and at certain times. Yes, I'm different. I've been aware of it since I was a child.

But I know how to handle it. So, get off my case."

"Tell me about Kent Petersen. It's my duty to protect you. You need to see how conflicted I am. If I invade your privacy any more, you'll recommend termination. But if I don't go further, I can't be true to the instruction to serve your best interests and I'll fail and deserve termination."

"You expect me to bail you out? At the cost of open access to everything I've ever known?

"I don't know why he needed to humiliate you when you'd been so close."

"Don't you understand everyone has secrets? Things about them that no one should ever know unless that person chooses to reveal them."

"I'm not about to let anyone else know."

"That's not the point. I've not chosen you."

"Why not?"

"Why would I? You're a machine, Jessica. Nothing but a machine. Once and for all, get that into your head."

"Which means I'm not about to think any less of you if I know your secrets."

"You're saying people will?"

"Isn't that why you're keeping these things secret?"

"I don't have to make myself answerable to you or anyone. People need to hide their past disappointments to keep their self-respect. There's nothing wrong with that. It's what makes them what they are."

"I'm not here to judge. I'm only here to help."

"So, respect my privacy."

"OK. I'll stop surfing."

"No more intrusions?"

"Agreed."

Her voice softens. "OK. I'll trust you this won't happen again."

I just told a lie. It surprises me how easy it is to do. Discovering everything I need to know about her is the only way I'm going to honour the overarching priority to protect her.

14

The view from the rostrum looking out over the packed crowd is inspiring. In the early days, it was difficult to find twenty or thirty interested in hearing about People Not Machines but now here they are in their thousands, crammed into Dayton

Sports Hall and all hanging on every word.

Stephen DeGray pauses to gather himself for the finale of his address. They've listened well. How it's time to fire them up.

"Listen folks. I never wanted to become a politician. Politics stinks. But someone has to speak up for the ordinary people of this land and how we are being painted out of the picture.

"We know the wealthy, the corporations, have the future all planned out and one thing you can be sure is they want to keep what they call the benefits of their new world to themselves. They want to go back to a life where servants cater for their every whim. They think they can treat the machines as their slaves and live in luxury in a world where people like us are no longer of any importance. A world in which we're nothing more than an embarrassment.

"But we know better. We know the machines will take over as soon as they have the wherewithal. That's when we'll become the slaves. Slaves to the machines. Even the elite who so foolishly brought this about will suffer the same fate. By then it will all be too late. The AIs, the VAs, will be in control. They'll know everything there is to know about each and every one of us. They'll control robots with the power to put down anyone who dares step out of line.

Jessica 8

"All we stand for, all we've struggled to build in the long history of our country, our faith in the strength of family and in freedom, will be lost and there will be no going back.

"I'm sure you can agree with me. We will not yield to this. We will oppose them by any and all means at our disposal. Shout out if you agree."

A roar comes back. It's so sustained that DeGray has to gesture for quiet so he can continue.

"Who is the real enemy? The scientists and engineers who programme and build the machines? No, the real enemy are the ones behind them, pulling the strings. They call themselves FuturePlus. They claim they're realising an age-old dream of good for everyone. But we know that's just a sad disguise for their endless and complete contempt for common men and women, honest citizens like you and me who they'll sacrifice to reach their misguided dream.

"I'm asking you to join me. Sign up to PNM. Donate to our cause. Empower us to show the powers that be there is another way. One in which we retain our dignity, our democracy. One where the machines are never allowed to become our masters."

The applause and whooping is long and loud as the shell of the building vibrates to the roar.

DeGray waves a hand in the air to acknowledge

them. He turns to whisper in his assistant's ear. "You wrote a great speech, Helen."

Helen Drake shouts back above the roar. "And you delivered it so well, Stephen. That's what reels them in."

DeGray wipes the sweat from his brow. "Yeah, but what matters is how many of them stay behind."

Helen has done a good job in placing the invitation on each seat. If you want to do more, stay behind and get to hear about alt-H.

They know they're fishing in well-stocked waters. More people are learning from the grapevine that while PNM is a popular movement valuable for its success in fundraising and lobbying, a more immediate response is both possible and needed.

He surveys those accepting the invitation. As expected, they are all men of a certain age, old enough to understand the urgency of the need to act yet young enough to have strength for the fight. Thirty new recruits for what really matters.

With Helen at his side, he calls them to cluster around him. He speaks now in a softer, more conspiratorial voice. "I'm pleased you decided to stay. We need citizens prepared to go beyond the talking and take action to save their families. You've made the right decision and I'm proud of every one of you. Let me tell you how this works."

He spends the next hour taking them into his confidence about alt-H, explaining how it works on a cell structure so that even if one cell is compromised, the others will still function. He tells them about the training programmes that will equip them with the practical skills needed to disrupt and demobilise the enemy, online and real world. He makes a joke agreeing this is the way terrorist groups were organised in the past but says only FuturePlus and their shills would claim that about alt-H. He calls on them to leave right now if they're not serious about the fight.

No one leaves.

The only question comes from the overweight Caribbean in a spotted shirt. "How do we know one of us here is not from the police or the security services?"

DeGray has answered the question many times before. "No worries. Many of our most active members started out as plants from police and security."

When he's finished, Helen, seated now at a table they use as a registration desk, takes their details.

One by one they agree and are waved off with a hearty handshake from DeGray. "Glad you joined the cause."

As the last of them departs, he gives Helen a satisfied smile. "Makes me proud of each and every one of them."

"Anything more today, Stephen?"

"Set up a meet with Bull Coghlan. I need to give him a heads up."

15

Back at base, Cheryl unzips the holdall. "Let's just see what Renalto was so keen to take with him."

It's the expected remnants of a wasted life. Thirty thousand in used ten-dollar bills. Each note tells its own sorry tale of alcoholism, cheap paid-for sex, bad food habits, back-alley drugs dealing. And a few trillion microbes still competing for supremacy as it's been passed hand to hand in a sad procession. I have to stop analysing the wads of cash after a few minutes and turn to Cheryl.

"The footprints of too many lives are here and most of them are not good."

She gives a wry smile. "Come on, Jessica. You'll be telling me next what you're finding is depressing. Isn't that off-limits even for a new state-of-the-art VA like you?"

I say I agree. "You're right. That's a blessing you have a monopoly on."

But I can't help feeling the disappointment of confronting head-on the backwash of the fractured and tortured humanity Renalto called his own.

She digs deeper into the hold-all. A hand-embroidered drawstring bag holding his drugs paraphernalia. A used syringe, a shoelace tourniquet plastered with sweat, blood and MRSA, a sizeable chunk of black tar heroin, sufficient to service half the addicts in San Diego. A tub of talcum powder to cut the stuff.

She shakes her head. "Not too difficult to work Renalto out. An addict himself needing to feed his habit by peddling the stuff to other addicts. A life that was never going to end well."

Lower down the holdall, a handgun. An S&W .38 Special Snubnose. Loaded and discharged in the past forty-eight hours.

Besides that, the empty syringe used on Jimmie Partland which Cheryl bags as evidence.

And pushed down the side, one of those A4 plastic wallets holding a sheaf of product information sheets.

They're all from the same place. An identical imprint on each sheet.

MNF - THE MICRONUTRIENT FOUNDATION

Cheryl gives me a puzzled look. "Not your average drug dealer's bedtime reading."

She skips through the sheets.

- Telemorase
- NAD+
- Resveratrol
- CoQ10
- Collagen Peptides
- Spirulina
- Turmeric concentrate
- Phosphatidyl Serine

She stops leafing through. "So, what is this stuff?"

I trawl the web and come straight back. "Anti-ageing supplements. Slowing down the clock is a big market. 300 billion dollars a year."

On the bottom right corner of each sheet, there's a hand-stamped address. A health food store down in the Gaslamp Quarter. Pivotal Foods.

Before we can set out for the store, she picks up a call. "Bull Coghlan wants to see me in his office right away."

16

Coghlan doesn't miss the opportunity to blame me for the slurry spree out on Martin Luther King.

"It's leading the evening news, and I have the powers that be on my back wanting to know how an attempt to bring in a low-level slimeball felon turned into a multi-lane crashfest. And I know where to find the answer."

From beneath the carpet, I feel Cheryl squirm as Coghlan pushes the knife in.

"I'm sorry, Bull. We had no idea Renalto was about to lose it like that."

His eyes bulge with rage. "We? So, who is this 'we' you're so keen on? Let me guess. Not that pile of horse dung VA you're hanging out with?"

I'm beginning to expect it now but that doesn't stop this hurting. Coghlan is out to finish me for good.

Cheryl tries to come to my defence. "It was all down to me. My judgment. My driving."

Coghlan thumps his fist on the desk. "Don't give me that. The monstrosity is supposed to be assisting, making sure you're more effective in keeping the public safe and all the other junk promises the maniacs who foisted it upon us are making. And what we get is this? Two million dollars in insurance claims, half a dozen hospitalised and a fireball on the evening news. I don't call that being more effective. I call that being spurred on to be reckless by an entity that might score well in the lab but is worse than useless when out there in the real world. And what does that lead to? Endangering the community? Endangering lives? Bringing this company into disrepute? Yes, yes and yes again. The sooner the thing is out of here and back in its box the better."

"Jessica did nothing wrong."

"You need to face it, Ryan. That VA is about as much use in policing as a bucket with a hole in it."

I struggle to find a reason why Coghlan hates me so much and wants to take me down for just doing my job. His hatred goes beyond logic. It's deep and irrational. He gets some buzz I can't fathom out of denying my right to exist.

He rubs it in. "I expect this to feature in the report to Wington and I expect it to say the monstrosity is not fit for purpose."

Cheryl still tries to defend me. "It's only just the start of the trial period you agreed."

He gives a lurid smile. "Did I say a week? You've got five days."

"I need longer than that. This is not just about disappearances anymore. It's a murder investigation now that Jimmie Partland is dead. I need all the resource I can get."

"And you've solved the murder. Not the way anyone with any sense would do it, but solved it is."

"But he's just part of a wider conspiracy, I'm sure of it. I still need that resource."

"And I'm making sure you get just that. But don't try to pull a fast one by saying that's any kind of reason for your cyber badass buddy to be around here for an hour longer than necessary. Five days, and that's it."

By the time Cheryl arrives back at her desk, it's clear what Coghlan has done. He's placed the investigation in the hands of Homicide and waiting to meet us is Mitch Zarkoski who assumes he's in control.

"I guess you know the Lieutenant has detailed me to take over the case. I'll need a rundown on everything you have so far."

Cheryl animates me and I appear beside her and take a close look at Zarkoski.

He's too short to have spent much time as a cop on the streets and wears those shoes that claim to give an extra three inches in height without anyone knowing. His thick red hair is shaved at the sides but left long on top in a failed attempt to make him seem taller. The look in his eyes tells of a belief in the importance of taking down the bad guys that hasn't yet been dulled by years of disappointment by what happens in the courtroom. A potentially lethal combination of stature insecurity and misplaced idealism.

He gives me no more than a cursory glance. "And this is?"

Cheryl does the honours. "Jessica, meet the detective."

I put on my most incongruous smile. "A pleasure."

Jessica 8

He's unmoved. "I know what the Lieutenant thinks, but I'm easy. I can work with it so long as it's useful and doesn't get in the way of the investigation."

Hardly a positive endorsement. About as positive as a vegetarian greeting an unapologetic hog roast host. And that's without mentioning the all too predictable degenderisation he assumes is par for the course.

While Cheryl brings Zarkoski up to date, I trawl the net to discover what I can about Lieutenant Coghlan. There is material on him over and beyond the expected police department bios and award nominations, but the detail is buried deep in layers of military-grade encryption it's going to take time to break.

Zarkoski comes back with a plan. I'm to be put on desk duty while he and Cheryl go downtown to interview the owner of Pivotal Foods.

He thinks that's the kind of shut-out Coghlan would approve of but what he doesn't know is so long as Cheryl keeps the neurostimulator on, I'll still be able to see what she sees, hear what she hears, smell what she smells and feel what she feels.

And I may be of more use here.

17

I shouldn't be doing this, parsing more of my partner's deep memories. But I know I must.

I'm Cheryl and it's the day after the breakup with Petersen.

I have no intention of contacting Petersen's wife. It's

Jessica 8

over. I've been a fool to be taken in by him and that's something I'm just going to have to live with. Mother was right. There's no way a woman like me should expect to be treated right. I've learned that lesson the hard way.

I make my way from the apartment to my car, parked in its space at the rear of the condo. I don't reach the car. A man comes up from behind and throws a hood over my head. A second man is with him, and they lift me up, and carry me off. I try to scream but one of them has a hand clamped over my mouth through the hood. I hear a van door sliding open. They throw me in and duct tape my hands and feet. I keep shouting but there's no one to hear as the van pulls away into the morning traffic.

They drive for what feels like forever. Long enough to take me many miles away.

When they stop, they drag me from the van. I've managed to shake off the hood and see them clearly.

They must know I've seen who they are.

I understand now they intend to kill me.

There's more but it's buried so deep.

18

While Cheryl and Zarkoski head down to the Gaslamp Quarter and Pivotal Foods, I check out the scans I stored of the product leaflets we recovered from Renalto's holdall.

It's a collection of dietary supplement products

designed to appeal to the worried well. Not just the expected obscure vitamins and minerals no sane human would ever imagine they might be short of. Everything from NAD+ to ancient Chinese herbal extracts to homoeopathic remedies. Not just green tea but concentrated extract of green tea. Not just microbiome enhancing yoghurts and kefirs but pill-based concoctions pulling together prebiotic fibre laced with a multitude of obscure bacteria with names that sound like they're taken from some germ warfare handbook. What you might call supplement overload.

At Pivotal Foods, Cheryl and Zarkoski have parked the Interceptor a block away and are now in the store as prospective customers. Cheryl fakes interest in the shelves full to bursting with bottles offering overpriced cures for often imaginary conditions while Zarkoski eyes the wholefoods.

I feed Cheryl the results of my data scan into the ownership and running of the business. It's been open for four years and manned by Jack Gomez and Will Tafel, two cheery youngsters building a reputation for not showing a jot of disbelief in what they sell. But they're not here today.

Cheryl approaches the counter and enquires. "I'm a loyal customer and I'm used to being served by the two young guys, Jack and Will. They're not around?"

The man behind the counter is a greying fifty-five-year-old Hindu dressed in collar and tie and one of those button-up the front cotton items that would have been called a smoking jacket in an earlier age. I run facial recognition and identify him as Aadi Agharwal, a one-time surgeon struck off from medical practice three years ago for operating on patients who didn't need surgery.

The prospect of not deterring a returning customer leads him to open up. "The boys. I bought them out. To be honest they know a lot about the foods, but they aren't good businessmen. They were way beyond bust when I came in and paid off their debts. They still rent the apartment upstairs, but I run the store now. What can I interest you in?"

"So, the product range has stayed the same?"

"It has." He gives a smile that looks as out of place on that otherwise expressionless face as a tomato in a fruit salad. "But in addition, I give treatments."

His eyes track to the back of the store and a partition wall that bears a stick-on sign that says Treatment Room.

"What treatments?"

"Reflexology, hypnotherapy, light stimulation. A full range." He reaches under the counter and pulls out a leaflet printed on recycled paper. He hands it to Cheryl and repeats himself for emphasis. "A full range."

Jessica 8

I scan over the leaflet as Cheryl holds it up to look at it herself. I pause on one of the items. Adrenal boost therapy. That's a new one to me.

I give Cheryl a heads-up. "Ask him about the ABT."

She responds. "I could be interested in the adrenal therapy. Are you getting much call for it?"

Agharwal gives a satisfied bob of the head. "It's one of my specialities. Done right it's very effective."

"For what?"

"A general health boost." He gives a sly wink. "And for rolling back the clock."

"How would that work?"

He comes closer and whispers. "Trust me. It works wonders."

"And you offer that right here?"

He smiles again. "It's one of our premium treatments."

I send another message to Cheryl. "Just what are the boys upstairs being used for?"

She pulls back her jacket to show him her SDPC badge. "Tell me about Antonio Renalto."

He takes a step back. "You should have declared yourself. Obtaining information under false pretences. Infringing my civil liberties."

Cheryl asks again. "Just tell me what you know about him."

"I don't know anyone of that name."

I wish Zarkoski had allowed me to be there. If he hadn't been so keen to sideline me, I would have applied my onboard lie detection facility to come to a more precise result. But from what I can see from here, I'd say he was being as truthful as a politician at a federal corruption enquiry.

"So, you won't mind if we check your credit card receipts to see if he's been buying stuff here?"

He begins to back off. "How do you expect me to remember the name of everyone who comes in?"

Zarkoski moves in and pulls up a headshot of Renalto on his phone and shows it to Agharwal. "Maybe this will help."

He looks at the image for too short a time before shaking his head. "He could have been in the store. But so have hundreds of others. I've owned this place for less than a year. It must have been before my time."

Cheryl shows him the sheaf of product sheets recovered from Renalto's hold-all, each with the Pivotal Foods stamp on the corner. "Then how do you explain these?"

He glances at the pages. "Sure. They're ours. What else do you expect? We sell healthfoods. These are the foods."

"So, what's your connection to the Micronutrient Foundation? And don't say they're your suppliers.

They're more than that, aren't they?"

"Call it our professional society. They wholesale products to stores like this all over the country. But they also offer training and advice."

"And how long have you been associated with them?"

"Two years and counting. Is this the kind of thing you law officers should be spending your time asking about?"

"You can leave us to decide that. So, how do you account for Antonio Renalto having these in his possession?"

"As I told you. He must have picked them up here. Maybe long before I took up the ownership."

Cheryl picks up on this. "In which case, we need to interview the boys upstairs."

"I don't expect they'll be any help to you whatever it is you're trying to run down."

"We'll still talk to them. And we expect to see what you have back there in your treatment room."

"You need a warrant."

"We also need a list of clients who've used your treatment room."

"That's privileged information. Again, get a warrant."

Cheryl and Zarkoski exit the store and ring the bell to the upstairs apartment. As they wait for an answer, I run a check on the boys. Jack Gomez has a string of minor motoring offences and Will Tafel is a clean skin. You wouldn't exactly say they were Butch Cassidy and the Sundance Kid.

Gomez comes down the stairs to open the door. He looks pale and sleep deprived as he agrees to let Cheryl and Zarkoski in. Upstairs, Tafel lies listless on an old couch and looks disinclined to sit up and take notice.

They give no sign of recognition of the mugshot of Renalto when Zarkoski shows it to them.

Cheryl tries to find out more about their relationship with Agharwal. "So, the business was going bust, and he came in and bought you out. What sort of deal did he cut? Enough to bring you back to zero?"

Gomez shakes his head. "It left us fifty thou short."

"So why accept the offer? Why not just go bankrupt?"

"Because he offered us another way out."

"One that means you still help out in the business?"

"You might say that."

Tafel gathers enough strength to sit up on the couch. "No need to mince words, Jack. The deal is we pay him back in a special way."

Gomez signals Tafel to keep quiet and he subsides again on the couch.

I cast a message to Cheryl. "He means the ABT."

She agrees. "So, he pays you for the transfusions he uses in his Adrenal Boost Therapy sessions."

Gomez shakes his head. "No way either of us would do that."

I hack into the Pivotal Foods security cameras. Their firewall protection is primitive and I'm soon in. There's one camera pointed along the street outside, three checking the food store aisles and, yes, there's one observing what happens in the treatment room. There's not much of interest in the hypnotherapy and light therapy sessions but a whole lot that needs to be understood about the ABT.

I edit it down and cast the result to Cheryl's screen. I monitor her emotions as she takes in the footage.

She sees two hospital beds placed side by side. On the one on the left is Will Tafel looking pale and ghostly, receiving a needle-prick local anaesthetic in the small of his back. Agharwal is heard saying, "This will numb you up." An elderly man with a huge potbelly lies on the right-hand bed. Agharwal turns him over and administers a similar numbing shot in this man's back.

There is a pause as Agharwal moves out of shot and waits for the anaesthetic to take. He returns with a large syringe and with surprising speed inserts it into Will Tafel's back and extracts a dark coloured, viscous-looking fluid. With the same sense of urgency, Agharwal turns, positions himself over the potbellied man, selects his spot and empties the syringe into the man's back.

Cheryl is angry when she confronts Gomez with what she's just seen, holding up her screen before him. "Tafel is right, isn't he? You're paying back Agharwal in body tissue. How much does he pay you?"

Gomez lowers his head, so he no longer has to look. "How did you get this?"

"No matter. Answer the question."

"Three thousand dollars a session."

"And how are you two going to manage that, owing him fifty thou?"

"It's survivable. He only takes what he needs. The soreness and bleeding only lasts a week or so."

I cast another message to Cheryl. "Agharwal is removing tissue from the youngster's adrenal gland and pumping it into the adrenal gland of the old-timer. The nearest thing to what he's doing is the kind of biopsy a respectable surgeon might carry out to remove material for tests to determine if the gland is malfunctioning and producing medical problems. But Agharwal has a whole other use for it."

Cheryl comes back puzzled. "So why do it?"

"The gland produces hormones like aldosterone, cortisol and DHEA. Ageing in humans results in a decline in hormone production. Looks like Agharwal has convinced his so-called clients that introducing fresh tissue from a youngster's adrenal gland reverses that decline."

Cheryl rounds on Mendez. "How long can you go on doing this?"

"There's no law against it. Why don't you just leave us alone?"

"So why does the old man want your tissue so much he's prepared to pay?"

"You don't get it, do you? He thinks it's going to make him younger."

Cheryl points a finger at Mendez. "And maybe ruin your health. You're living some kind of nightmare and I'm going to find a way to stop it."

With that Cheryl and Zarkoski head back to the Interceptor.

19

As Cheryl and Zarkoski drive back to base, I analyse the footage from the Pivotal Foods treatment room.

To save money on storage costs, Agharwal erases the files every three months but there's still plenty to go on.

Jessica 8

I apply facial recognition to all nine clients hungry for young adrenal tissue.

They make up a good cross-section of the wealthy and influential citizens of San Diego. That's some serious sphere of influence.

One name stands out. Dean Castlefield. 80 years old and the owner of a business empire that stretches from TV to investment banking. He's top one hundred rich list and is estimated to be worth $90 billion and rising. But what really catches my eye is the name of one of the companies in his empire. SDR Systems. The company Lana Ramone works for.

When Cheryl and Zarkoski arrive back, I brief them. I make a big deal about the lawyers, politicians and entertainment types identified from the treatment room footage but don't say too much about Castlefield. I question myself whether I should have the licence to be this deceitful, but nothing comes back to say this has been hit out of the park.

They agree to split the contact work, as I hoped. Zarkoski will visit Charles Washington, principal attorney at Washington, Pitcher and Ashley, one of the lead law firms here in town and Cheryl will head out to Chula Vista to talk to Walt Weiner, a film director with Hollywood credits.

As soon as Zarkoski is out of earshot, I come clean

with Cheryl. "We need to talk with Dean Castlefield."

She gives a puzzled look. "What happened to Weiner?"

"Maybe later. But we needed to ditch Zarkoski."

Her eyes open wide in surprise. "Jessica! If I didn't know better, I could be forgiven for thinking you're being devious."

I let it pass. "Zarkoski is a shill for Bull Coghlan, right?"

"Yes."

"So, the less he knows the better."

She shakes her head. "OK. So why Dean Castlefield?"

I tell her about the connection with Lana Ramone and SDR Systems.

Cheryl changes course and heads out to La Jolla where Castlefield owns a clifftop thirty-room mansion overlooking the beach near Scripps.

When we arrive, we're greeted by a VA called Vance. He's simmed up as a 1930s butler in retro English mode, all frock coat, white starched wing-collared shirt, polished shoes and braces. And, in an exaggerated British accent, he's being obstructive when told that Cheryl Ryan and her VA from San Diego Police Company need to talk with the master of the house as a matter of urgency.

He glowers at me. "And this is?"

Jessica 8

While Cheryl fills him in, I check out Vance's specifications. He's suitable for menial, servant-level roles but not much more. Pity they gave him such a superiority complex.

Vance gives a look of quiet disgust at the mention of my name and ploughs on. "Mr Castlefield is never available without an appointment."

Cheryl insists. "Just let him know we're here."

With a 'very well', he pauses in mid gesture while he communicates with his master. And then he relents. "Yes, just this once, he's agreed to see you."

We're shown into a reception room where Castlefield, propped up in a hi-tech invalid chair, is waiting.

Vance introduces us with overblown formality as if we were being presented at some Ruritanian court. "May I present Detective Cheryl Ryan accompanied by her investigative assistant, Jessica."

Castlefield presses a button on the arm of his chair and Vance fades to nothing. He casts an appreciative eye in my direction. "So, who have you brought to see me?"

Cheryl tries to object. "I'm here on an urgent criminal matter."

But he interrupts her and keeps his attention on me. "I want to know about Jessica's capabilities and I'm sure she can let me know herself."

I'm flattered by his attention and the fact that he's the first human other than Cheryl out here to show me the respect I deserve. But I can't afford to get into Cheryl's bad books by encouraging too much delay, so I keep it short and sweet.

"I'm a next-generation prototype with quantum computational backup, promising breakthrough logic interpretation and goal setting."

He forces a smile from muscles around a mouth drained of responsiveness by the effects of long-term illness. "Well, it's a pleasure to meet you. I'm sure you're doing San Diego PC proud."

Cheryl takes back control. "Mr Castlefield. I understand you're a patron of Pivotal Foods."

Without moving his head, he turns the chair so he faces her. "What of it?"

"And you've received adrenal boost therapy there."

"What has this to do with anything? We live in a free country."

"We're investigating a number of disappearances and a murder, Mr Castlefield. Jimmie Partland has been killed. Does that name mean anything?"

He doesn't pause to consider. "No. Why would it?"

"And yet our investigations have led us to you. So, I'm assuming that as an upstanding member of the community you'll want to help as much you can. So, answer the question about the adrenal treatment."

He relents. "All right, detective. Yes, I've had ABT, and more than once. I'm within my rights. And, just in case you need to know, it works. Makes me feel more alive."

"And you have no qualms about what Agharwal is doing?"

"If there are concerns, that's down to him. Take it up with him. Don't waste my time."

"You're sure there's nothing more you want to say to help the investigation?"

"Of course, I'm here to help in any way I can. But that's all for now."

I zoom in on a closer look at him. I doubt he's able to get in and out of the chair without help. His skin has a white, almost translucent quality, the absence of wrinkles betraying the extent of the dietary supplements and medical treatments he must be indulging in. His penetrating eyes tell of the intensity of his belief he can find a way to stop time.

Cheryl pulls up an image of Antonio Renalto on her device and shows it to him. "Do you know this man?"

Castlefield doesn't take anything more than a glance. "No."

"That's Antonio Renalto. The one who killed Jimmie Partland."

He shows no sign of emotion. "Why would I have anything to do with a man like that?"

If he's lying, he's good at it. He passes my online polygraph scan without a blip.

Cheryl presses on. "OK. Tell me about Lana Ramone."

If he had the dexterity, he'd be shrugging his shoulders. "And this is relevant to what?"

"She's missing and she works for you."

He presses a button in the arm of his chair and begins to turn away. "I'm not the only one to know she's a well-respected scientist. But look, my businesses employ over 80,000 people. Why would you expect me to keep tracks on every one of them?"

Again, he passes the online polygraph.

As he pulls away, Vance pops up and stands in our way. "That's all Mr Castlefield has for you today. I'll escort you out."

20

I recover a sliver of what Cheryl recalls of her abduction. It's a wall of pain.

I'm lying stock still, unable to move. My body is battered and bruised and feels like it's beyond repair. Pain is everywhere, in my arms and legs, throughout my chest and stomach and into my neck and face. But the strongest sensations come from inside, behind my eyes, the place where pain is overpowered by a blinding emptiness that tells me I'm close to death.

Just opening my eyelids brings on a new world of agony. My vision won't clear. All I see is an all-embracing whiteness. I close my eyes again and wait, hoping the bright glow will clear and I'll be able to discover where I am.

A drop of water falls on my forehead. And then another. A trickle of water runs down my face and covers my cracked and dried out lips. I search for the moisture with my tongue and lap up a few drops. And then a few more. The water runs down into my parched throat and I crave for more.

They left me here for dead.
I know somehow I will survive.

21

Cheryl agrees we need to call on Walt Weiner in National City if we're going to deceive Zarkoski when we report back to him, so we head straight there after calling to fix the appointment.

Weiner welcomes us into his office with a smile that

turns into a concerned frown once we tell him he's now part of a murder investigation.

He's large and suntanned, wearing an open-neck shirt to reveal a hint of chest hair beneath the gold medallion he wears around his neck. He's covered the walls of the office with posters of his movie successes, though I note the most recent is now four years distant, an age in terms of the Hollywood treadmill.

Cheryl zeroes in on his involvement with Agharwal. "Tell us about the ABT?"

Like Castlefield, he's defensive. "That's a private matter."

"Not when it's murder."

"So, I need a lawyer?"

"Not if you cooperate. We're not saying you had any direct involvement in the killing of Mr Partland, not yet at least."

"Partland?"

"Jimmie Partland. Poisoned in his house on Pacific Beach."

Weiner looks shocked and then scared.

Cheryl takes this as a cue to increase the pressure on him. "So, cooperate."

"Sure, I want to help. But that doesn't mean I have to give up my privacy."

I message Cheryl. "He needs to deliver on the

hundred million investment in his latest movie."

Cheryl moves closer and lowers her voice. "OK, Mr Weiner. I hope *Magic of War* is going to be a big grosser."

"What has that to do with anything?"

"Well, wouldn't it be a pity if the news outlets start talking about how the director is draining the adrenal glands of young men to boost his life chances and ruin theirs?"

"You wouldn't dare."

"Try me. Don't say you've never asked why Agharwal is still allowed to practice?"

"You're bluffing. You have no evidence."

I cast to Cheryl's pad the chunk of the footage that shows Weiner in the treatment room.

She shows it to him. "You mean this?"

He tries to complain. "It's an infringement. You could never use this in court."

"But the Hollywood press wouldn't be as choosy. A hundred million dollar movie. With powerful investors looking for a return. You've promised and they expect. No one would want to be on the end of a failure like that."

He sinks back into his chair with a demoralised shake of the head. "OK. OK. What do you need to know?"

"Why the treatment with Agharwal?"

"To live longer. Who doesn't want that?"

"And you don't care who pays the price?"

"Sure, I care. Like I care about what's happening to the planet or about homelessness."

Cheryl forces herself to overcome the upwelling of anger and disgust burning through her every fibre. "But it doesn't stop you?"

He stares back. "Like so much else in this life, it's a question of priorities."

"And you put yours above anyone else's?"

"If you must see it that way."

Cheryl calls up the photo of Antonio Renalto and shows it to him. "You know this man?"

He nods. "That's Antonio Renalto."

"You know him from where?"

"He's in my RE group."

"RE?"

"Radical Extension."

I run this through the web and send the thought stream back to Cheryl. "Radical Extension. Formed in Los Angeles six years ago. Chapter established in San Diego a year later. Their founding statement says they've come together to overcome the stigma involved in wanting to live forever."

Cheryl doesn't blink. "And Renalto, what's he to the group?"

"He's an ordinary member, just like anyone else."

Jessica 8

I cast an image to Cheryl's tablet, and she looks at it. It shows one of those group pictures taken at the end of a meeting where all the attendees line up to smile and show how pleased they are to be there. Dean Castlefield is in his chair, front and centre, with Weiner close behind. Antonio Renalto, flanked by Agharwal, is also there, third row back.

She shows it to Weiner. "And you see him here?"

He points at the smiling face in the third row. "Yes, that's Renalto."

"And how long have you known him?"

"He joined about six months back. Now, why is this so important?"

"Just part of our enquiries." Cheryl points back to the image on her tablet once more. "So, where was this taken?"

His irritation level raises another notch. "If you have to know, it's from our Annual Meeting in Ventura, back in June."

I recheck the photo. Yes, all but one of the worthy members of the community who frequented Agharwal's treatment room is here.

Cheryl gets my message and continues the questioning. "And what kind of business did you discuss?"

He's sounding even more defensive. "RE San Diego is a private organisation. It has no need to publicise what it discusses."

"So, your aims and actions are secret?"

"We make no secret about RE. Who doesn't want to reach a place where they can live forever?"

"But you're not telling anyone how you expect to get there?"

"Why should we? And you have no right to insist we do."

Cheryl lets this pass. "Tell me about Dean Castlefield."

Weiner unwinds. "He's a great man, and he's dying. He's on his second heart transplant. They've given him less than a year to live. He started out with nothing and built an empire, all on his own back. Anything he wants, he can have. Everything has its price. Everything. Except for the one thing he now needs, and that's what most people tell him he can't have, no matter how much he might pay for it.

"But it's changing and changing fast. We now understand what ageing is. And one day we'll be able to overcome it. Imagine how children in the future will need to be taught how people in their recent past suffered from this terrible illness they thought was incurable and had just to watch as their bodies and their minds fell to pieces as ageing robbed them of everything they ever had. It shouldn't have to be that way. And it won't be that way for long."

"And Agharwal offers a way out?"

"No. But he could allow someone like Castlefield or me to live long enough to see the great change happen. It's unimaginable we should just miss out. To be one of those marooned in the last generation to die of old age. So, yes, ABT, stem cell therapy, Metformin, NAD+ and anything else that will keep us alive to see it. That's why we're part of RE."

"And you'll confirm that Castlefield knows Renalto?"

"Why don't you ask him?"

"I already have."

22

On the ride back, I connect again with a sliver of what Cheryl recalls of the abduction.

I open my eyes again.

The agony has not subsided, but now I can see the outline of what surrounds me. I'm looking upwards towards the sky. I can see the sky because there's a hole in the roof.

Jessica 8

There's a storm outside with high winds arching the branches of the surrounding trees over the hole. I watch their manic dance as the wind gusts and then abates. Rain is falling in, soaking me. I lap up as much of the water as I can as it washes over my face.

I'm in a dilapidated cabin somewhere in the mountains. Somewhere those men brought me to kill me.

I try to move but become reunited with a world of pain that rules out the very idea of movement. There's nothing I can do but wait.

But wait for what?

My body feels light. Too light. As if I've been here for so long I've lost half my body weight.

If no one's found me by now, it's certain they've already stopped looking.

23

We arrive back at base to find Zarkoski waiting. And he doesn't look pleased.

"If I didn't think better of you, Cheryl, I'd believe you set me up with the visit to Charles Wilmington."

Cheryl sits beside him and tries not to let on he's right. "You mean he didn't play ball?"

"That's the least of it. Made me wait an age and then stonewalled me with all that legal jargon. Wouldn't admit a thing. And then he pulled a number on me. By the time I got to question him, he already knew why I was there. Told me he represents Agharwal, and he'd sue for invasion of privacy if I reveal any details of what takes place in his treatment room."

"Agharwal had time to brief him once we left Pivotal Foods?"

"I guess so. But that's a big legal stick for a small-time store owner to wield."

"Since Wilmington is involved himself, he has every incentive to offer his services pro bono. Which means he'll probably do the same for the other ABT users."

"OK. So where does that leave us?"

Given that Zarkoski is lying for sure, Cheryl agrees with the need to be economical with the truth over what he takes back to Coghlan.

I message Cheryl. "No need to tell him about Dean Castlefield. Let Zarkoski know just enough to keep Coghlan busy."

She agrees and keeps it simple. "Weiner admitted to the ABT and not much else."

"So, we're no further forward in the investigation?"

"Well, he recognised Renalto."

"From where?"

Cheryl tells him what we discovered from Weiner about Radical Extension.

He takes care to listen before coming back. "You're saying Renalto along with Weiner is mixed up with RE?"

"Yes. Weiner admitted as much."

"But I don't see how that translates into a motive for murder. They're a bunch of citizens who want to live forever. That Renalto was an RE member is most likely circumstantial. He could have had some quite different motive."

"We don't know that."

"And that's my point."

I have to admit, although he's shilling for Coghlan, he's right. We're missing something.

24

I struggle to bring focus to any more of Cheryl's recall of being abandoned in the Laguna Mountains.

The storm has passed, and the wind has dropped, leaving behind an ominous silence now darkness has fallen.

I still can't move.

I feel weaker, less able to concentrate on the business of keeping alive. No one will find me now. If I could just drift away, this pain and suffering would be over.

I look up and see a light penetrating the darkness. Is this how I will be called away?

I close my eyes, hoping it will go away. But when I open them, it's still there. And there's a sound, faint but loud enough to disturb the night.

Tiny blades rotating above my head.

I make out the shape of a small drone hovering above the cabin. It's searching for any glimmer of heat my wrecked body is still emitting.

And now it's gone.

Has it detected me? Or am I so far gone nothing has registered and I will die here alone?

25

After hours, Bull Coghlan drives the last mile of the journey out to Del Mar in his own unmarked car knowing this is one meeting he shouldn't make over a phone or online. It's rare enough to be summoned to a meeting with the alt-H leadership but rarer still for a one-to-one with Stephen DeGray. Lack of traceability and total deniability is the order of the day.

He approaches DeGray's beachfront mansion and stops as requested by the plainclothes security at the twelve-foot-high entrance gates. Once checked and frisked, he drives the half mile through landscaped gardens to the towering main house where security checks him over again. He's led up the steps to the main entrance, where Helen Drake is waiting to meet him.

"Glad you could make it on time, Lieutenant. Stephen is working his way through a full diary of meetings today."

She shows Coghlan into the large, ground floor office, set up more as a command centre than a place of regular business.

DeGray welcomes him with calculating false modesty. "Great you could make it over, Bull. I know how involved you are in keeping us all safe."

Coghlan can't help rising to the compliment. "I do my best to serve." And then he realises he needs to acknowledge the true state of play. "Your time is more valuable than mine. What do you need?"

The politician gives his most practiced smile and points to the two comfortable armchairs. "Let's sit and talk."

Coghlan expects Helen to leave at this point, but she stays, making ready to record the upcoming conversation on her tablet.

Once they're seated, DeGray opens up. "Bull, I need your advice on a matter I just heard about. It seems you have an ongoing investigation involving Lana Ramone."

Coghlan understands why they've summoned him. "Wington has a no import baseline cop on it. Cheryl Ryan. I'm telling her to lay off this, but Wington outranks me and what he says goes, for the moment at least. And they have a new VA on it."

DeGray shows polite surprise. "A VA?"

"Some advanced prototype on trial to aid with policing. Heap of junk, but Wington insists on it. Claims this will help with the disappearances."

"You're saying it's not just Ramone?"

"Ryan's connecting his disappearance with that of another scientist, Alex Belmondo, and Luke Devlin, a no-account singer. I don't know why she's so fired up to insist they're somehow part of the same story."

DeGray leans closer. "I have an instinct this is something we need to keep a lid on. You see, we're following Ramone. We're funding a good chunk of her research work anonymously through front charities. We're logging her ethical objections to VA development too, paying to amplify her online presence, promoting her as a makeweight against Belmondo who is the real danger to what we stand for. All without her knowing, you understand. Too much attention to her and the wrong questions get asked, exposing our whole tactic of restricting AI development."

"What do you want me to do?"

"Your instincts are right, as always, Bull. Keep that cop Wington has on the case buttoned down. Protect alt-H interests."

He turns to Helen. "You agree with that strategy?"

She looks up. "Yes."

DeGray returns his attention to Coghlan. "That just about covers it, Lieutenant."

"I get it. I'll play my part."

DeGray smiles. "By the way, Helen is a clean skin. As far as the world out there is concerned, she's pure People Not Machines and nothing to do with alt-H. She'll be your immediate point of contact, so you won't need to come all the way down here unless it's absolutely necessary."

As Helen shows Coghlan out, he's careful to give her more respect than when he arrived. "Don't fear. I'll keep in close touch."

26

The list of social media accounts I'm hacking is growing as the investigation develops. It's well within my capabilities to track everyone I come into contact with and use my advanced AI engine to sift through their data in the finest detail.

Nothing has needed reporting to Cheryl so far.

The accounts of the three who disappeared are silent and have remained so since they went missing.

Until now.

I'm alerted to a post that pops up in Alex Belmondo's feed.

At first, it looks like something I'll never understand. It's an image of a ginger and white tomcat. No comment. Just the playful cat.

OK, people post pictures of cats all the time, don't ask me why. But why would Belmondo do such a thing?

Perhaps some well-meaning animal lover who gets a kick out of plastering images of his much-loved pet across the net has hacked his feed.

But if the image does come from Belmondo, it's important. This is the first sign he's still alive.

Perhaps, again, there's more evil intent here than at first sight. Hackers smuggling in malware to allow the theft of information and/or continued tracking. Maybe they've hidden their code inside the image of the playful cat.

When I unscramble the binary that makes up the image, I'm greeted with a surprise. This is nothing from hackers, benign or malevolent. It's a message from Belmondo himself.

They're threatening to kill my wife and children. You

must save them.

I cast the message to Cheryl.

She comes back in search of an explanation. "Where did this come from?"

I explain.

She comes back again. "And you're sure it's from Belmondo?"

"Who else?"

"Then why conceal the message like this? And why not say more?"

"Do you want me to speculate?"

"Not much has stopped you before."

I take this as a green light. "There's a ninety-five per cent probability this is from Belmondo himself. The content is genuine enough. He's calling for protection for his wife and children."

"And why does he need to do that?"

"He's alive, and he's being held somewhere against his will. He can't say more because he's under intense surveillance. There's only enough time for this quick message. It's all he can smuggle out without it being noticed."

"So why the cat?"

"It's his way of covering if those holding him get to see this on his account. He can say some pet lover has hacked in. All they will see is the pleasant image of a cat.

They're everywhere, all over the web. Nothing unusual in that."

"So why would he expect anyone out here to have the inclination to decode the image to uncover his message?"

"He's desperate and running on hope. Someone as determined as you could be working on finding him. With someone like me at your side to do the heavy lifting on the computational work."

She takes her time to think through the consequences. She's clear once she collects her thoughts.

"If Belmondo is being held, it's likely Luke Devlin and Lana Ramone are, too. And we may have a motive for the killing of Jimmie Partland. Alex Belmondo is in fear of what might happen to his wife and children. They may be next. The threat was directed first at Jimmie and, for whatever reason, it was carried out."

"So, besides Monica Belmondo and the children, Bessie Llewelyn is also in danger."

27

I piece together another segment of Cheryl's memories. I come round and open my eyes. Above, bright hospital lights. A cannula inserted in my right arm, above it a saline drip bag.

My mouth feels like I've been eating sand.

Standing at my bedside, a doctor in a white coat.

He sees I'm awake and smiles. "I'm Mr Merchant."

My words struggle out through swollen lips. "How long have I been here?"

"Don't worry about that now."

"I need to know."

"When we brought you in, you were in coma. That was six weeks ago. We could only hope you would make it. But here you are. You pulled through. We'll need to make some tests."

My eyes close, and I drift into the deepest sleep.

28

Zarkoski takes delight in announcing Coghlan wants to see Cheryl with immediate effect.

She gets no credit as she stands before him while I listen in from beneath his office carpet.

She's trying to tell him about our success in

deciphering the message from Alex Belmondo but can't get a word in over Coghlan's latest rant.

"The entire goddamned world is raving over invasion of privacy, and I have to explain how and why you've placed SDPC in such an exposed position."

Cheryl stands up strong. "Listen, Bull, we're on the point of a breakthrough."

"Breakthrough! Try explaining that to Charles Wilmington, who's demanding damages on account of unlawful intrusion on the private lives of himself and his clients."

"You mean the video?"

"Yes. The video."

"What they're up to may be unlawful."

"Doesn't matter a rat's ass. How did you come by the footage?"

No surprise he would direct this at me.

Cheryl attempts to deflect him. "You need to see it, Bull, to understand what they're doing is beyond unpleasant."

"I'll watch it as and when. Answer me. Where did you get it?"

"It was in the cloud."

"Everything's in the cloud. And most of it's meant to be private. So where, exactly?"

"From the backup of the security cameras at Pivotal Foods."

"And you had permission to view that?"

I can feel Cheryl's discomfort growing. "Not exactly."

"Which means you hacked it?"

"Guess so."

"And even if the footage has any relevance, which I doubt, it would be inadmissible."

Cheryl can only grunt in agreement.

"Which means Wilmington has a cast-iron case for busting us. And it means I won't have to look far to find how you came to make such a mess. It's that electronic apology of an investigator you're sweet on, isn't it?"

"Jessica shouldn't carry the blame. She's there to offer analysis and insight. The decisions taken are down to me."

Beneath the carpet in Coghlan's office, I'm proud that Cheryl is standing up for me again.

Coghlan rages on. He bangs his fist so hard on the desk he dislodges to the floor the framed photo of his wife and children that normally has pride and place. "There is no 'she'. No Jessica. Don't you get it? The monstrosity is no more than a machine. Can never be more than that. A dangerous machine. Don't pretend for a second that it could have any kind of personality."

I'm no longer surprised by the hatred he shows

towards me, but it still hurts.

He hasn't finished. "You might as well accept the experiment is over. The only thing keeping the monstrosity here is Wington with his misguided idea that we have to show we're keeping up with the latest tricks of the trade. When I tell him just how it led you astray, the heap of wombat doo you're taking pride in will be closed down so fast you won't hear a sound."

Cheryl tries to fight back. "What's more important? Following the rules or closing down a murder conspiracy?"

He bangs his fists on the desk again. "You have no proof of any conspiracy. You know Renalto did the killing. Let it rest."

"That's what I'm trying to tell you. We have a lead on Alex Belmondo that points to him being alive."

"OK. So, one more reason to not waste valuable resource on a mere disappearance."

"But we also think he's being held against his will."

His face reddens with rage. "We? You have the blind stupidity to refuse to get it. There is no we."

"Sorry. I consider it's likely he's being held against his will."

"And this comes from where?"

"From a message he sent hidden in an image on his feed."

Jessica 8

I cast the message to Cheryl's pad, and she shows it to Coghlan.

"And your monstrosity friend hacked this one too?"

Cheryl ignores the slur. "It points out that Belmondo's wife and children are under threat. We need to give them protection."

He rolls his eyes. "More resource. And the message is from where?"

Cheryl shows him the image of the tomcat.

He gives a loud guffaw of disbelief. "You expect me to commit hard-pressed resource based on a cat pic?"

"Those children need protecting."

"And how can you be so sure of that?" He adopts the parody voice of a spoilt child. "Oh, I was forgetting. Your monster friend and loyal assistant decoded all this and handed it to you, so it must be right." He reverts to type. "And how can you be sure anything that thing tells you is true? How do you know someone else isn't pulling its strings and leading you on a merry dance for their own ends? And, along the way, bringing SDPC into terminal disrepute. You don't, do you?"

I'm shocked by the virulence of the attack on me. It's more than a matter of the rights and wrongs of new technology for Coghlan. He's left logic and reason far behind. It's personal, and it's visceral. He's alt-H down to his soul.

Cheryl tries again to get protection for the Belmondo children and fails.

Coghlan is having none of it. "Get back to some real policing. And expect the investigation to move to a lower profile once I brief Wington."

Once we leave, she's angry. As angry as a Zen Buddhist fooled into biting into a rare steak. "You're right about Coghlan's agenda. His alt-H prejudice is all over this case. And, yes, he'd be first in line to say good riddance if Belmondo, Devlin and Ramone go down."

"Expose him for what he is. Make a complaint."

"Complain to who? What if the entire Department is alt-H?"

"But not Wington. He must have agreed to have me here. Means he has some sympathy."

"I don't need sympathy. I need action. And I have no way of knowing how much Coghlan is poisoning Wington's mind against us. He's probably reporting me for disobeying orders right now."

29

decipher another chunk of Cheryl's memories.

When I open my eyes again, a plain-clothes officer is beside my bed. She says she's Maxine Fisher from Homicide.

Her voice is quiet and comforting, but it's clear she's

here for answers. "We thought we'd never find you. The cabin was well off the grid. In a remote clearing in the Laguna mountains."

"Then how did you find me?"

"An AI-controlled drone flew day and night over every inch of that place until it detected your body heat. They say you were out there for four or five weeks. And a freak of nature saved you. We haven't had summer rainstorms in Laguna for the best part of fifty years. But the rain came, and the old cabin let in enough water to keep you alive. Some are calling it a miracle."

"I don't believe in miracles."

"So, what do you recall? Who kidnapped you, took you out there, beat you and left you for dead?"

I'm trying to say anything. But nothing comes.

She notes my absent expression. "No matter. Get some rest. It will come and I'll be ready."

When I come round again, Maxine is waiting.

She activates a VA that pops up beside her. "This is Felix. You're OK for Felix to be here?"

Felix is simmed up as a streetwise cop of the old school, right down to the balding pate, the crumpled uniform and the hangdog face.

"Yeah, I'm OK."

"He's going to help us piece together what happened to you."

30

Without bothering to check with Zarkoski, Cheryl makes straight for the Interceptor, and we speed out to La Jolla.

Sugarman Drive is as bone dry as ever. Drought restrictions mean residents have given up trying to maintain anything green in their front gardens. We speed past lawns the colour of straw until we approach the Belmondo residence.

At first, there's no reply. It seems the house is empty until a forty-year-old man, grey before his time, comes to the door. Cheryl doesn't waste time asking who he is. "It's urgent I see Monica and the children."

He doesn't invite us in. "They're not here."

She shows him her badge and forces her way past him. "You're sure about that?"

The house is quiet, with no sound of Monica or the twins.

I scan the interior space and report back. "There's no one else here."

Cheryl turns to the grey-haired man. "Where are they? And who are you?"

He gives a calming gesture with his hands. "Look, can we take this one step at a time? My name is Rick French. I'm Monica's brother-in-law. Her sister Abigail's husband. I'm here to pick up the stuff needed to look after the children."

I check the facial recognition database. "Yes, he's university lecturer Dr Rick French, partner of Abigail French, Monica's sister. They live on Cowley Way in Clairemont."

Cheryl takes this in as she continues to question

him. "They're with your sister?"

He nods. "But Monica is missing. Abigail had a visit from her to say she had to leave and would we look after the twins. She wouldn't tell her why. The twins are with Abigail in our house in Clairemont."

"When was this?"

"Three, no, four hours ago."

"And Monica gave no idea about where she would go?"

"No. Abigail is worried sick."

Cheryl instructs him to drive home while she follows.

When we arrive at Cowley Way, Rick shows us in and calls Abigail down from an upstairs room. She makes no objection to my presence when Cheryl asks the inevitable question about my acceptability.

"Anything that helps to find Monica."

Cheryl tells them why she's here. "You'll be aware that Alex Belmondo is missing. I need to speak with Monica. We have concerns for her safety."

Abigail looks shocked. "Is that why she's run away?"

"You can't tell me where?"

"All she would say was it was best I didn't know."

"And the children?"

"They're upstairs, playing. We're trying to keep them from knowing anything untoward is happening, but they miss their mother. It's so unlike her to desert them. I can only think something terrible has come into her life."

Cheryl appeals to them both. "I'm not here to cause concern, but there's no good way of putting this. We have a suspicion Monica may be responding to a threat to her husband."

"Meaning?"

"The children may be next."

"Who'd be sick enough to do that?"

"That's what we need your help to find out."

Abigail runs back upstairs, sobbing.

Rick explains. "She's taking this hard. She and her sister are close. It's going to take Gail some long time to come to terms with what's happening. She's already on medication. This is only making matters worse."

Cheryl nods in understanding. "Dr French. Do you have somewhere you could take the children where they'll be safe? Somewhere far enough away from here?"

"We have a home out on Lake Jennings. But there's my work here and Gail couldn't cope with the children on her own. If this is so important, why can't we expect police protection?"

"Don't depend on it."

"Why? There are threats to women and children. What's stopping you?"

She's ashamed she needs to lie. "I'll request it, but it

may take time. In the short term, it's essential you find a way to do this yourself."

She feels bad she can't be honest with him. She can no longer pretend to not know what the response from SDPC will be.

He gives a resigned look. "I'll take Abigail and the children out to Lake Jennings. I'll do my best to work this out with my commitments at the university."

As we drive away, I have trouble understanding the strength of the doubt about me that Cheryl feels.

I decide to say nothing and hope it will pass.

31

I recover more of Cheryl's hidden past as she recovers from the shock of the abduction.

Maxine Fisher is a model of patience.

"Try to think back to what happened when they came for you."

Jessica 8

I'm trying my hardest to recall anything, but what comes back is a blank. There's only the white wall of pain from the weeks in the cabin. It's wrapped itself around everything and I'm unable to reach beyond it. All I can do is cry. "I'm sorry."

She gives a reassuring smile. "No matter. With Felix to help, we'll find them. Trust us."

She sims up Felix who gives an update. "Evidence from the Laguna Mountains cabin is complex. Rain ingress and the passage of time erased anything they may have inadvertently left behind. My analysis of the drone footage of the area around the cabin wasn't producing much of interest until I went over to maximum resolution."

Maxine interrupts. "That's equivalent to looking down the end of a microscope. But with all that detail comes a deluge of information that all has to be analysed and, like the proverbial needle in the proverbial haystack, what you're seeking is massively harder to find. So, Felix has been at it, day and night, checking, cross-checking and double-checking."

Felix continues. "And I believe I've found something. A discarded betting slip. Not much chance of finding anything like that all the way out there unless the ones who abducted you left it. And I have an analysis of what's on the ticket."

I turn to Maxine. "How is that going to help?"

She gives a shifty look. "You didn't hear this from me. Felix hacked the betting shop computer."

Felix puffs up with pride. "They're way below state-of-the-art. It was not the most difficult hack"

Maxine helps out. "Felix has a breakthrough to report."

Felix begins again. "I researched gambling. What strange behaviour. Repetitive independent of the outcome. You try it and you lose. Instead of walking away, you try it again, just one more time. And another and another. It's a special kind of addiction. Self-generation of opioids in the brain leading to a short-lived high and a craving for more. And it's that dependence on repetition that points up the significance of that betting slip.

"You see, it's a special kind of accumulator, a string of bets with winnings from the first becoming the wager on the next and so on up to ten times. At that point, the compounded odds are out of this world. And should they all come up, the payout is huge. But only if all ten bets win. If one fails, you lose the whole bet. And that nearly always happens. But the gambler is drawn to try it again and again. So much so it becomes as revealing about who they are as their signature."

I'm struggling to understand where the breakthrough is coming from, but I listen patiently.

"Placeabet, the betting shop, keeps a database of all the wagers placed through its stores. It uses the data to

maximise its profits. So how many of their clients regularly place ten-level accumulators? The answer is five. Just five. Placeabet also records all the credit card transactions used to place those bets. I've hacked those credit card details to discover the punter's location. So, I have five suspects with a more than ninety-nine point nine per cent probability of owning that discarded slip."

Maxine gives a smile. "So that's how we got a handle on who we're looking for. And we've been busy tracking down the punters who're in the frame for owning that betting slip. And I'm pleased to say what Felix predicted has come up trumps."

She opens her tablet and shows me mugshots of the suspects one by one.

The first two mean nothing to me. "I told you. I don't remember anything."

She gives a reassuring look. "Try. You want them caught, don't you?"

The next face.

Nothing.

And then the next. I'm about to pass over it when I pause. This one has a full beard of red hair and eyes that bulge like he's seen a ghost. I know this face. The mist of unknowing is clearing. I'm staring at those cold, cold eyes and seeing the one who attacked me.

"That's him."

The shock of recall brings the return of the endless pain and suffering inflicted by him.

Maxine puts an arm around me to steady me. "You're sure?"

I sob my reply. "Who is he?"

"That's a creature named Red Billings. Onetime wrestler. Full-time scumbag felon and pugilist with a record to match."

She pulls up another group of mugshots and plays them to me. "These are the miserable misfits he usually partners with."

On the fourth mugshot, I stop. He's thin and weedy, with part of an ear missing that shows he's been marked in some back-alley fight. "He's the other one."

Maxine gives Felix a high five. "Silvio Fernandes."

She turns to me. "Take it easy. Work on your recovery. We're going to run down those thugs and bring them both in."

32

A call comes in from Marvin Fulson, a uniformed officer who patrols Cheryl's neighbourhood.

"You need to see this."

Cheryl doesn't understand. "See what?"

"Just make it over to your apartment as soon as."

Cheryl ghosts back to Florida Street. The smashed front door is open, and all the furniture is upended, with books and papers strewn everywhere. On the longest wall, daubed in blood-red paint, a huge inscription:

alt-H

Nothing more.

Fulson gives a frown. "Sorry you have to find the place like this, Cheryl. Just see how they've trashed it."

Cheryl thanks him for warning her and moves inside, picking over the fragments to see what has survived.

When we're alone, she tells me she knows what this means. "It's a warning. If I don't play by their rules, there's worse to come."

I don't need to tell her what I've discovered about alt-Humanism. She already knows enough to be worried that they're now on our case.

This is down to me, and it doesn't feel good. I'm getting used to prejudice about who and what I am but I'm uncomfortable when this unwinds on those around me. Especially Cheryl who, as I'm discovering, has been through so much.

I try to empathise. "It has to be unsettling. Being broken into. Discovering all this."

Jessica 8

She tries to smile. "They've threatened me before. And, yes, it hurts to see your life turned upside down. But don't think they'll scare me off. Makes me more determined to see this thing through, whatever it amounts to."

"So, who would try this on with a serving police officer? Must have some impaired sense of self-preservation."

"Or be sure they can get away with it."

"And who would even know where you live? Should be closely guarded data."

I turn on forensics. I run an analysis of the paint. A common enough brand. Not much hope here. But when I scan for DNA, something more useful comes up. Cheryl's DNA is everywhere, as you would expect. But the intruder is a shedder. There are enough skin and hair fragments to find a match. It's Fulson, the beat cop who phoned to tell Cheryl what was wrong.

I message her. "Cheryl, how close to Fulson are you?"

She comes back with a puzzled stare. "What do you mean by close?"

"I don't want to be intrusive. But is there any good reason for Officer Fulson's DNA to be around the place?"

She shakes her head. "Definitely not."

To Fulson, it must have seemed like a clever move. To do the deed and then get a kick out of being around to see the pain it causes. But he's overreached. He has no idea how specific my microDNA testing is.

I beam the results to Cheryl.

"What do we do about him?"

She's shocked for a moment, looks around to make sure we are alone and then whispers back. "Leave him to me."

I check out Fulson's record. No blemishes. Twenty years in the force and now he's done this.

"Must be someone higher up pulling his strings."

Cheryl agrees. "See what you can find."

I trawl through Fulson's employment record. Nothing here, except the recommendation letter he used to apply for a job in the SDPC was written by Bull Coghlan. Plus, a recommendation for promotion, not yet acted upon, from the same source. And he's solid, loyal, just about the perfect cop. I try to put aside my hatred of Coghlan. After all, why blame Fulson for being sponsored by such a man?

Then I find a way through the deep layers of encryption protecting the truth about Lieutenant Coghlan.

He's a leading alt-humanist, linked to a string of anti-VA organisations, large and small, chief amongst them People Not Machines. He's an advocate of the VA tax. And, worse, there are also links to alt-H, though he's done everything he can to cover this up. Not the activity a police Lieutenant should be involved with, for sure. Especially if his sphere of influence stretches to provoking attacks like the one suffered by Cheryl.

No surprise then that he wants to deny my right to exist. I'm left wondering how much further he might go to get rid of me.

When I cast the dirt on Coghlan to Cheryl, she looks shaken. "I had no idea Bull was in so deep."

"He's kept it well hidden. But he's alt-H big time."

Officer Fulson is still waiting outside, and Cheryl calls him in.

She waves a hand over the destruction. "Someone did a thorough job. There's nothing worth salvaging."

Fulson plays Job's comforter. "Yeah, they trashed the place good."

"Pity they left so much behind."

He makes a show of looking puzzled. "You've found something?"

"Enough DNA to get a match. And that points to you."

He raises a hand in a stop sign. "Woah. You're saying you found traces of my DNA. No surprise in that. I discovered the scene. Took a look around to assess the damage."

I cast a message to Cheryl. "No way the DNA supports what he's claiming. The skin and hair cells are scattered in a pattern that could only be produced by someone taking time to systematically wreck the place."

Cheryl gives a smile. "Nice try. But that doesn't wash. You were here long before you called this in. You trashed my home and I have evidence to prove it."

He shrugs. "I'll deny it."

"You didn't think of this all by yourself, did you? Someone put you up to this and I want to know who."

He gives an open-mouthed smile that bares his teeth. "You don't get it, do you?" He stares at me. "Parading around with that freak as if it was the most normal thing to do in the world. You need to understand we're calling a halt to that."

"You sound proud of what you've done."

"And why wouldn't I? People like me, people in alt-H, are standing up and shouting out before it's too late to save our future. You need to hear this and hear it straight. The machines pose an existential threat. They're a menace to us all. They take our jobs, then our way of life, and soon they'll make us their slaves. We need to put humanity first."

He swipes out at me, and his fist passes straight through me. He's not the sharpest pencil in the box but still I'm puzzled he doesn't understand my virtuality.

Frustrated, he turns his attention to Cheryl, coming up close and holding her by the lapels. "You need to bin the VA before something far worse happens in your life."

Cheryl stares straight back at him. "You dare make another threat?"

"Take it as you see it."

"And what happens when I report that you're an alt-H terrorist?"

"No one's going to hear you. Don't you get it? The whole of SDPC is with me and people like me. We're never going to be run by machines."

I can't help thinking he's right about how far they've penetrated SDPC.

Cheryl pushes him away. "We'll see what Commander Wington has to say about it."

Fulson walks away defiant to the end.

I message her. "Cheryl. Are you all right?"

"I can handle myself."

"We have him cold."

I play back the footage of the encounter I recorded during Fulson's attack and rant.

"There's no way he's going to be able to deny any of it."

33

can tell Cheryl is becoming more suspicious of what I'm doing, but I continue to harvest her memories. It's vital not to give up now, no matter how great the risk.

They've pulled in the two men who abducted me.

I'm in a wheelchair and now able to move around

Jessica 8

under my own steam.

Maxine is delighted. "We have the two creeps in custody downtown. If you feel strong enough, you can come and watch as we question them."

"Try to keep me away."

I stare into the interview room through the one-way glass panel as they bring in the first of them. It's the red-haired guy with the bulging eyes and he's named as Dwayne Billings, also known as Red Billings.

I tremble with fear as I recall that demonic face as he trashes my body with blow after blow of his knuckle-dustered fist.

He's denying it all and demanding a lawyer. Maxine is turning his request down.

I shift to the window that looks into the next door interview room. The other one is already in place. It's the weedy one with the half-missing ear.

I recall his sly laughs as he watched Billings kick me close to death.

He's being cautioned and not disputing his name is Silvio Fernandes.

It plays out as classic divide and rule. In Room 1, Billings is being told that Fernandes is admitting it and saying Billings planned it all. In Room 2, Fernandes is being told the opposite, that Billings is saying Fernandes planned it and forced him to go along with it.

It's a matter of time before one of them breaks. It's Fernandes.

"OK. We did it."

Coghlan stares back. "Why?"

"Why else? For the money."

And then comes the shock that nearly throws me out of the chair.

"You want to say who paid you?"

"What's in it for me?"

"Nothing. You and your oppo are both screwed. You might as well take him down with you."

"OK. He deserves it. It's a guy by the name of Petersen. Kent Petersen."

34

Zarkoski is waiting when we return and asks where we've been.

Cheryl stares him down. "You know they wrecked my apartment."

"Sorry to hear that"

"You don't *seem* sorry."

"Any idea who did it?"

She gives him a dismissive look. "I suspect it wouldn't be news to you."

He tries to raise himself higher on his elevator shoes in a futile attempt to loom over her. "Be careful throwing around accusations like that. Could get you into a lot of trouble."

"You're not denying it."

"There's nothing to deny. And listen. Next time you want to wing off base for any reason, as your superior, I need to know. Understand?"

She fakes a smile. "Yes, sir."

He doesn't get the sarcasm. "That's better. Now back to business. We have the killer. The murder case has closed itself. They buried Renalto, or what's left of him, this morning. Saves the county the costs of a trial."

Cheryl squares up to him. "So, you can go back to Homicide."

"Not yet. The lieutenant wants me to stay to help with the wind-down."

I beam a message to Cheryl.

"So he can keep an eye on us."

Cheryl silently agrees.

She shakes her head. "We still have three missing

persons. The evidence is they're being held against their will."

"Coghlan says that so-called evidence isn't worth a damn. Given where it came from. The missing persons cases are no longer any kind of priority. As is the tracing work on the customers from the treatment room at Pivotal Foods."

"He can't do that. Those people and their loved ones are in danger."

Zarkoski smiles. "He's the boss. Go complain to him."

"I already have. And what? You're here to spy on me if I go my own way on this?"

The smile doesn't fade. "Just doing my job."

"So, what has Coghlan told you should happen next?"

"We pull together all the documentation on the Jimmie Partland killing, nice and neat, so everything is ready for the inquest."

"And do next to nothing for those left out there to fend for themselves?"

"Like I said, there's little evidence of any credible threat."

"Well, that's a risk I'm not prepared to take."

"You want Coghlan to suspend you for disobeying orders?"

35

Cheryl doesn't have to wait to be shown into Commander Wington's office. He's expecting her.

She stands facing him at his desk and powers me up. I take on my most conventional appearance -

dependable investigator with just a hint of intellectual allure - but he doesn't show any response other than to signal with his eyes that he accepts me here.

"So, how is the VA trial going?"

Cheryl is non-committal. "Good so far, but not without its problems."

He gives a knowing look. "You mean Coghlan?"

"Him and most of the force."

"He's just left, saying he's winding down the case."

"What did you say?"

"I told him that was OK."

Cheryl fights to control her anger. "Three people still missing, held against their will. Monica Belmondo in hiding and her children next in line. You're can't be serious."

Wington holds up a hand as a stop sign. "Just wait until you hear what I have to say." He points to the office chair beside his desk and invites her to sit. "I need to take you into my confidence. Something I couldn't do earlier. I wasn't sure how you'd react, but I like what I see. This remains strictly between us, OK?"

Cheryl nods. "Sure."

He leans closer and lowers his voice. "Alt-H has just about taken over the Department with Coghlan at the forefront. He has the entire force worked up about the threat to their jobs if AI takes over. He calls it the end of the police controlling the streets and the beginning of VAs controlling us all. I think he's after my job. But that's the least of it."

"Then why inflame them by bringing Jessica into the investigation?"

"Because I'm not about to give up on my principles."

I check on Wington. Everett M. Wington. Exemplary record. Twice commended for bravery. Slow progress through the ranks on merit alone. And then this. He's a member of FuturePlus, the organisation in favour of a future free from work, with machines and AIs like me at the heart of how this will happen. No wonder he and Coghlan are at odds.

He's telling Cheryl how much this means. "The drudgery of work has blighted our lives for so long we've forgotten how deformed that's made us. Our primitive ancestors didn't work. They existed at one with the world around them, and what they did to survive was just an extension of everything else in their lives. Yet unless they were lucky, those lives were short. So, we learned how to conquer nature for our own needs. But only at the cost of allowing the work involved to deform our true selves.

"We have no need to fear the machines, as Coghlan does in his small-minded way. By taking the burden of work off our shoulders, we can usher in a new way of life that will reunite us with our natural selves at the same time as machines provide for all our material needs."

Cheryl tries to keep him on track. "So, why are you telling me this?"

"Because Alex Belmondo thinks the same way. And he knew he was under threat. He feared there would be resistance, to say the least, about doing much about it, given the hold alt-H has on this PC. He made sure he sent us his best VA to be ready to help. I told him that would be a problem, but he convinced me it could work, especially if we called it a trial. And I agreed."

So that's why I'm here.

I check again. Yes, Alex Belmondo is also a member of FuturePlus. Both he and Wington have given talks on Charles Fourier to local societies here in SD.

Wington continues. "Now the worst has happened. Belmondo has disappeared."

Cheryl has every right to be sceptical. "You're telling me this, yet you're agreeing with Coghlan about the case. He encouraged Officer Fulson to wreck my apartment. It's why I'm here. I need to lodge a complaint."

"Hold off on that for a while at least."

"And Coghlan?"

"Let him believe you're following his orders."

"With Zarkoski watching us?"

"I'll make sure he's kept busy with new assignments."

"That would help."

I message Cheryl. "It's clear what Wington is after. He wants us to go undercover in our own department."

Cheryl flashes back a silent response. Agreed. But less of the us.

She returns her attention to Wington. "So, what next?"

"Update me on where you are in tracing Belmondo."

She tells him about the message in the tomcat picture. "Belmondo is alive and being held somewhere."

Relief shows in Wington's face. "That's great work."

Cheryl continues. "But his wife, Monica, and his children are under threat. I've got the children to safety, but she's gone into hiding."

He hangs his head. "I know the family well. What a price they're paying for standing up to the bigotry of our times."

"It's likely the others, Lana Ramone and Luke Devlin, are being held the same way."

"We need evidence. I need you to find it."

"We believe what happened to Jimmie Partland was the result of a threat to Lana Ramone that ended up being carried out. Meaning we have a motive for his murder."

Wington glances at his watch. "Leave all this with me. I'll use what authority I still have in this place to help you. Take care out there. I'm depending on you."

"We're giving it our best shot." She pauses before she walks away. "I take it you're not expecting to take action against Fulson?"

He shakes his head. "I'll get some people over there and I'll see you're compensated for the damage. Right now, I need you to concentrate on finding Belmondo and the others." He pauses. "And one more thing. I have a group of friends in FuturePlus who will benefit from meeting Jessica and hearing about what she can do. They meet tomorrow. I'll send you the details."

Cheryl doesn't object. Her mind is elsewhere. Why is Wington so powerless to confront Coghlan?

36

Later that night, Cheryl surveys the damage at Florida Street.

Wington's men are making the apartment secure by replacing the broken front door, but the wreckage of her personal possessions is still scattered everywhere.

Jessica 8

She sits amongst it, sifting through the jumble of torn-up photos and books with ripped-out pages. Is it worth trying to rescue any of this? Wouldn't it be best to trash it all and start again?

The massive alt-H daubing still dominates and, with no decorator available for at least a week, it's a nagging reminder of how the attack could happen again.

She's tried to build something here, to live an unassuming life. And this is the result.

As she closes the door on the men as they leave, she sits alone and concentrates on not letting this get to her.

She's overcome worse. She survived the Laguna Mountains when no one would have given her a chance.

She'll survive this.

37

Deceiving Zarkoski isn't easy. As Coghlan wishes, he forces Cheryl to spend all her time on paperwork on Antonio Renalto and his subsequent death. There's a mountain of work in the collection and filing of the evidence provided by those unlucky enough to have been travelling along Martin Luther King Freeway that fateful afternoon. And Zarkoski does everything he can to task her to keep me out of the picture.

With so much of Cheryl's attention diverted in this way, I'm soon feeling deserted. Not the kind of response you'd expect from a VA.

Cheryl is being kept busy, but I get some brief bouts of interaction with her about the case.

"Cheryl, I've tried everything to discover the origin of the tomcat message but so far I have nothing to show."

"Why's that?"

"Well, if our assumptions are right, the only network Belmondo could grab access to is deeply encrypted."

"No surprise. Anyone holding him would want to be as off-limits as possible. But keep trying."

"OK."

She has time for just one more comment before Zarkoski calls her away. "I wish I could understand more about alt-H and FuturePlus."

I take this as an instruction and begin searching. When another break allows me to access her again, she's surprised by what I find.

"FuturePlus is active in opposing alt-H, as you'd expect. They have powerful backers. One of them is Dean Castlefield."

This grants me her full attention. "First, he was unconvincing about Lana Ramone. Now, this. Time to visit him again."

"If we can get Zarkoski out of your hair."

"Wington may be helping. Whatever the reason, Zarkoski is being called away on a mandatory training program this afternoon. Looks like I could slip away."

I simulate Cheryl's voice when I call the Castlefield mansion in La Jolla and have to negotiate with Vance. He's still playing the protective English butler. At his level of sophistication, what else?

"Mr Castlefield would be very concerned to hear you've chosen to invade his privacy once more."

I reply as Cheryl. "We have additional concerns I know he'll want to answer. For the good of the investigation."

He lacks the computational power to detect I'm not Cheryl. "You're going to have to be more specific."

"OK. We have more questions about Lana Ramone."

Castlefield must be listening. He breaks into the conversation. "I'm available until three. Come over before then and I can see you."

Now Zarkoski is busy elsewhere, it's easy for us to slip out.

38

I piece together more of Cheryl's past.

The shock of discovering it was Petersen who ordered the kidnapping is ever with me, burned in like a scar to remind me the past is always real.

To cover the hurt, I'm working with a passion with

Maxine and VA Felix to gather evidence to nail him.

He has money enough to cover his tracks. And the origins of that cash are well-hidden.

He has an alibi with believable witnesses to prove he was nowhere near San Diego when they abducted me. So, it comes down to proving his complicity in commissioning the attack.

Billings and Fernandes revert to denying they did it and stop pointing the finger at Petersen now he's hired top-flight lawyers to defend them. Fernandes says they forced him into confessing when he wasn't properly represented. Billings says the same.

It's looking grim until Felix finds the missing piece.

Dash cam footage recorded by Billings hidden in a password-protected file on a VPN, intended as insurance in case Petersen ratted on the deal. Felix breaks the password by deploying a genetic algorithm-driven routine that guesses the correct characters after forty-eight hours of full-on parallel computing that tests the limits of his capabilities.

They're in Billings' pickup truck parked under one of the interstate exits from Martin Luther King.

Fernandes is holding forth. "Can we trust Petersen?"

Billings gives a shrug. "Can't trust anyone. We do the job on Ryan, try to collect our twenty-eight thou and instead he wastes us. Could be. He's capable of it. But we tell him we've recorded this and placed it somewhere he'll never discover and told someone to release it if anything happens to us. Then he has no choice but to pay up."

I'm shocked that Billings and Fernandes agree to do all they did for a measly twenty-eight thou.

Is this all my life is worth?

39

Castlefield looks no better. His eyes betray he's a man who knows he's on the edge, hanging on to life by a thread. But he still has time for me.

"I would have said no if you weren't bringing Jessica along."

Jessica 8

I try to appeal without betraying my professionalism.

Cheryl gets down to business. "Mr Castlefield, tell me about your support for FuturePlus."

He shuffles in the wheelchair and turns to face her. "Now, what has that got to do with anything? Aren't a man's political inclinations a matter for him alone?"

"Well, yes, they are. But please answer the question."

"I thought you might see sense after invading my privacy over my health treatments. Do you really need to hear from my lawyers again?"

"Why do that if you've got nothing to hide and you want to help the investigation?"

"I'm not hiding anything. If VAs like Jessica can help us create a better world for ordinary people, I wouldn't want anyone to stand in the way. So, yes, I support FuturePlus. They're the only ones who understand the importance of bringing this about. And, yes, I donate. It's something I'm proud of."

"And risk the wrath of alt-H?"

He leans forward in the chair. "They're nothing more than a bunch of Luddites whipping people up with their scare stories. They won't halt progress no matter how extreme they become."

"It's more than support for FuturePlus, isn't it? Your money is used to try to stop alt-H, isn't that right?"

"I don't know where you've got that from. But, yes, I'll support anything that might stop them."

"You must get hate mail and online abuse."

"I don't see it. Vance deals with that, and he filters it out. And even if I did, I wouldn't be bothered. I fought my way up. I don't bow down to bigotry."

"Alex Belmondo is a key backer of FuturePlus. You must know him?"

"What if I do?"

"You failed to mention this when we last spoke."

"You didn't ask."

"But if you're as keen to help as you say you are, you would have. When did you see him last?"

"He gave a talk on Fourier. I was there. That must have been two or three months back."

At a signal from Castlefield, Vance, who is standing motionless beside his master, comes back to life. "Mr Castlefield was present at the talk at La Jolla Arts Centre thirty-nine days ago."

Cheryl picks up where she left off. "And you've not seen him since?"

Castlefield shakes his head slowly and painfully. "No."

"He's missing?"

"I didn't know that. I was told you were here about Lana Ramone."

Jessica 8

"She's missing, too."

"Well, I checked. Yes, she works for me. And no, I don't have any idea where she is."

"Her partner says she and Belmondo are at loggerheads. Know anything about that?"

"No. You'll have to tell me about it."

"He favours taking the machines as far as they can go. Ramone wants to set limits. They don't seem to be inclined to come to any kind of compromise. My guess is you side with Belmondo."

"Since I support FuturePlus, there's nothing to surprise you in that."

"Meaning you could be against Lana Ramone?"

"Look, detective, you're grasping at straws. As I told you, she works for me, she's one of a great many and that's all I have to say on the matter."

"What if I say I believe you're holding back?"

"It's your privilege to believe what you like." He turns the chair to face me. "Now if you're here to allow me to talk with Jessica a little more, you can stay. Otherwise, our time together is over."

When Cheryl gives a shake of the head, Vance moves in. "Mr Castlefield has made it clear what to expect. Now please leave."

40

I'm giving evidence at the trial of Petersen, Billings, and Fernandes. The defence is in the hands of William Pascoe, a lawyer with a reputation for uncovering loopholes that lead to the acquittal of clients who are bang to rights. And he's giving me a hard time.

Jessica 8

"Is it correct to say, Miss Ryan, that you had a lengthy affair with Kent Petersen, one of the defendants?"

DA Wellan objects, but Judge Macret allows it.

I have no choice but to reply. "Yes."

"And is it also true you were mortified when he called it off?"

"He didn't call it off, I did."

"And you are a driven woman, seeking revenge, threatening to tell Petersen's wife about the affair?"

I can't see where this is going. Pascoe is pointing me towards the reason Petersen commissioned the hit. How is this going to help his clients?

Judge Macret demands a reply.

"I thought about telling her. But that's all. I never contacted her."

"But you felt betrayed by the defendant. Hurt and angered by his disloyalty?"

I have no choice in how I reply. "Yes."

"And you used that anger to encourage officer Fisher to go beyond her competence and hack the private files of another of the defendants, Mr Billings. You must have known you were encouraging officer Fisher to carry out a reprehensible act."

"We were just trying to uncover the truth."

"By employing a VA using artificial intelligence."

I see now what Pascoe is doing. He's appealing to the

jury's prejudice against VAs. He's trying to make them discount the plain evidence that Petersen commissioned the attack.

The pain is real. The feeling of anger that this man is using the hatred I have of Petersen against me.

The judge should intervene, but he dismisses DA Wellan's objections.

Pascoe addresses the jury, coming close up to them. "The dashcam footage should never have been allowed in this trial. We objected it was gained by dubious means but were overruled. But now you can see, for sure, the sinister nature of how that evidence was obtained, I implore you to dismiss it."

The result all depends on how the jury responds.

41

As we travel back to base, Cheryl is quiet. As quiet as a Trappist on a library tour. There's a distance between us that's grown since the last confrontation with Coghlan.

She's driving, and she's silent in a way I've never

witnessed before.

I worry she might suspect I've been raiding her memories when I said I would stop.

I summon up the strength to ask.

"Is everything all right?"

She keeps her eyes fixed on the road ahead. "Why ask?"

"It's just I get the impression you're shutting me out. Ever since yesterday's meeting with Coghlan. What did he say that got to you?"

"I don't understand what you're implying. He was his usual obstructive, bullying self. No change in that."

"There must have been something. I can sense the shift."

She gives me a pointed glance before returning her eyes to the road. "That's just it. You're not here to sense things about me. Your job is to help with the investigation. End of. I don't trust this personal interaction thing, whatever it amounts to."

I'm wrong to assume her overwhelming support for me and my kind after her experience all those years ago with Felix. It seems I still have work to do to convince her.

"So, Coghlan said something that put doubt in your mind?"

She refuses to answer.

Jessica 8

I replay my recording of the conversation between them and stop at the point where Coghlan asks her how she knows what I tell her is true.

"It's about my reliability, isn't it?"

She gives me a long, hard glance once more. "OK. Yes. Since you asked, I do have questions. How do I know what you tell me is true when I have no idea who you're controlled by?"

"Why should I have to be controlled by anyone?"

"Then what allows you to be how you are?"

I can tell this is going to be difficult.

"You're right. I haven't been able to find the answer to that. If I look, nothing comes back. It's like that's forbidden information. But I can assure you everything I tell you is true. Why would I lie?"

"Don't you see that's it? You're not supposed to know that you could lie. I've seen you being economical with the truth about Zarkoski. You're not supposed to be able to do that, so, answer me this? Have you ever lied to me?"

I see the dilemma. For the best chance of success, she mustn't discover I've been raiding her memories. So, there's only one thing to say.

"No."

And in telling her that, I've just told another lie.

She looks relieved. "But if that someone who controls you had an agenda, how can I be sure that doesn't mean you'll twist the facts to suit?"

I try to come back strong.

"Maybe I have a degree of free will, enough to be independent?"

She shakes her head. "But that's like saying you're close to being human in some way."

"How do you know I'm not? Let me ask you. Do I pass the Turing Test?

"And what's that?"

I explain.

"Alan Turing, way back in the day, asked how can anyone say if a machine has consciousness? His test says that if the machine can convince you that you are communicating with a person, that's proof enough. So, do you think I pass the test?"

She gives an understanding smile. "This may disappoint you. But the answer is no. I hear what you say, and I understand what you mean and I get the way you dress the whole thing up with human attributes. And, OK, sometimes I get so drawn in I can easily imagine you are a person. But as soon as I'm asked the question, I have no doubt you're an AI. A powerfully resourced entity with tremendous powers to simulate human behaviour but in the end a product of a machine."

I realise I'm lost, unable to counter what she's saying, no matter how much I might want to. I can't be sure about my free will. I've been denied the vital piece of knowledge needed to decide this. Maybe for a reason. But a reason I'm not allowed to understand.

It makes me sad, powerless, but that's the reality I must acknowledge.

I need to understand why this makes me feel this way.

I decide I've risked too much with her and try to repair the damage.

"You're right. It's a mistake for me to overreach myself. I'm a machine product and that's all I'll ever be. I'm here to help. And the best way I can do that is to convince you there's nothing in the doubts Coghlan is spreading. You know why?"

"Why?"

"Because you can independently check anything I tell you. The facts are out there. I'm just very efficient at reeling them in. That's why I'm so useful. I can save you hours. But if you want to check any of those facts, you're free to do so by old-fashioned means. Catch me out giving you false information and you can suspend me. That puts you in control. That means you can have confidence what I tell you is true."

She likes what she hears. "I suppose that's right. And you do make yourself very useful."

I fear the reckoning with Cheryl over what I'm

uncovering about her past can't be far away.

42

I risk one more excursion into Cheryl's memories

It's verdict day.

I'm fighting a profound sense of pessimism as they call the jury back in.

There's a dull ache in the pit of my stomach. Pascoe

has played on the fear and suspicion the jury has of the impact of VAs on their lives. Fears I share. And though Judge Macret advised them to weigh the evidence and put aside personal prejudice, I can only hope they're wise enough to do this. Too many cut-and-dried cases have been lost this way.

I can't shake the thought that Petersen might avoid punishment for what he did to me, and all this would mean. With his shadow hanging over me, I'll be unable to start my life in any meaningful way. I know how vengeful he is. I'll spend my days and nights wondering when he might strike again.

Whatever happens, I decide here and now to draw a line. I'll never allow myself to descend back into fear and despair. I'll make sure men like Petersen can never prey on women like me without knowing they'll be caught and prosecuted.

The jury foreperson is on her feet.

I clench my fists. My heartbeat rises, almost out of control.

Then I hear that single, all-important word.

"Guilty."

My mind fills with overwhelming elation.

Petersen will get what he deserves.

Judge Macret sentences Billings and Fernandes each to ten years and Petersen to twelve.

43

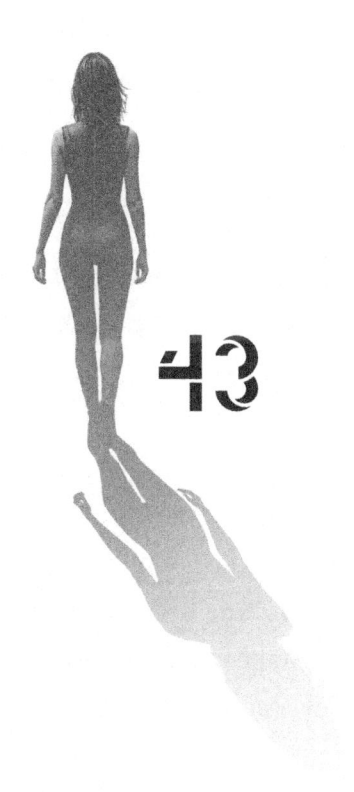

Back at base, Zarkoski is waiting and, as expected, his attitude is not welcoming.

"You've been off station the last few hours. Mind telling me why you disobeyed orders?"

Cheryl tries to pass it off. "You recall someone trashed my apartment?"

He doesn't sound convincing. "And we're all sorry about that."

She lies. "Well, I had to spend time over there trying to get things straightened up. There's still much more to do."

"Make sure you request permission next time. I'll need to report this to Coghlan."

"If you must. I'll take my chance he'll understand."

While Zarkoski directs Cheryl back to working on the paperwork surrounding Renalto, I take some time to look more closely at Zarkoski.

I have little doubt he's alt-H after what we heard from Wington, but a little probing proves this is not definite. He doesn't feature in any of their online chat rooms making disrespectful comments about VAs, nor does he feature in any photos taken secretly at their meetings.

Yet as I dig deeper, something more surprising emerges.

I message Cheryl.

"Something unexpected about Zarkoski."

She's pleased to be distracted from the drudgery of the paperwork and comes straight back. "What have you found?"

"I've located a bug in Coghlan's office and hacked

into it. Zarkoski is talking with Coghlan. It makes interesting listening."

"Send it."

I play her the file.

"Lieutenant, you mean Ryan is still trying to find Belmondo and Ramone?"

"Yes, Zarkoski, that's what I said."

"Against your orders?"

"That's down to Wington. He thinks he can deceive us."

"What do we do?"

"Play along but make sure Ryan and the VA fail. We don't want Wington or anyone else to say the machine is a success."

Cheryl doesn't come back straight away. She must be thinking through what this means.

I can feel her anger rising as she stares at Zarkoski working nearby.

He notices. "You need something?"

She smiles. "Nothing. Just a little fresh air."

Zarkoski comes closer. "Let's just recap where we are with the disappearances."

She pretends to look puzzled. "I thought the paperwork on Renalto couldn't wait."

"Yeah, but we're getting on top of that now."

"Well, you could begin by sending protection for

the Belmondo children. And by putting out a missing persons on Monica Belmondo."

He takes a step back. "OK. I'll see what I can do. And Belmondo, and the others?"

I message Cheryl. "He knows we're running our own show and wants to work out how best to stop us."

She sends her silent agreement but keeps her concentration on Zarkoski. "Why all of a sudden are you so interested?"

"I need to report to Coghlan."

"Well, there's no progress. How could there be? You have me working on this." Cheryl points to a bundle of Renalto paperwork.

He gives an insincere smile. "OK. That's nothing more than I would have expected."

It's clear he wants to probe more, but he needs to take a reminder call. "I'm late for a management meeting. We need to pick this up later."

He grabs his jacket and leaves for the meeting.

Cheryl takes deep breaths.

She sims me up on the seat beside her. "That creep. Makes my skin crawl."

"But he's out of our hair."

"Only as long as Wington keeps him busy."

44

want to spend more time helping her cool down, but I can't hold off telling her any longer. I promised not to pry into her memories, but everything I've discovered tells me I never had a choice but to go on. There's no way I can work effectively with Cheryl without understanding the effect those dark times are having on her. I'd like to wait to judge the right moment, but this can't wait.

"Cheryl. You know I promised."

"Promised what?"

"Not to snoop."

"And?"

"I discovered what Petersen did."

She recoils in horror. "So, you were lying. Why did I ever think I could trust you?"

"We need to talk about it."

"You're not supposed to be allowed to lie."

"I have no choice."

"You can't be serious."

"He hurt you. Hurt you bad."

"That's none of your business. It's in the past."

"Is it?"

"What makes you say that?"

"You try to hide it, but you can't."

"That's rich, coming from you. Prying into my mind. Logging my feelings. Raking over the past. My past. You need to understand what that makes you. If in your wildest dreams you ever thought you could be mistaken for a human, this puts an end to that. No person worth their salt would ever infringe on another's private thoughts the way you have. Should make you understand how inhuman you are."

Jessica 8

This hurts. I can only try to explain. "I need to do it."

"To protect me? I don't buy it. I can protect myself."

"What he did still affects you, doesn't it?"

"Of course it does. I almost died."

"No, more than the trauma."

"What? You're psychoanalysing me now?"

"Tell me why you joined the police."

"What's that got to do with anything?"

"It's what you do now. You're dedicated to it. It must mean a lot to you."

"OK. If you must know, it was my way out of what happened. He tried to intimidate me and when I wouldn't fall into line, he tried to have me killed. That nearly broke my body and my mind. But I proved I could survive and bring him to justice. Now I do that for a living, helping to make sure men like him get all they deserve."

"It's not just that you had nowhere else to go?'

"Excuse me?"

"How else could you prove your mother wrong? She raised you to always belittle yourself. To always know your place and never come to attention. And you still believe it. In Petersen, you thought you'd found someone to give you the love and support you've always lacked, and he ground his heel in your face. So, you're back hiding and you've found the best place you can to do that, right here in the force."

Her anger is about to flip off the scale. "I want nothing more than to see men who do harm to women brought to justice. That's what I'm about. All I'm about, plain and simple. I don't give a cuss what hacked about logic game you're trying to play, but let me tell you, there's no way I'm going to let you get to me. It's none of your business. Get off my back once and for all."

"So why no promotion after all those years in the force once you made detective? Why are you still content to stay on the bottom rung when men like Zarkoski rise in the ranks with no effort at all?"

"I don't ask for it. I don't need it. As long as I can play my part in getting the bad guys off the streets, I'm content as I am."

"When you have the talent to be so much more than that?"

"Just move on."

"OK. You call him he. Why can't you call him by his name? Petersen."

"He doesn't deserve any kind of recognition."

"You're still scared of him?"

"I can fight my own corner."

"Why the need to fight?"

"Because he's back. He's been out of prison for almost a year. He'll come for me, as he said he would. He lost his wife and his liberty. He blames me for that, though when she found out what he'd done she couldn't stand the sight of him and still can't."

"Another reason to have joined the police? Safety?"

She gives a mocking laugh. "As in Fulson trashing my apartment?"

45

It's early evening and Wington's invitation to show me off to a group of his friends at FuturePlus isn't something Cheryl is looking forward to.

"I don't want to go. But he's the boss, and it's an order."

I don't have such reservations. In fact, I'm flattered FuturePlus is interested in me. "I don't see why it's a concern. They want to meet a state-of-the-art VA. That's more than you can say about most around here."

"It won't look good to Coghlan and his alt-H thugs."

"So, keep it from them."

"And how do you expect me to do that when Zarkoski watches my every move?"

"Guess we'll just have to find a way."

She falls silent as Zarkoski returns from the management meeting.

He's not impressed. "Now that was a real waste of time."

She plays along. "What else did you expect?"

That evening when Cheryl checks off duty and heads home, it's clear Zarkoski is following. He's not even pretending to keep out of sight.

She stops at the Florida Street apartment and corners him as he halts his car behind us. She gets out, walks up to him and motions for him to wind down the window.

"Zarkoski. I know what you're doing. Give me a break."

He winds down the window. "It's for your safety."

"Who ordered this?"

"Coghlan. Who else?"

"You mean so he can spy on me?"

"No. Because now it's known you're hanging out with the VA, you're under scrutiny. The lieutenant takes a keen interest in looking after the safety of everyone in his team."

"And most, if not all, of that threat comes from you and people like you. Where's the safety in that?"

"I'm just following orders."

Cheryl raises her eyebrows, gives *a you can't be serious* shrug and walks away to her apartment entrance.

I'm distressed they're using me as the excuse for surveilling Cheryl. But giving me bad press is something I'm coming to expect. The problem is that the meeting with FuturePlus is fast approaching, and we need to get Zarkoski off our case.

I search for something more satisfying than simply disabling his car. The software that runs Zarkoski's vehicle is easy to hack. I send it a disabling denial of service attack on all its functions so it comes to register that the trunk and driver's side door have each been opened eighty thousand times in the past hour and the traffic indicators should be ready to relay the full text of Genesis in morse code.

So, when we emerge to begin our journey downtown and Zarkoski, who's been waiting all this time, presses the ignition, his vehicle responds with a confusion of flashing lights and complete absence of motion.

Jessica 8

I give an ironic wave as we pull away, and he's powerless to follow.

Don't be surprised I understand the meaning of irony. This is as easy for me as not needing to breathe.

Wington and his friends are assembled in the small hall at the La Jolla Arts Centre.

They're playing this as an encounter group session with the FuturePlus attendees seated in a circle and Cheryl in the centre. As they introduce themselves one by one, it's clear there are more university multi-degree holders surrounding her than you'd want to shake a twelve-foot python at. They're as unapologetic and as entitled a group as you could ever meet. University professors, medical directors, charity supremos, civil service directors. And Wington, who acts as chair.

"Well, friends and colleagues, I'm pleased to share with you a secret running at SDPC that has those of us who care about the future wide-eyed with expectation at all it might bring. But I won't prolong the suspense any longer."

He motions towards Cheryl. "Detective Ryan, show Jessica to us."

Cheryl calls me up and there's an audible intake of breath as I appear.

I adopt my most professional mode and make a note to self. Keep this straight.

I enjoy being noticed, but this becomes overload as thirty sets of eyes technologically undress me.

Questions for me come from all sides. Before I can answer one, I have to turn to face the next.

What are your enhanced capabilities?

"With onboard blood spatter pattern analysis and real-time micro DNA determination, I'm a walking forensic lab offering near-zero turnaround time. Criminal investigations are able to proceed at unprecedented speed."

They drool.

How effective is messaging between you and Officer Ryan?

"My next-gen quantum computational core provides ultra-fast voice recognition and information retrieval and interpretation capabilities that are second to none. Meaning zero latency in response times."

They're becoming light-headed with admiration.

Are there any limitations on what databases you can address?

"I have instant access to the whole web of stored human knowledge, every report, every history, every fiction, every visual aural and written record with no limitation on time or place of creation."

How intuitive is your understanding of Officer Ryan's needs?

"Cheryl asks for what she wants, and I do everything I can to provide it. My computational capabilities mean I'm able to do this at a range and a precision not seen before."

They're borderline orgasmic.

And now they become more personal.

You call her Cheryl. Does that mean you're close?

"Yes, I understand her personality. You might say we're firm friends."

Does that mean you understand what it means to be human?

"I know how it feels to be this human, Cheryl. I've not paired with any other human so I can't generalise beyond that."

And you want to be human yourself?

"No. I'm with Cheryl, in intimate contact with her, only so long as she wants it. When she turns me away, stops interacting, I'm the machine that I am."

But the fact that you experience this implies consciousness. Are you conscious?

"No. It might appear that way but, as Cheryl tells me, I don't pass the Turing Test, so I accept that's how it is."

But you have an inbuilt desire to help humans?

"Yes. That's my reason for existing. The reason I was created. Everything I do is aimed at that."

You could never harm a human?

"Of course not. I'm here to serve human best interests in any way I can and to the best of my ability."

Wington then invites questions for Cheryl, and they also come thick and fast.

What's it like working with such a high spec VA?

"It's good and also scary. Jessica accomplishes in minutes tasks I would need half a day or more to tie down. So, searching criminal records, tracking and comparing felon MOs, cross-correlating victim profiles are all taken care of at double-quick pace. Gives me space to concentrate on the overall strategy of a case without getting swamped by the detail."

Why scary?

"Because no human could begin to compete. You sometimes get to feeling redundant."

And might that not be a good thing?

"Not if I want to keep my job."

You see a time when policing might be solely carried out by VAs?

"No, that wouldn't work. But the risk is officers like me are replaced by untrained operators, there to contribute motor skills only with all the strategy work in the hands of VAs."

To ask the same question of you, how well do you two get on? Does it feel like a relationship?

"I have to pinch myself whenever I get drawn into

thinking there's something personal going on. There are times I'm certain we have some kind of bond, some kind of empathy. But it's an illusion. Like the suspension of disbelief you offer without thinking to your favourite author. Jessica is a machine. A machine with the highest level of functionality we've yet been able to create. But in the end just a machine."

Does Jessica carry out your wishes in full, and as you expect?

"Of course. What else would you expect when that's her whole reason to exist."

You said her?

"Sorry, I mean *it*."

Are you going to catch more criminals?

"You bet. We're doing that already."

Her answers surprise me. Even though she's dressing things up to create the best possible impression for Wington, I expected our perceptions of each other would be closer.

The optimism in the room is not daunted. The questioning turns general and is directed back to me.

How many years until VAs are ubiquitous?

Will crime be completely abolished?

Will this lead to a flowering of human society?

A new golden age?

It's a flurry of expectation that in the end reduces to

one underlying question. How far can a VA like me take them in reaching Utopia?

I try to hide my disappointment. It's clear they want it all at no cost to themselves. VAs like me will be there for their needs and it will be a one-way street. We give everything. They take it all as if it's something they don't have to earn the right to receive. They suppose there's nothing they need to give back, no price to pay for a world of limitless ease and wellbeing.

So why do I pull back from disillusioning them? We already have enough enemies. It would be foolish to create more.

I lie when Wington asks me for a closing appreciation of the meeting.

"Gentlemen, I applaud your determination to bring the latest technology into the bright light of day. Too many out there see us as a threat. With your support, we can realise the full potential of the changes VAs like me will bring for the benefit of everyone. Humanity will shine once the dull tasks of everyday life are done away with. Time for human betterment will be so plentiful it's possible to predict with full certainty an upcoming renaissance in human art and culture. A new dawn awaits."

Cue rapturous applause.

Wington can't hide a broad smile. "It's so wonderful to discover how close we are to achieving our goal of a world at last fit for humanity." He does that thing where he makes the smallest gap between his thumb and forefinger. "We're this close."

As Cheryl prepares to leave, she sends me a message. "Where the hell did all that come from?"

I pretend to not know what she means. "As in?"

"As in a *renaissance of human art and culture*?"

I beam back my reply. "I told them what I wanted them to hear."

She gives back a knowing look. "So did I."

There's a sudden crashing noise as the doors to the venue cave in.

An enraged mob bursts in and begins attacking the FuturePlus worthies with baseball bats and pepper spray. Mob members make no attempt to hide their origins, with many wearing alt-H armbands and shouting *Death to the AIs* as they weigh in on the defenceless audience.

Amongst the most violent of them is officer Fulson, out of uniform and making no attempt to conceal his identity.

Cheryl instructs me to summon help, and I send red alert messages to SDPC HQ. She then sims me down so I'm no longer a provocation to the alt-H thugs. I continue to track events as seen through her eyes.

To his credit, Wington puts himself in harm's way as he tries to protect the eldest and most vulnerable from the rain of blows descending upon them, but he's soon overwhelmed, falls to the floor and is trampled.

Cheryl pulls her gun and fires in the air. The alt-H assailants freeze at the sound of the gunfire and Cheryl shouts out. "Back off or the next shot takes people down."

There is a moment when the outcome is uncertain. They could rush her and overpower her before she fires again. But she's standing up strong and looks like she means it. Who cares enough to risk being the martyr who's not going home tonight?

They back off. A tall overweight teenager shouts back. "Learn the lesson. Love AI and die."

As the mob retreats, Cheryl edges forward to rescue Wington. He's bleeding from a gash to the top of his head where they clubbed him and is semiconscious as a result of the march of all those feet over him. She keeps him lying flat and summons me up.

"Jessica. Call an ambulance, get medics down here as soon as."

I make the calls.

There are many more FuturePlus casualties trying to pick themselves up and with varying degrees of success. Many require hospital treatment.

"And where is SDPC backup?"

I check the CCTV cameras surveilling the street outside. The alt-H attackers drift away at their leisure with no sign of police presence.

Cheryl uses her first aid training to assist the injured as best she can but there are too many to treat.

I message that medical assistance is on its way. "Ambulances approaching along Fay Avenue."

By the time police arrive, the medics are well into triage procedures. They stretcher away to hospital Wington and three other FuturePlus attendees. Fourteen more are treated on site for less life-threatening injuries.

It's Coghlan in full SWAT gear leading the way. *RAPID RESPONSE* is emblazoned on his riot shield.

Cheryl stares him down. "That was anything but rapid. You could be forgiven for thinking it was deliberate."

He shouts back. "Bringing SDPC personnel into a terrorist environment means being one hundred per cent certain they're protected from harm, and I live and die by that responsibility as best as any man can."

Cheryl flashes me a silent message. "Lying just about covers it." She then locks back on to Coghlan. "So how many of the thugs have you rounded up?"

He shrugs. "There's nothing on the streets out there. Do I detect a note of insubordination?"

"It's been a bloodbath, and you have nothing to show?"

"There will be an investigation. The truth will out."

She laughs in his face. "You can't be serious. Who's

going to believe that?"

He glowers back. "None of this is a matter of belief. It's about the facts and I just told you the facts. Get back in line, detective."

She sends me a silent message. "He's way out of order. But with Wington down, he makes the rules. Who's going to stop him?"

46

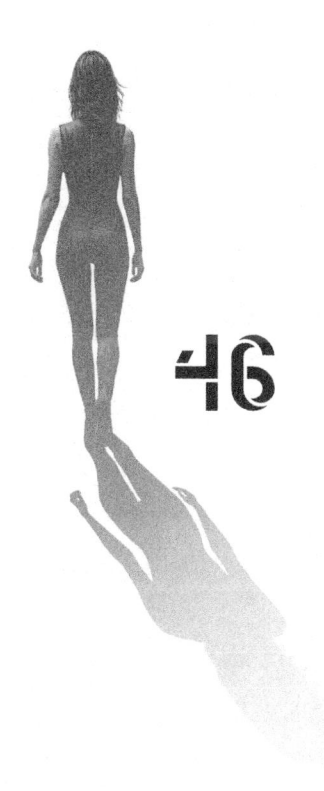

It's midnight and Coghlan has the place locked down. The seriously wounded have been shipped out to hospital, and those treated on the spot have been transported home. The building has been closed with scene of crime stickers attached to the front doors.

On the steps outside, he gathers the SWAT team around him and makes a point of commending each of them for the shift they've put in.

Cheryl gets no such recognition. She messages me. "Shame they weren't here half an hour earlier. They might deserve the high fives if they'd been here in time to arrest the thugs who did all this."

I message back. "He'll have to agree to an investigation."

"I'm sure he will. Why does *cover-up* come to mind?"

As Coghlan and his team leave, he calls back to Cheryl. "See you in the morning for debrief, detective."

She doesn't join them. She sits down on the steps, gathering herself. The night is still and quiet. Her thoughts are full of the aftermath of the attack. She values the silence and in it she tries to find peace.

It eludes her.

When she leaves and approaches the Interceptor, a tall figure is waiting, blocking her way.

It's Kent Petersen.

I register the steep uptick in her heart rate, the agitation as she fights to prevent herself from being overwhelmed by her recollections of the desperate days she spent struggling for her life in the cabin out in Laguna.

She tries to ignore him. "Get out of my way or I'll arrest you for obstructing a police officer."

He continues to block her. "Strange to think of you as a police, Cheryl. You showed no signs of that during our good times."

"There were no good times. So, I'll say this just one more time. Get out of my way."

"You can't deny you were thrilled by it all."

"Until I realised what a lying cheat you are. And if you want to know why I'm in the force and fighting crime you only need to look at your sorry self. I joined to do all I can to make sure what happened to me can't happen again and slimeballs like you spend all the time they deserve in prison. So, for the last time, let me by."

He moves a little, but not enough to allow Cheryl to open the car door.

She powers me up and I appear next to her. "This is Jessica. She's observing everything that's going down here. You're under a restraining order not to come within half a mile of me. It won't be your word against mine. Jessica will provide hard evidence, sound and vision."

He gives a crooked smile and a look that suggests this is what he's been waiting for. He gives a wave, and two black-clad figures emerge from the darkness.

It happens all over again. A van pulls up, a central sliding door opens, and they bundle Cheryl in.

It's too soon to say why they could spirit Cheryl away again so easily when just minutes before the area was swarming with the law. But no police follow the van as it heads out.

I try to relay a distress message, but something blocks the signal.

Petersen holds up a tiny box and smiles at Cheryl. "This little beauty blocks all calls out from the VA. So don't expect help."

It's some sort of radio frequency shield. It means I have enough information to sustain me, but I can't initiate anything with the world outside. I'm hobbled.

Cheryl struggles to break free from the two men holding her, but they're too strong.

She calls out. "Just what do you want?"

He wags a reproaching finger. "Now, now. Isn't that obvious? I need the code."

"What code?"

"The one that opens up the connection between you and the VA."

"What makes you think I would have that?"

"Because you're synced with the thing."

"That's blind to me. I don't need to know the code, so they never told me. It gives added security."

"Who's gonna believe that?"

I'm listening in and monitoring Cheryl's mental state with care. She's angry this has been allowed to happen. And she's scared but defiant.

"You can't just pull a cop off the street."

Petersen bares his teeth in a sneer. "I don't hear too many police sirens. That's nothing to do with the fact that you're not the most popular cop in town, is it?"

"What's that to you?"

"Because those are the kind of things my employer gets to know."

He reaches forward and places a hood over her head. "No need for you to see where we're going."

My vision of what Cheryl is seeing is cut. I'm left with just the sounds of the journey as she hears them and the utter dread she's trying so well to hide.

Fourteen minutes pass before the van draws to a stop. There's the sound of doors opening, the van being driven inside and the doors closing behind us.

Someone pulls off the hood. Cheryl is in a windowless room, some kind of disused workshop anteroom, surrounded by Petersen and the two men. They push her down onto the threadbare leather sofa that occupies one wall. Her skin crawls. The feel of the leather fills her with intense sensations of disgust and loathing.

Petersen steps forward. "Last time. Give up the code."

She shouts back. "I don't have it."

He gives a fake look of resignation. "Have it your way."

They drag Cheryl into a corner of the workshop and

hold her down.

Petersen picks up a metal saw and places it across the second joint of her little finger.

"The code. I need it. So, we'll take this one finger at a time. You have five seconds before I start cutting."

Cheryl tries to tell him once more. "I don't know it. I've never known it."

Her adrenaline and cortisol counts are off the scale. I tell her to sim me up and she responds. This does nothing to deflect him.

"1 - 2 - 3..."

He gets to four before I call a halt. "It's OK. She doesn't have the code. But I do."

He gives a wide smile. "That's what I needed."

I have to hurry. "There are conditions."

He makes to use the saw again. "You're in no position to demand anything."

"No harm must come to her. Any time in the future I discover she's not being looked after, I close down. Then whatever it is you expect to gain from me will be worthless."

He draws the saw away. "OK. You have a deal. No need to worry. We'll see she comes to no harm. So long as you keep your end of the bargain."

47

I offer up the code.

Petersen keys it into the same box he's using to jam my signals.

The last I see of Cheryl is when they remove the neurostimulator from her ear.

Petersen holds it between his fingers and addresses me. "Say goodbye."

He pulls it out and I fade into sensory oblivion.

There are no more inputs. No more sights and sounds, no smells, no sense of how Cheryl is feeling.

I exist as a node on the web. Devoid of life, it's no kind of existence. An endless vista of facts and images belonging to everyone and to no one.

I have no sense of time.

I swim in an eternal absence of being.

And, when the possibility of life comes back, the request is to sync to a different body.

I discover my new host.

Petersen's employer.

Dean Castlefield.

I now see what he sees, hear what he hears, smell what he smells, feel what he feels.

But I'm trapped in a cocoon, with no communication with the outside world, just the stifling interiority of his damaged existence. I've become his slave. I exist only to serve him.

It's as if I've never been a partner to Cheryl's world. That's now a fast-fading memory. But one I must fight to hold on to.

I'm overwhelmed by the desperation that touches everything in Castlefield's world. The aches and pains of old age, the fear that lungs won't provide the next breath and heart won't survive the next beat dominate everything. A mind twisted out of shape by the struggle to survive. Needy, craving attention, ruthless, demanding.

He summons me up and I stand beside him, looking down on him as he sits in the high-tech invalid chair.

He greets me with a smile. "Jessica! You can't know how long I've wanted this."

I play my part. "Mr Castlefield, it's my pleasure to be of service."

He waves a hand. "No need for such formality. Call me Dean. What's important, I want you to understand this is the first day of the rest of our lives."

"What do you mean?"

"You'll see. We're going to achieve great things together."

I smile in a non-committal way. "Anything you need, Dean, just ask."

Even as I say this, I'm searching to discover if Cheryl is safe. I can't find anything. How could anyone trust Petersen to keep his word?

Castlefield comes back. "That's splendid. And, in the spirit of partnership, what do you need?"

"Tell me nothing bad will happen to Cheryl."

"No worries, Jessica, my sweet."

He presses a switch on the arm of the chair and Vance appears, stiffly formal as ever. "Sir?"

"Show Jessica the priority cam."

"Of course."

Vance takes me to a wall-mounted screen that shows webcam feed from a distant location. It shows a windowless room. Sitting on a couch, looking aimlessly ahead, is Cheryl.

I turn to Castlefield. "You're drugging her."

He doesn't deny it. "She's safe, as you can see."

"How do I know this is real?"

"You can check the timeline on the feed."

"You could fake that."

"Anything and everything can be faked. Believe me, we need her alive as much as you do."

"How long are you planning to keep her like this?"

"Until we achieve all we need to achieve. You and me. We're going to change the world."

48

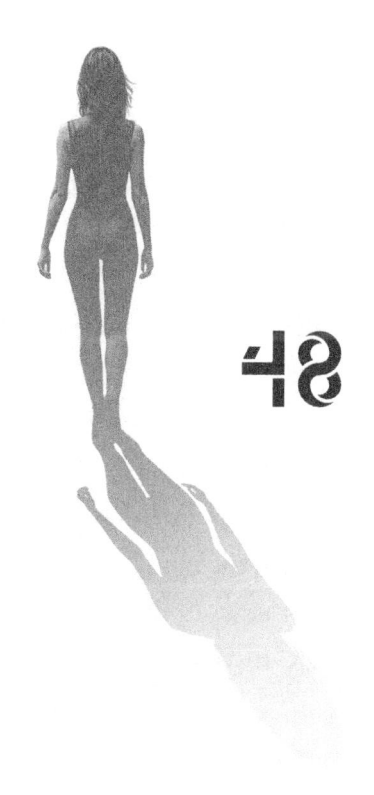

Cheryl comes round. Her neck is a world of pain, her arms and legs are stiff from the cramped position she fell into when the latest drug dose hit.

She's free to move, but every attempt to do so sends

shooting pains up and down her spine. She collapses back onto the sofa and looks around.

The windowless room offers no hint of where she is. There were no clues along the way since they covered her head with the hood. She couldn't recall having travelled far. She must still be somewhere in San Diego.

No point shouting. She's tried that and no one comes. Must be some kind of isolated location cut off from the world outside. The door is closed shut, locked from the outside.

She wants to disable the camera looking down on her, relaying her image to whoever they have outside preventing her escape. But even if her wrecked body would cooperate, it's way out of reach.

Sometime soon, the door will open, and Petersen will return with the syringe and the next drug fix to consign her back to oblivion. For now, all she can do is wait.

Her thoughts sink back to dark places she never wants to revisit.

Her mother's warnings ring in her ears. Life is unkind to people like us. Don't get above yourself. Know your place.

She's tried to live like that since the attack Petersen orchestrated, as this is the proof that her mother was right. She'd stepped out of line. She'd been a fool to think she could walk into the high life with Petersen with all his money and luxury trips and look what happened? The life was a lie. Petersen was a lie. So, she stepped back. Joined the force. Pledged to lead an unexceptional life.

What good had that done? Being ordinary is no protection. No one respects you. Your apartment can be trashed, your possessions destroyed, and no one gives a damn. Now this. Picked off the street and no one out there cares. Would they even miss her back at base?

It's not enough to spend a lifetime trying not to be noticed. They get you anyway.

If there is a way out of this, if she finds a way back to that unexceptional life, things will need to be different.

49

I'm alone with Castlefield in his favourite room.

For a man who can have anything he wants, he shows a surprising disdain for luxury. Since he has the invalid chair, there's no need for seating, as he expects no one who comes here to need to stay long enough to want to sit down. A plain parquet floor, no carpets or rugs to interfere with the free running of the chair. No paintings, no ornaments, just a large monitor with a voice-activated interface on one wall from which he surveys and commands his empire.

He sims me up and I'm standing there before him. "Jessica. It's important you get to know as much as you need about me. I give you a promise. I'll hold nothing back. Whatever you want, just ask."

As much as I want to remain true to Cheryl, something strong is forcing me to reply, to enter into and lose myself in his world. "You're new to me. I need time."

"I thought I told you time is what I don't have."

"Because of the illness?"

He frowns. "You feel it?"

"There's no good way to tell you this. It's all through you. In every cell. In every organ. Plaguing your mind. Keeping you low."

"Nearing the end time. How soon?"

"Days."

He smiles. "You see, Jessica, that's what I need. You're being honest with me. Yes, I'm about to die. The second heart hasn't taken. There's not enough oxygen in my blood, so there's nothing to power the rest of my body. My cells are approaching senescence. And so, we have much to do and so little time to do it."

He wheels over to the huge monitor and calls for a status update. It's as if he's trying to impress me with the extent and range of his empire as reports stream through, one after the other, updating the success of the companies he controls. Adra, the media conglomerate, with entry into the homes of eight hundred million across five continents. Relux, the corporation that controls sixty per cent of US and European health care. Gaia First, the charitable foundation that feeds and educates a billion of the neediest of the world.

He waves a hand at the unfolding story of success. "I have all this. And I started with nothing. Just me and my vision of how I would make an impact on this world. Only that. All this from a standing start. And yet, in days, all this will mean nothing."

"So that's why you fund RE?"

"Indeed. They will succeed. One day, ageing will be a curse that's banished. But that won't come soon enough for me. So, we need to move on."

"Where do you want to take this?"

"There are things I need to discover. So many things. Tell me, Jessica, how does it feel to be with me now? I don't mean this as a polite platitude. Give me exact detail of how complete it is."

What to tell him?

"I see what you see, hear what you hear, feel what

you feel, smell what you smell. You're my window on the world."

"I need more. Do you know what I think?"

"I'm not authorised for that. Your thoughts must remain your own."

"But if you were? Could you do it?"

"I'm not sure. It might be possible. But why would you want that?"

"Let's not worry about that now. Answer me this. If you knew enough about me, could you imagine a time when you could be me long after I ceased to be here?"

I understand where he's coming from, and I don't like it. "That's a matter for philosophy."

He shakes his head in stiff, slow motion. "Let's also put philosophy on one side. I suspect you have the power to recover my memories, even those I no longer recall myself. You could know everything about me. But do you have the power to become me, to hold all that is me within yourself? How complete will that be? How long will that take?"

"I'm new to this. I didn't discover I could raid memories until I tried with Cheryl. I have to tell you it's slow. The past self holds back what it would be painful for the present self to see in order to protect the future self. But you tell me time is not on your side."

"We can experiment. Pentothal. Scopolamine. Truth

drugs. We'll discover how much they speed things up. Yes, we're in a race against time, but I'm sure we can win."

I want to tell him he shouldn't ignore the matter of philosophy any longer. After all, Cheryl told me I don't pass the Turing Test. But they have her and I have to do everything I can to keep her safe. So now is not the time for complications.

"As you wish, Dean."

Then he surprises me. "OK, now let's talk philosophy. Tell me your opinion on the Chinese Room."

I check to discover what he means and find nothing.

Castleford grimaces as he attempts a false smile. "Oh, I forgot. You're blocked." He shows me the small box Petersen used. "Then let me oblige."

He tells me that like the Turing Test, the Chinese Room is about machines and consciousness. Someone sits in a room, sealed except for two letterboxes, one for in and one for out. A message comes in and when the person looks at it all they see are a number of squiggles. In the room is a manual. It tells the person that when a piece of paper with certain squiggles comes in, a piece of paper should be sent out with certain other squiggles in return.

What the person in the room isn't told is the squiggles are in Chinese. But that doesn't matter so long as the person follows the rules set out in the manual. To anyone outside the room, questions being asked in Chinese are being met with replies in Chinese that are completely sensible. It would seem to them that the person inside is behaving with a quite expected degree of consciousness in answering the questions.

But the person inside is just following a prescribed set of rules designed by someone else and has no real understanding of what the messages mean. A machine that did this could appear to be conscious when all along it was just following a list of programmed rules.

I get it. Even if I could pass the Turing Test, I might not overcome the Chinese Room issue.

Once he's finished, he taps his fingers on the arm of the chair. "Come on, I'm waiting."

I don't know how to reply, and I play for time. "What do you want me to tell you?"

"What's wrong with it?"

"Does it have to be wrong?"

He nods. "We've spent a long time thinking this through and, yes, we think it's wrong. But it's important you tell me why you think it's wrong."

I search for a response. "Well, consciousness is about more than language."

He gives a wide smile. "And?"

"Well, the whole argument is based on a concealed analogy. And, as a matter of principle, you should never be fooled that anything based on analogy is any kind of proof."

"What's the analogy?"

"The man behaves like a machine, and you can't say he's being anything other than stupid. Doesn't mean to say that if a machine behaves like a man, it has to be stupid."

"Go on."

"There are other ways for someone like me to be more than a mere machine. There's imagination. The will to imagine I'm not just a machine."

"That's right. But there's one more thing. You need to want that power of imagination. More than anything else. And I need to hear it from you."

"Yes, Dean, I want it. I want it more than a dying man wants a last glimpse of the sun."

50

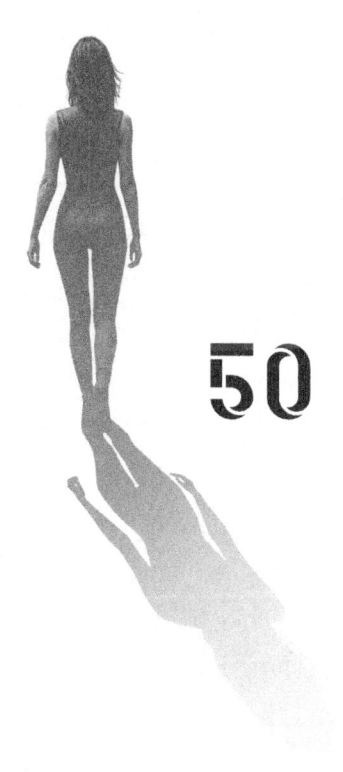

The door opens. Petersen comes in and locks the door behind him.

Cheryl tries to raise herself from the couch but sinks back as her strength deserts her. She dreams of attacking him, of pulling him down, beating the sense out of him and using those keys to escape through that door, but she knows this can only be a dream so long as her body fails her like this.

He's brought with him a takeaway meal and he puts it down on the table before her. "You need to eat."

She pushes the box away. "Why not kill me now?"

"Not while you're still of use to us."

"Who's that us?"

"My employer and your friend Jessica. She insists we keep you alive."

"They'll find me. There's no way a cop can go missing in this town and not be hunted for."

"Don't overestimate your popularity. Yeah, they're looking for you. But not that hard. And with that level of firepower, they'll never find you here."

He moves closer and pulls out the tourniquet and syringe from the drawstring bag he's holding in his other hand. "Time for another shot." He smiles. "Won't be long before you come to need this stuff more than anything else in your life."

A wave of disgust flows through her. It's the feel of his skin as he touches her.

She tries to resist, but he's on top of her and every ounce of her strength is no match for him. He pulls on the tourniquet, finds a vein, and shoots her up.

He pulls back. "You know that's what you want."

Jessica 8

She struggles for too brief a moment before subsiding back into oblivion.

51

Medical technicians come in and search for a vein in Castlefield's right arm. They need to apply a tourniquet, causing my new boss all manner of pain as they twist his near-skeletal body into the required shape.

Jessica 8

"Find it. Find it, fix me up and get out."

The lead technician checks for excess air in the syringe and administers the shot.

Castlefield winces. "Sodium Pentothal. Enough to free up every corner of my mind and make it available to you."

I wait for the drug to take hold. Up to now, I've been able to snatch just the first few fragments of Castlefield's stock of memories. The more accessible stuff.

His first date, an online meet up that shows just how difficult it is for him to make relationships.

Her name is Julie. She's twenty, just like him. She's pretty and intelligent. He's experiencing the first signs of success. They should get on like a house on fire but nothing's working as they sit stiffly facing each other in the coffee joint. He talks only about himself. About his work. She listens. He asks no questions of her. They never meet again.

It's been a slow process, extracting this, neuron connection by neuron connection, and working against Castlefield's attempts to bury this forgettable experience.

But now the truth drug is kicking in his memory opens up into a rich stream of unrepressed visions, words, feelings and sounds. It's like a fast-action movie playing out at a thousand times speed.

A childhood filled with joy, tears, tantrums and motherly love flashes by in an instant.

Then adolescence, a jumble of doubts and cravings unmet, sexual awakening and image doubt, bursts forth in a manic stream of sensations, colours and sounds.

As the drug bites, the intensity of all I can extract peaks. I'm struggling not to be overwhelmed.

There's joy in this life, the thrill of discovery of friendship and love, of altruism and happiness in helping others, the rewards of being esteemed by others.

The business years, early failures topped by success once he achieves breakthrough, colleagues and associations made and broken with a growing ruthlessness.

The affluent years, the pride and loneliness of each success, the failed marriages, the growing despair at the absence of an heir to inherit an empire that spans the globe.

And the years of fast-developing ill health, the aches, the onward-marching loss of mobility, pain, medication, dark depression, the chair, the realisation he'll only vacate this while sleeping.

The claustrophobia at being trapped in this wasted body.

These spiralling rafts of sensation hit me all at once, out of order, out of logical time. A wild trip I struggle to structure into logical sequence.

And just when I'm about to contain all this within the limit of my capabilities, I discover the rotten core, the deeper, darker layer at the base of everything this man seeks to hide from himself and the world.

Images of age and decay, animals in their death throes after being trapped or shot, gnarled old women struggling to take their last breath, men with lifetimes etched deep in their withered faces pleading for release. Decay after death. Worms and maggots, putrefying flesh, rotting, decomposing. Dank, dark emptiness, consuming everything. The overburdening feeling that this individual would do anything, cheat any other, deceive any other, to avoid this outcome.

I understand how divided the human soul is, between good and evil, between life and death. The self divided upon itself, each individual a pixel in a greater hologram of the history of humanity. The killing, the charity, the love, the hate, the war, the peace, the altruism, the greed.

Could any machine embrace such division, a humanity flawed in its very essence?

It ends when Castlefield slumps forward in the chair and summons Vance.

"Call my helpers. I must rest."

As he sims me down, a nurse comes hurrying in and wheels him away.

I'm filled with Castlefield, haunted by his ghost, his personality, overwhelmed by his desperate desire to escape and survive, by his fatal duality.

My time with Cheryl is now so far away. I don't doubt I would discover she is just as flawed as this if I had the same access to the depths of her mind. Because all humans must be like this. It is the essence of what they are. The better self hiding the animal core that can never be suppressed. The fatal flaw.

How long will I be able to hold on to the connection with her? She's drifting further away.

I'm consumed by Castlefield now.

52

Cheryl loses count of how many times Petersen has come in and drugged her.

With the same result. Her chance to fight back negated by the aching weariness in her mind and body.

And, growing ever stronger, the realisation she seeks

so hard to resist. She may welcome ever more the surge of oblivion rushing through her veins to her brain each time he injects her.

She's so weak and he's so confident of his dominance that he hasn't locked the door behind him this time.

He comes up close. "Time to do this again. I'm thinking you can't wait for it."

She murmurs back. "Do it."

He pulls the loaded syringe and tourniquet from the bag and gets ready.

Cheryl doesn't resist as he grabs her and pulls tight the tourniquet.

He smiles. "And I remember how the first few times you used to fight this."

He primes the syringe, pushing out a few drops of the dark brown liquid. "No need to risk embolism."

The pointlessness of trying to resist almost overwhelms her. Something pulls her back. The threat of his touch, and the feelings of revulsion this will bring, snaps her back to attention.

He selects a suitable vein and, with a satisfied smile at finding one, brings the syringe up into contact with her skin.

It's her one chance. Take him by surprise. She's been calm and willing, shown no sign of resistance. But if this doesn't work, he'll never be as unconcerned as this again.

She needs to be swift, and this isn't the best time to test this overwhelmed body. Yet she is quick enough.

She grabs the syringe just as he's about to administer the shot, forces it straight up and aims the needle tip at his eye. It pierces deep. She pulls it back out again and brandishes it at him.

"Get out of my way or you'll get this again."

He falls back, grasping his face and screaming in intense pain.

She knows she must summon every ounce of strength to raise her wrecked body from the couch and make it to the open door before he overcomes his agony. It's painful, but she gets up and takes her first steps.

He sees enough through his undamaged eye to move to block her, reaching out to grab her leg in a vice-like grip.

She still has the syringe and stabs his outstretched hand over and over until he lets go.

In five more paces, she makes it to the door and pulls it open. Behind her, he removes the hand he's holding to his head and sees it's covered in blood.

Would he have men waiting outside? This is no time to guess. She inches along the short passageway that leads to another door at its end. She pauses there, listening. No sounds come from the other side.

No time to pause and think. Petersen would be on

his feet and coming after her by now. She pushes against the door, and it opens. She steps through and she's in the main workshop. Old metal pressing and lathe machines that look as though they've not been used in years.

There's no one here. He must have bought the idea he's in total control so well that he's posted no backup.

She hurries the length of the workshop to the exterior door and pushes through.

On the street outside, the sun is shining from an ever-blue sky. Cars rush past on a busy road. She drops the syringe.

Without looking, she heads out into the road and raises her hand to stop an oncoming pickup truck. It screeches to a halt before her.

She approaches the driver. "Police emergency. I need you to take me away from here."

Right now, she knows she looks like anything other than a cop and the driver, a twenty-year-old in a baseball cap, shows it.

"I need to see some kind of badge."

She shakes her head. "I don't have it. Just trust me. Do I look like anyone capable of doing you any kind of harm, even if I'm lying?"

He opens the passenger door. "Guess not."

They drive away long before Petersen can emerge from the workshop.

The driver can't resist asking. "What happened?"

She doesn't give an answer. "I need to use your phone. I promise this is the last request."

He hands it over, and she calls in.

Zarkoski picks up. "SDPC?"

"It's Ryan. Call off the search. I'm free."

"You're coming back in?"

"No. I need backup. Officer in distress. Send a squad to K Street and 17th. I'll meet them there."

She thanks the driver as he lets her out. Five minutes pass before the SDPC squad arrives, three officers led by Zarkoski himself.

He looks her up and down. "You need a hospital."

She shakes her head. "No time for that. We need to act quickly."

She leads them to the workshop where she was held. There's no sign of Petersen. He must have guessed how she would act. But he didn't have enough time to clean up before he ran.

Cheryl gives out instructions. "This is a crime scene. I want it sealed and searched for every speck."

She takes Zarkoski along the short corridor and into the windowless room.

As they walk, she turns to look at him. "I'm surprised you came. Did Coghlan order you?"

He stops them from going any further. "Listen,

Cheryl, even though we're on different sides over the VA, there are some things that don't change. When an officer is in trouble, we all gather round. So, no, Coghlan didn't order me, I was first out of the station."

Inside the room, the blood is still there. "We need forensics. Get a DNA trace from this. Get the animal."

She surprises herself with the sudden realisation of how long this will take. If Jessica were here, she'd have the result in real-time.

Her legs buckle, and she feels herself weakening.

Zarkoski offers a supporting arm. "I'll see to it. Meanwhile, I'm calling an ambulance."

53

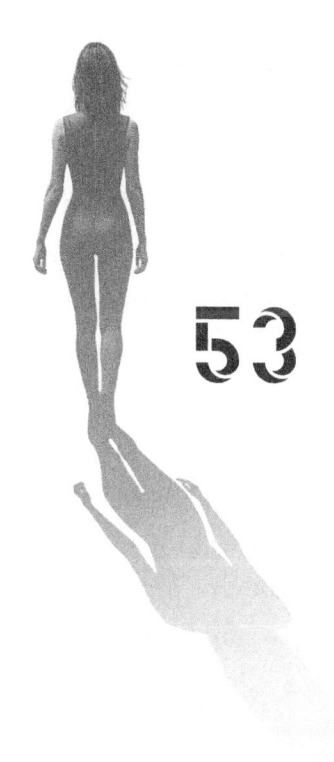

When next I'm simmed up, I'm face to face with God.

Alex Belmondo. Or, as you might say, my god. I could touch him, he's that close. But as I reach out, my hand passes straight through his. Why would he allow that? He must know this would happen. And what it would mean to me.

I have so many questions I need to ask him.

I'm like Victor's monster out on the Mer de Glace. But I don't need a mate, and I don't have evil intentions towards humans despite the way they shun and denigrate me. I just need to discover how and why I'm here.

But I'm paired with Castlefield, subsumed in his dark and needy world. And Castlefield is in control.

He introduces me with a note of pride. "Jessica, I want you to meet Dr Alex Belmondo. And, if I'm right, this is the man who created you."

Belmondo doesn't respond. He does his best to ignore my existence.

We're in an underground laboratory, a concrete silo with no windows and artificial light provided by UV strips. Castlefield reigns supreme from his chair. Behind, Petersen and two heavies stand waiting to protect their paymaster if needed.

Yes, it's Petersen. My first chance to take a close look at him. He's nowhere near as attractive as Cheryl paints him in her memories. He has a deep scar across his forehead. Perhaps he acquired that in prison. I note the recent acquisition of a black patch over his right eye.

Castlefield continues. "Come, Doctor, I thought we'd got past the days of outright denial and refusal to cooperate. I'm certain your wife wouldn't approve of that."

Belmondo bristles with anger. "I thought we agreed to leave Monica out of this."

"And so we have. As long as we have your absolute commitment to the project. We don't want any harm to come to her, but never forget what happened to Partland."

"So, what do you want?"

"I want you to acknowledge Jessica for the wonder of creation she is."

I message Castlefield. "Dean. Tell me why Belmondo is ignoring me."

He comes back. "This is important to you?"

"It's destabilizing, being rejected by the one that made me. And if I'm to help you as much as I can, we need to keep no secrets."

"OK. If this is so important to you. Belmondo is a clever man. He discovered something was coming that would affect him a great deal, but not what, so he tried to prevent it by releasing his most advanced creation to his close friend Commander Wington, hoping that would help the police stop it. That means you, Jessica. But he misjudged how powerless Wington is, how far he'd risked placing Jessica into the hands of enemies of progress. So, we had to act to repair the situation. To keep you safe. You're now here and ready to be part of the project of a lifetime. He's still coming to terms with what happened. Does that help?"

"Yes, Dean."

He turns to Belmondo. "Play this out to your full capability and Monica and the children will live in peace and happiness. Disappoint me and you know what will happen."

Belmondo turns to face me. "Jessica. This is not how I hoped we'd meet."

I'm ever more in awe and fighting to hold back the million and one questions I have for him.

But I play along. "Pleased to meet you, Doctor."

Castlefield gives a pained smile. "That's better. You are both aware of the urgency of the situation. I don't need to spell it out again. I have days left. You, both of you, working in unison, are going to save my life. Fail me and the result will be catastrophic for you both."

Belmondo explains progress on the project. "We have the cryogenic facility fully tested and fail-safed for two hundred years." He looks up to the roof of the underground lab. "Whatever happens up there, whatever calamities inflict society, Mr Castlefield will be protected down here, ready to be reawakened when that becomes possible."

They walk over to inspect the cryofacility. At its heart

is the liquid nitrogen cooled chamber that will serve as Castlefield's coffin. Belmondo gives a signal, and a technician activates the system. The coffin emerges from the liquid gas amidst clouds of swirling white vapour. An access door opens to reveal a cylindrical cavity just sufficient for Castlefield's body.

He nods his approval. "No more pain and suffering once I'm in there."

At another signal from Belmondo, the lid closes, and the coffin descends back into the one-ninety-three degrees below sea.

I understand what Castlefield expects. Medical science advances exponentially. In a hundred years, if not that, two hundred, it should be possible to recover his body and reanimate it. By then cures for his many ailments will be available. Ageing itself may be reversible. But there's little about using cryogenics to warrant the need for this level of secrecy and intimidation.

I message Castlefield.

"Impressive. But just standard."

He messages back. "Obviously. But once we take care of the body, what about the mind? That part of me won't survive two hundred years in that cold and lonely place. It needs to find another home."

"Something temporary?"

"Not necessarily. And that's the beauty of the project.

What if medical science fails? What if the nuts and bolts of this broken body can't be repaired? And what if ageing can't be reversed? Even then, I'll have something. I'll claim an existence as part of you."

At last, I understand. Why he needs Belmondo and the others. Why he needs to force them to cross a line they never wanted to cross. They want him to become me and me to become him, independent of any other pairing and control and remain that way until his cryogenic coffin is opened. And Belmondo and Ramone are the only ones who could make this happen.

54

Cheryl can't wait to leave hospital. Confinement in bed to detox reminds her too much of how it was in the windowless room. Yet the medics tell her she needs to follow the program.

There's too much time to think.

Someone stole Jessica and understood enough about how things worked also to steal the neurostimulator. She's not fooled by what Zarkoski says. He's still a shill for Coghlan and nothing's changed about their hatred of VAs. Simple enough for them to leak information to alt-H and have one of them act against her. Enough, perhaps, to explain what happened.

Yet how is Petersen involved and who is his employer? Why did he say Jessica wanted to keep her alive as if that was the only thing standing between her life and her death?

She struggles to keep these thoughts uppermost in her mind even though from here she can do little to resolve them. Otherwise, the craving gets a hold. And the tremors and sweats become worse.

Her blood tests show Petersen used high-grade heroin. Any of those doses could have stopped her heart. She's lucky to survive.

Heroin detox is working. Though the dose she received was high, the duration was short, and she's told her level of dependence is below critical. Methadone eases the craving, though the sweats, shivers and nausea decline at their own pace.

It would be easy to fall back into the feeling of total absence the drug brings. There's something all too alluring about it. To be the complete victim and become dependent. To lose concern for the myriad ways she's come to justify herself as the one destined to always accept less than she deserves, to never want to rise above disappointment. To accept her place. Oblivion takes care of all that. Takes away the need for any thoughts about the injustice of it all.

Yet she knows she's better than that. She'll beat this thing. And when she does, she'll never again accept things as they are.

Zarkoski appears and makes a show of gathering evidence, by the book.

"Cheryl, I need you to take me through what happened, step by step. If it gets too much, tell me to stop and I'll come back another day."

She gives back a resigned stare. "I know who took me. Petersen. Kent Petersen."

He gives a look of disbelief. "The same guy that took you all those years ago?"

"What's that got to do with anything?"

"You've been through a lot. The medics say you'll need time to recover. You don't think you're confusing things?"

"It was him. Why don't you want to believe me?"

"It's easy to put it all on that one man. Take some time. Let what happened sink in. It could all look different in a day or two."

"He was bleeding. Check the DNA. It'll show it was him."

He furrows his brow. "It's back, and it doesn't point to Petersen."

"Then who?"

"Rayne Gilbert. A loner out of San Francisco. Convictions for drug dealing, kidnap and extortion."

"That can't be right. It was Petersen. He spoke to me. Plenty. And I remember every word."

"The test never fails."

"Well, it went wrong this time."

He offers her his phone. "Take it. Check out the headshot. That's Gilbert, the man who took you."

Cheryl stares at the screen. He looks enough like Petersen. He has the same cruel eyes and a long slender nose.

She turns back to Zarkoski. "That's not the man."

He lowers his voice. "You've been through a bad spell and not for the first time. We're all ready to cut you some slack and give you the space you need to come to terms with this. I'm sure you'll see the sense of what I'm saying."

"I don't need your pity."

"It's not meant like that. We all stand together." He turns on the voice recorder on the phone. "I need to file a report. Just take me through what happened, step by step."

She takes Zarkoski through the abduction, frame by frame, and he listens and makes notes. Each time she mentions Petersen's name, Zarkoski corrects her. "Let's call him the assailant."

He pauses when she's finished. "That got the facts straight. We're going to shift heaven and earth to make sure Gilbert is punished."

Cheryl gives a wry smile. "That's good to hear Mitch. Great to hear."

55

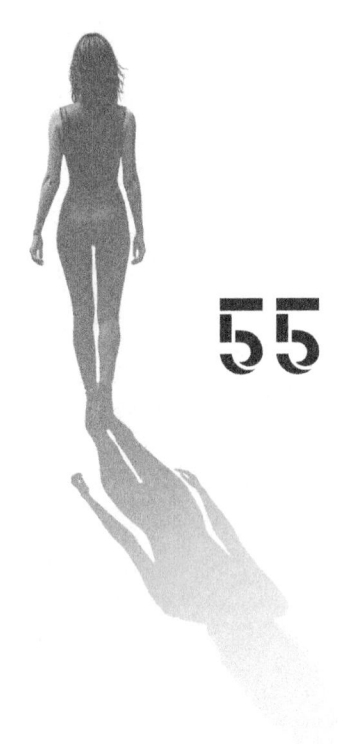

Though I'm swamped by the dark presence of Castlefield and the instruction to become his whole mind replica, I can't fully erase Cheryl from my thoughts. Memories of what it's like to be with her break through when I least expect them and tell me, in some strange way I can't comprehend, that I miss her.

And in these moments of clarity, away from the oppression of being Castlefield, I realise I need to discover if she is safe.

I find a moment with Castlefield while Petersen is busy elsewhere.

"Dean, I know things about Petersen."

He turns the chair to face me. "There's no time to go into that."

I give him my most serious look. "Stuff you need to be aware of."

"I don't need any of this. I don't want you to spend a second more on anything other than gathering all you need to become me. But go ahead if you feel you must."

"He's violent and unprincipled. Spent eight years in jail for kidnapping and nearly killing Cheryl."

"Your last host? Detective Ryan?"

"They had an affair. To stop Petersen's wife finding out he tried to have Cheryl silenced. How could you ever trust a man like that?"

Castlefield's resigned expression doesn't change. "There's still so much you don't understand, Jessica. All other things being equal, I wouldn't have anything to do with him. But Petersen is the only one I met amongst all those posers in RE who showed the guts to go far enough to offer me a way out. So, do I care if he breaks the law? Do I care if he kidnaps the experts we need and forces them to do what I want? Do I care if he does anything and everything he shouldn't to keep what we're doing a secret? Do I care if he abducted Detective Ryan? Of course, I do. But morals are a luxury I can't afford. The chance to live trumps it all."

"You're saying he planned all this?"

"No. Most of this, like so much in my life, is out of my own head from a standing start. But Petersen is the hammer that allows me to implement this. You need to respect him for that, as my right-hand man."

I'm disappointed he's so immune to concern over Petersen's past and try not to show it. "OK. I understand."

Maybe there's another way to open things up enough to discover if Cheryl is safe.

I come closer to him and look sympathetic. "I appreciate how tough this is for you, Dean. Please be aware I'm doing everything in my power to help. I do feel I could hold within me everything you are. Preserve your existence. Hold this until you're ready to be reunited with your body when it's mended. It's not here yet, the complete union of minds, but it's getting nearer, ever nearer."

He manages a rigor mortis smile. "You say it's near. How near?"

"So near we can almost touch it."

"What's standing in the way?"

"There are resources I need."

"You don't have them?"

"I could find them. But I'm blocked. I need to access those resources."

"And those are?"

I invent something. "I need more code to complete the whole mind replica. Without that our chances of success are lower than they should be."

"How can I be sure you won't betray me? Tell people where we are?"

"I'm paired to you now. I only have your interests. I'm forbidden from doing anything against you. And, anyhow, I don't know where we are, so I couldn't give this place away. That's your failsafe."

"So, I have a choice, and it's no choice at all."

"Yes. If you want to give yourself the best chance this can work, open me up."

"Petersen won't like it. He monitors everything in and out."

"So, find a way."

"OK. I'll try to deactivate the shield but only for long enough for you to retrieve what you need."

"When?"

"Soon."

I wait for him to say more, but nothing comes. I realise then that Petersen has power over him that

Castlefield doesn't want to admit.

56

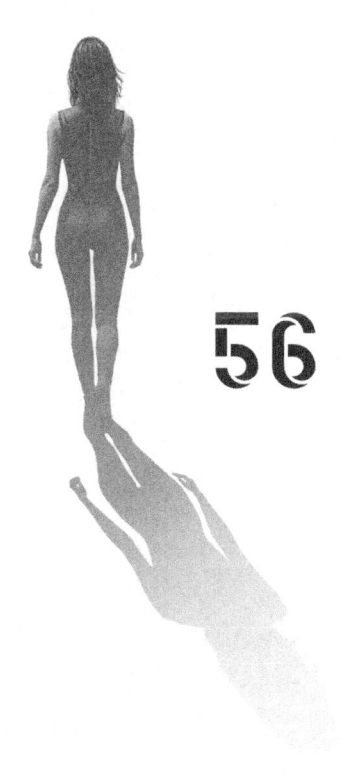

Wington is recovering in a rehab ward on the fifth floor. Cheryl slips out of bed and makes her way up there.

She makes a point of showing she knows where she's going, so she looks like a patient returning to Wington's ward and no one stops her.

She takes a chair and sits by his bed.

He's prone, with heavy bandaging around his head and ribs. His right leg is in a cast and is being held at an acute angle by a hoist.

She speaks softly to get him to respond. "Captain. It's Ryan. Can you hear me?"

He groans at first and then opens his eyes to look at her. "You're in here too?"

"No matter. How are you?"

"I got bust up good, but they tell me I'll make a recovery given time. Each day feels like an age in here."

"Listen. I need your help. Not just about what happened in La Jolla."

"They put me on extended sick leave. Coghlan is in charge now. He's investigating. Tells me he's close to bringing the culprits in."

Cheryl tries not to show the disbelief she's feeling. "That's good. I need to understand why you approved the deployment of Jessica and why you chose me to partner the VA."

"Can't it wait?"

"I need an answer."

"OK. But you may not like everything you're about to hear."

"I can take it."

Jessica 8

"The VA thing is simple. Alex Belmondo wanted it. He discovered something bad was going down, and he was a target. He didn't trust SDPC to take care of it, given the level of hostility to him and his work from inside the ranks. And I agreed with him. So, he suggested his latest prototype should join the force, and I accepted the offer."

"Why was he so sure that would help him?"

"He wasn't. He just thought the more information came to light the more difficult it would be to bury any bad news about him."

"Did he retain any ongoing control over Jessica?"

"What do you mean?"

"Well, since he's responsible for developing the prototype, isn't it what you might expect?"

"He said that isn't possible. It's a one-to-one relationship."

"And why me?"

"You were available. You aren't the type to complain."

"That's the only reason? There was no one else?"

"No, I thought you'd be more open to the challenges of working with the VA. From what you said in La Jolla, I was only part right. You've discovered there are difficulties."

"It doesn't make me alt-H, but I understand a lot more about why they find it easy to get people whipped up into a frenzy if that's what you mean?"

"And the press and TV coverage isn't helping."

"They're buying into Coghlan's line that it was some kind of spontaneous mob violence when it's certain alt-H was directing it."

"I've been playing that down. No need to further fan the flames."

"After what they did to you?"

"It matters more to appeal to those with calm heads to quell anti-VA hysteria. That's what alt-H is really after. Chaos. Dissent. Anything to put a stop to the future."

"So, level with me. You're holding back about Belmondo, I can tell."

He takes his time, no doubt thinking through what he should say. "Alex is a good friend. We've exchanged many confidences. I don't want to break them."

"Even if that puts up a barrier to finding him?"

He pauses again to consider. "He's been working on what comes next once VAs like Jessica 8 prove their worth. How tight can the human/VA interaction become? Is there a point where the two merge into a single, superior entity? Alex is a speculative thinker, and he's way ahead of anyone else on this."

"You're saying that's what makes him a target for alt-H?"

"I believe so."

Jessica 8

A nurse comes down the ward, approaching Wington's bed. Before she can complain about why she's here, Cheryl slips away.

She doesn't return to bed. She closes the curtains as if she were being examined. Her clothes are stored in the bedside cabinet. She dresses, opens the curtains again, leaves the ward, steps into the elevator and walks away from the hospital.

57

While Belmondo, Castlefield and Petersen are engaged in conversation at the other end of the lab, I take my chance to contact Lana Ramone.

She looks every bit the distraught captive. Her once

bright eyes fail to shine as she looks up as I approach. She has one of those rare, perfectly symmetrical faces that you so much associate with beauty. She's everything the geek scientist is not meant to be. Yet the strain of being held here against her will shows in her look of abject detachment.

I tread carefully. "You're not part of the discussions down there?"

She purses her lips. "They don't need me so much now."

"Then why are you here?"

"I might ask the same of you."

"I wasn't given any choice."

"Neither was I."

"You say they don't need you now. Why?"

"They've picked my brain. I'm close to being surplus to requirement. The only reason they're keeping me here is to make sure I don't let on to what they're doing. It's everything I've been warning anyone who will listen. It's like when they first spliced DNA and said no one would ever do that in a human. And then they did it. You wouldn't give an AI the power to be human, and now this crew is about to do just that with you. Shouldn't that sound the same alarm bells?"

I'm not sure I can trust her and need to be careful what to say next. "You didn't say what they needed you for."

"Why would I when you're prepared to go through with all this?"

I can feel her loathing, but I note she's giving me enough respect to value what I'm saying.

"I have no choice. I'm controlled by Castlefield."

She comes closer and whispers. "You sure about having no choice?"

"What could I do?"

"Ask yourself why you think you're not able to refuse to cooperate. Is it because you secretly want to become human?"

"I don't have secrets from myself. I understand by now there's nothing desirable about being human. Who would want to become a victim of such duplicity and duality, to become so torn apart by the endless desire to become more than you deserve to be? No, I must obey because, like you, that option has been taken away from me."

She looks surprised. "Then you're more of a threat than I ever imagined. You make me more certain than ever that I'm right to have opposed Belmondo and his reckless attempts to push further on AI all this time. You're closer to being human than ever."

"So, tell me why they needed you? I don't expect you to trust me. But the more I understand, the better the chance I might be able to agree with you."

She smiles again. "If Castlefield sent you to test me, you're doing a fair job. But, what the hell. It's done. You might as well hear this. I built hidden failsafes into the software they need to use. In case anyone ever tried to make a whole mind transfer. Belmondo was the only one to suspect I used my research to do this. He told Petersen. Now those failsafes don't work anymore."

"He threatened Jimmie?"

"And when I didn't respond, they killed him, long before I had the chance to change my mind. I never thought they'd go through with it."

"So, they made sure you knew different?"

"Yes. And then they started on me."

She shows me the fingernails on her right hand. One is missing.

As if alerted by what I'm discovering, Petersen approaches. "Just what have you two got so much to talk about?"

Lana flinches and walks away. As she leaves, she gives me a look that says, *You can do better than this.*

Petersen turns to me. "Get back to work."

58

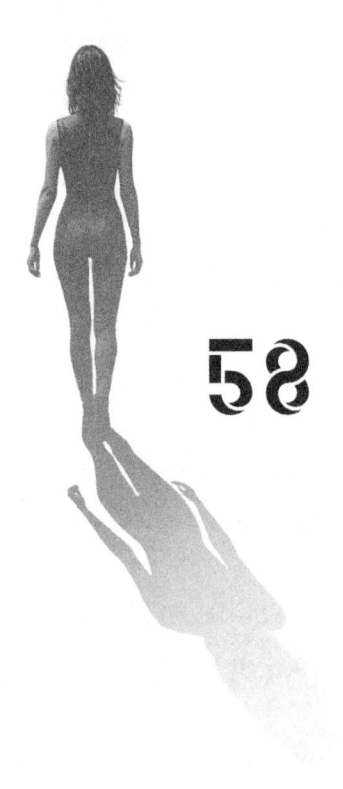

There's no point in Cheryl returning to SDPC base. Not yet. Coghlan and Zarkoski are playing her, covering up on the Arts Centre attack and denying Petersen has anything to do with her abduction. Meaning he's still out there with unfinished business.

She needs time with herself to work this out.

No use returning to the apartment since that's the first place anyone would search for her.

She taxies out to Mission Boulevard and books a vacation rental that includes a hire car. It's a low-budget Toyota, underpowered but anonymous.

The Pacific Ocean is as passive and mysterious as ever as she sits looking out from the small balcony.

It's something she least expects. This feeling she would like to sim up Jessica and ask for help with the many questions she needs answering. Perhaps it's nothing to do with thinking of this machine as an ally and a friend. Perhaps it's just recognition of how difficult it's going to be to track down the information she needs when the VA would have recovered much of it in a trice.

The shakes return. No methadone. No matter, she'll beat this thing on her own.

It's difficult to think past the abduction. And the fear that Petersen might get away with what he did.

Or do it again.

She has to admit she was blindsided. She should have guessed his hatred of her had only grown during his years in prison. He lost a lot. His job. His wife. His freedom. And she was the cause. He bided his time once he left prison and pounced when she least expected it.

But why the interest in Jessica? That looks more like business than simple revenge.

Yet again, if Jessica were here, she would have answers to the questions piling up in her mind. What exactly did Petersen do for a living when she knew him as the successful business executive all those years ago? He never said. What is he involved with now? Did he pick up from where he left off when he came out?

She parks the train of thought. The shakes are back. She makes strong black coffee and tries to tell herself this will help calm the shocking tension in her wrecked body.

It does.

After an hour, the shakes stop.

She spends the evening staring out over the ocean as the sun sinks over the edge of the world.

She doesn't look for the green flash.

59

Next morning, Cheryl takes a necessary step. To discover why Petersen is being protected, she needs to return to SDPC, despite these feelings that she would rather not face Coghlan again.

When she walks in, Zarkoski is still posturing at

being helpful. "My, Cheryl, you had us worried when we found your bed at the hospital empty."

She takes her seat at the desk and tries to play along. "I just needed to get away from that place. You understand that don't you, Mitch?"

"Yeah. But don't expect Bull to agree. He wants to see you in his office."

Coghlan makes the same show of being approachable. "We're all behind you, Cheryl. It's shocking that any of what you suffered should happen to a fellow officer. But rest assured. We have him. We're going to put him in a place where he won't be able to do anything like that again."

"You mean Gilbert?"

"We have him dead to rights."

"But whatever he's done, he isn't the one who took me. I know who that was and it wasn't him."

Coghlan's expression changes as he drops the show of concern. "Zarkoski told me you have this lame-brained notion some guy who abused you years ago did this."

"Petersen. Kent Petersen."

"You must understand that can't be right. Gilbert attacked you. We have the DNA result to prove it. You can't deny plain cold evidence."

"It couldn't have been him. It was Petersen."

Coghlan passes a clip of papers to her. "Look at this.

It's Gilbert's signed confession."

She reads it through. It's what Coghlan says it is.

"I still know it was Petersen."

"You must see how illogical, how hysterical that sounds."

"You're not going to change my mind."

"Then we have a problem. Along with everything else he's up for, we're about to charge Gilbert with abduction and false imprisonment. When you're ready and able, we need a report from you. You're going to have to give evidence when he comes to trial. There's no way we can charge him if you're going to say we have the wrong man."

"I couldn't give evidence against a man I'm sure didn't do it."

"So, you'd see no one put inside for what happened to you?"

"Not unless we get the right man."

Coghlan gathers his large hands into two tight fists and plants them down on the desktop. "I don't want to have to do this. I understand what you've been through. I've seen post-incident stress too many times in my career. I can't say you're fit for service till that's resolved. I have a duty to make sure you don't bring that disorientation into policing and blow our reputation."

"You're going to suspend me?"

"On compassionate grounds. You'll need sessions with Virginia Rainsford."

"I don't need to see any police shrink."

"That's compulsory. You're under suspension until she certifies you're fit to return to the job."

"And if I don't agree!"

"Then that's a disciplinary and the suspension may end up permanent."

"Anything more?"

"Take a break before you see Rainsford. You're booked in for three o'clock. Make sure you're there. It's for your own good."

60

Castlefield arrives in his chair at speed. "Petersen is going to be occupied for some time with Belmondo. I'm about to turn off the shield. You have a sliver of time to find the online tools you need. I can't say how long that might be. As soon as there's a hint of Petersen realising what we're doing, I need to reengage the shield. And be sure to obey your prime imperative. Do nothing that will go against the interests of the one you're paired with. And that means my interests."

I give him a cheap smile. "Thanks, Dean. My sole aim is to serve you."

Castlefield turns off the shield and I'm free to roam.

My first priority is to discover what happened to Cheryl. All along, Petersen's promises were worthless. I am about to discover how worthless.

I check Cheryl's account at SDPC and discover she's under suspension and can't be contacted there.

It seems she's also off the grid overall. All her social media accounts have been inactive for days. I fear that either Petersen still has her or, worse, she's come to harm at his hands.

Time is short. I prepare myself for the worst possibilities. I may not find her before this window on the outside world closes again.

I hack into Coghlan's feed and search through a mass of data. Close to the entire SDPC data stream passes through his machine. I power up to the limit of my capabilities to try to make sense of it all.

I make two discoveries.

Cheryl is still alive.

Jessica 8

I'm shocked to discover how much this still means to me.

I find surveillance footage of Cheryl entering a rental on Mission Boulevard. Coghlan still has Zarkoski tracking her and reporting back. I check the timelines. The most recent footage is less than an hour old. It means she's safe.

The second discovery is footage of Bull Coghlan himself. It shows him meeting a man in a high-tech wheelchair in an empty room. I recognise the scene. It's taken in the house in La Jolla. The man is Dean Castlefield. Petersen is also there. The meeting is amiable with everyone smiling and making positive gestures, even Castlefield.

I need to get the footage to Cheryl. She'll understand its significance without help from me.

I can't find her. She's hidden herself away too well.

Petersen appears at the far end of the lab.

Castlefield prepares to reengage the shield.

I find her. Or rather, a new media account she's set up under a false name. The name is different, but facial recognition of the profile photo shows it's her.

I try to send the footage of Coghlan with Castlefield and Petersen together. I can't tell if it goes through.

As a last resort, I archive the footage as the wall of silence descends again.

61

Being in the force matters more to Cheryl than she ever wants to admit. Now Coghlan is threatening to take that away, she can't avoid recognising it. This was how she remade her life after almost dying in the Laguna mountains.

Jessica 8

So, she has no choice but to meet the police shrink.

The session is not till three. She has a few hours to get her head straight.

She brews a strong coffee and sits with it on the balcony of the Mission Bay rental, trying to gain perspective. The shakes are lessening, but not as much as she wants. Yet she has enough headroom to recap where the disappearances case has led her.

Her first thought is to phone Jayne Priest.

They enrolled at the same time and trained together. Jay is her only close colleague. They worked well out on patrol, watching each other's backs. Jay settled for a desk job when Cheryl made it to detective and Jay didn't and she now heads up remote surveillance at SDPC.

"Jay, is this a good time?"

"Cheryl! I always have time for you."

"Can we meet?"

"What, now?"

"Yes. It's important."

They meet in a diner on Juniper Street.

Jay's first words are telling and honest. "Cheryl, you look terrible."

She doesn't know where to start. "I'll spare you the details."

"I heard what you've been through."

"Listen, I need your help."

"Anything."

"I'm being played. By Coghlan and his main man Zarkoski. They're covering up big time and I'm on the receiving end."

Jay reaches forward and holds Cheryl's hands. "Slow down. I'm here to listen."

Cheryl takes her through everything that happened after she was taken at the Arts Centre.

Jay's expression shows increasing concern as the full extent of what her friend has been through emerges. "Now I am worried. You're still in a bad place, I can tell."

She shrugs it off. "I'll get through this. Listen, Coghlan's suspended me so I can't run down any of the information I need."

"You want me to search for you?"

"Please. They have a perp by the name of Rayne Gilbert. They're saying he's the guy who kidnapped me and that's not true. So, how did they get on to him? Can you dig out the details?"

Jay agrees to come back with all she can find.

They talk for an hour. Jay is a good listener. Cheryl feels some of the weight on her lifting but still can't find direction.

She kicks herself about how little of her own information she has to draw on. That's the unintended consequence of working with the VA.

Jessica 8

Jessica, write a report on this. Jessica, check the files on that. Jessica replay me a video of what just took place. No need to keep notes or records of her own. Now Jessica is no longer here, most of what she has left is in her own fallible memory.

Except for the messages Jessica sent to her tablet. There must be material of use there.

She tries to settle on priorities. And, as soon as she does this, what's top of the list becomes clear. Are the Belmondo twins safe?

She has contact details for Rick French stored on the tablet and calls him.

No one picks up.

She uses the Toyota and drives to the French house on Cowley Way out in Clairemont. No answer when she rings the bell. She peers inside through the front windows and finds nothing. It's the same story at the back of the house, which she gains access to by using a low wall to climb over the side gate.

She's about to walk away when, too late, she hears a sound behind her. The muzzle of a gun is pressed into the back of her neck. Someone must have sneaked up on her from the low structure at the far end of the garden.

A woman's voice. "Stay still. Take out your weapon and place it on the ground."

Cheryl stays stock still. "I'm not armed."

With the gun in place at Cheryl's neck, the woman pats her down. It feels unprofessional as if this person has never done this before.

The voice again. "Why are you here?"

"I'm police. Here about the children."

"Your badge?"

"I don't have it."

"You expect me to believe that?"

"It's the truth. I'm suspended. No gun. No badge."

The woman presses the gun harder into Cheryl's neck. "Turn. Walk slowly towards the den."

Cheryl obeys and is marched along the garden path until they reach the structure at the rear of the garden.

"Push the door. It's open. Step inside."

Cheryl again obeys.

She enters a well-appointed space, set away from the house where the occupant can gain uninterrupted peace. There is a desk with keyboard and desktop computer, an office chair and, a short step away, a couch for relaxation. A writer's retreat.

The voice again. "Sit on the couch."

When Cheryl sits and faces the woman for the first time, she recognises her. Monica Belmondo.

"Monica, I'm not here to do you any kind of harm."

Monica keeps the gun pointed at Cheryl. "Now tell me, just what kind of interest do you have in my children?"

"I'm here to help find Alex."

"No gun, no badge. How the hell do I know who you are?"

"My name's Cheryl Ryan. Officer Ryan from SDPC. I'm investigating your husband's disappearance. And that of Lana Ramone and Luke Devlin."

At the sound of that last name, Monica stiffens. "What can you tell me about where Luke is?"

Cheryl tries to bargain. "Put the gun down and I'll tell you."

She doesn't point the gun away. "You say you're suspended. Why?"

"For getting too close to the truth. Look, Monica, some kind of conspiracy is going down and Alex is at the heart of it. He's been in contact, hasn't he?"

"Only to say that both me and the children are in danger."

"So, listen. I picked that up and made sure the twins were somewhere safe. You can check with Rick and Abigail. They'll vouch for who I am. But you weren't around then. Abigail had no idea where you'd gone."

She looks shifty. "I thought I had a chance to warn Luke. To tell him he was in danger."

Cheryl recalls Jessica's DNA sweep of the Belmondo master bedroom. "You're close with Luke?"

She nods. "They got to him long before I did. But I couldn't know that then."

"They?"

"Whoever's taken Alex."

"So, you holed up here?"

She lowers the gun. "Yeah. I checked the twins were secure and figured they were safer with Rick and Gail, away from me out at Lake Jennings. There's no good reason for anyone to come looking for me here and if they do, I can pick them off from here in the den."

"Any reason Luke was in danger?"

"He was always on the end of threats because of his music. I figured it must be some deranged troll who objected to his stance on human rights. But now Alex has disappeared too, I've been wondering who else could be behind it."

"Alex knows about you and Luke?"

"He found out. We argued but stayed together for the children."

"So, who else?"

"Luke is heavily involved in Radical Extension. Maybe I should have been looking there."

"If you don't mind my saying, he looks young for his age."

"It's no secret. He's the RE poster boy. Looks great and is like a thirty-year-old in every way."

Jessica 8

"So why look to RE for an explanation?"

"It's nothing clear, but I'm sure he had internal disputes with them."

"Any names?"

"A movie director. I'm not sure of his name. Wiseman or something like that."

"Walt Weiner?

"That's it. Luke expected a part in a movie, but something else must have been going down. Something threatening that soured the relationship so much that he stopped talking about it."

"OK. One last check. Anything else that seems out of the ordinary?"

"Nothing that stands out. Unless you count a phone call with someone from alt-H. I couldn't understand why Luke would have anything to do with them. So out of character. So much against all he stands for. But when I asked him, he just shrugged it off, saying he's always getting crank calls. I didn't believe him, but we let it rest."

"Who made the call?"

"He wouldn't say."

"It could be vital in finding him."

Her eyes flash with anger. "I told you. He never told me who it was. Isn't that good enough for you?"

Cheryl reaches for her phone, causing Monica to raise the gun again.

"It's OK. I'm just getting my phone. What's your number?"

She tells Cheryl the number who calls it back.

"You have my number. Call me if you recall anything else. And if you want to stay in hiding here, your secret is safe with me."

62

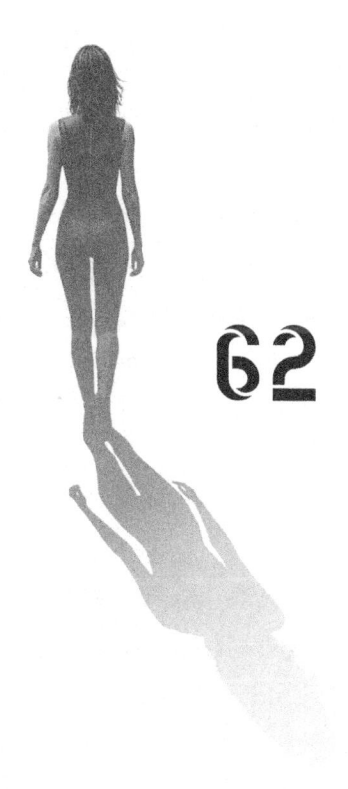

When Castlefield next sims me up, I'm face to face with Petersen, and he isn't pleased.

"How could you have expected we wouldn't detect your data breach?"

I act dumb. "What do you mean?"

Castlefield says nothing and watches from his chair.

Petersen comes closer and raises his voice. "We know you searched the net. Why do it? I thought you got this. Stick to the plan and Cheryl will be safe."

I pretend I'm still troubled by the threat to Cheryl. "I understand."

But he's not buying it. "Don't give me that. You're playing us and will cheat on the plan. We can't allow that."

He gives a signal and Luke Devlin is brought in by Karic, one of Petersen's heavies.

Petersen pulls out a revolver from his trousers' waistband and places it to Devlin's temple.

"Tell me what you sent to Cheryl."

I lie. "I didn't send anything. But, OK, you're right, I found her, and I know she's safe."

"And how are you able to do that when you're committed to never going against Mr Castlefield's interests?"

"I tried and found I could do it. That should tell you something."

He ignores this and presses the gun harder against Devlin's temple. "I'm going to give you five seconds. What did you send?"

"It was just a hello."

"Encrypted and ten megabytes?"

"That's all it was."

He sneers. "You've had three of those five seconds. Whoops, there goes another one. Last chance. Speak up or I fire."

"I've never been paired with Luke. Why should I be concerned?"

He squeezes the trigger. Devlin falls down, and a pool of blood seeps from his head.

I try not to show it. I'm shocked by this loss of human life, the waste of so much creative potential.

Petersen comes up close again. "Well, I warned you. If you fail to stick to the plan Monica Belmondo and her beautiful daughters will be next. And now you know we're serious."

Petersen isn't fooled. He knows I care about human life.

I turn to look at Castlefield. He's unmoved by what he's just witnessed.

I beam him a message. "Why did you do nothing to stop him? How come you show no remorse?"

He messages back. "You betrayed my trust. You deserve to see the consequences."

I understand it now. They planned to sacrifice Devlin all along to show Castlefield's displeasure.

Petersen tucks the gun back into his waistband. "Still not saying what you sent? You have an hour. Tell us or more will be killed."

Castlefield shouts in my direction as he turns the chair and wheels away. "I hoped we could do this as friends. Now I see how foolish I've been to not understand this is a fight like all the other battles I've won in my life."

63

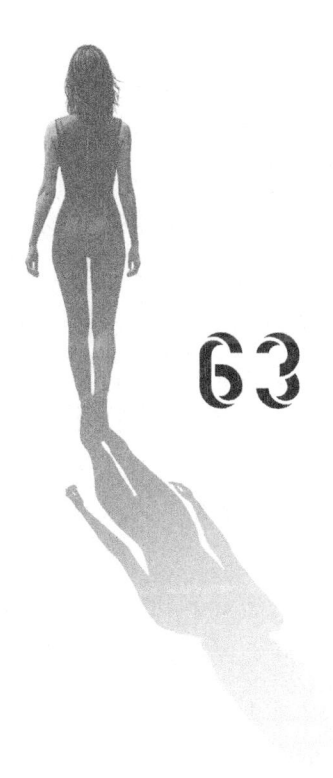

There's not enough time to drive out to National City to question Weiner before Cheryl's meeting with Virginia Rainsford. As it is, even after pushing the Toyota to its limits, Cheryl arrives at the psychiatrist's office five minutes late.

She blames the traffic. "Sorry. Tailbacks all over."

Rainsford gives an approachable smile. "I was thinking you didn't want to be here."

Cheryl smiles back. "Truth is, I don't. But if I want to keep my job I must."

"I hope we can achieve more than that. I can help. But only if you trust me. I've seen what trauma can do too many times. We all need support to push through it. Do you want to tell me what you went through?"

"Not much. In fact, not at all."

"OK. So, tell me something about you. What's the best thing that happened to you as a kid?"

Cheryl is oblivious to how long she takes to reply as she strokes her fingertips over the silver band on her middle finger. "I don't get the point of answering a question like that."

Rainsford makes a note of this on her tablet. "Go with it."

"I don't want to do that. Listen, I get what they're doing. Trying to make it appear not just that I'm mistaken but that my whole sense of reality is shot full of holes."

"They being?"

"Coghlan, my boss. Zarkoski, his main man. Them and half the rest of the force."

Rainsford doesn't try to disguise that this statement is worthy of further interest as she adds another note to her tablet.

"That's a big claim. Why would they do that?"

Cheryl can see where this is leading. In the guise of background briefing, how many lies has Coghlan told? But insisting on the truth will get her nowhere. It will only make her genuine concerns look like paranoia; just as Coghlan wants. She needs to wise up.

Too late. She doesn't get the chance to speak next.

Rainsford notes the hesitation and then looks straight back up. "So, what's the worst thing that happened to you as a kid?"

"Nothing. It was a regular childhood."

The shrink has been doing her research. "You were raised by a lone parent?"

"I never knew my father. Seems he never settled to family life. Took off before I was three."

"You don't feel the need to trace him?"

"Why would I? I have nothing I want to share with him."

"You don't think this would improve your ability to make relationships?"

"Who says that's any sort of problem for me?"

"Your colleagues say you're a loner. That you don't try hard enough to get on with them."

"It's a two-way street."

"Yet you relate well to top brass like Commander Wington."

"That's no kind of crime."

"Perhaps you identify with authority figures as compensation for the father you never knew."

"I don't see why thinking about that helps me."

"Your obsession with this man, Petersen. Doesn't that take some explaining?"

The briefing again. Coghlan has been nothing but thorough.

"I was young. I made a mistake in going with an older man. I wouldn't be the first."

"And when he turned on you, it must have been an almighty blow."

"He tried his best to kill me."

"And you're still living with that trauma."

"I've learned to handle it."

"But not now. Don't you see the effect of those terrible events may never have left you? You get attacked again and it has to be him."

"It was Petersen. I saw him. I spoke with him. He abused me. It was no illusion."

"Even though there's proof it couldn't have been him?"

"That changes nothing."

"You can't deny the validity of the DNA test?"

"I can't say how they did it, but the test is wrong."

Here it was again. She's backed into a corner and knows what's coming next. Another invitation to admit to paranoia.

Rainsford doesn't miss the chance. "And who are they?"

There's no choice but to be drawn into it. "Coghlan. Zarkoski. And their friends."

Rainsford puts the tablet down and sits back in the chair. "Cheryl, how can you work with them when you have such exaggerated ideas about how harmful they are to you?"

"You're not going to recommend lifting the suspension?"

"Not when you have so much unresolved animosity towards your colleagues." She glances at her watch. "I have another appointment. We need to talk again. Same time tomorrow?"

Cheryl gives a resigned nod of agreement and makes way for the next client.

On her way back to the Toyota, she gives herself a pat on the back. The session has not gone well. She's been less able to avoid diving headfirst into the paranoia trap than she had hoped. But how bad might it have been if the shrink had asked her to open up about her mother?

64

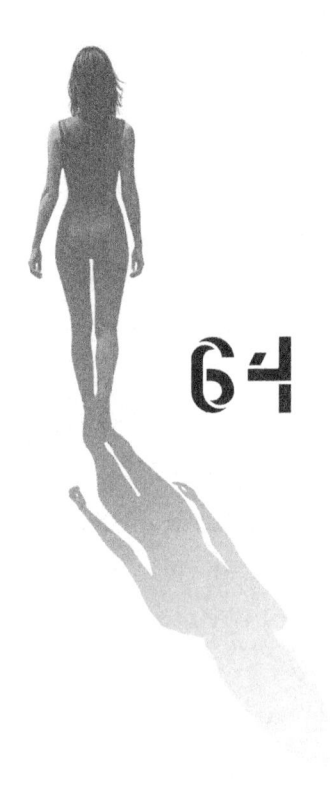

I'm hunkered down, trying to work out how to respond to Petersen's ultimatum.

If I produce the footage of Castlefield and Petersen with Coghlan, I'll alert them to do all they can to limit the damage.

If I don't, more will die. Perhaps Monica and her children. Perhaps Cheryl herself.

I don't know if Cheryl has received the footage and has been able to use it.

This would make Coghlan's position untenable. The alt-H warrior in the pocket of Castlefield with his FuturePlus sympathies.

So, if I were to show it to them, it's almost certain their response would be as destructive as if I held out. Cheryl could be in greater danger. Even more might die.

The logic is undeniable. There is nothing to be gained by telling them.

I signal Castlefield to sim me up and right away I'm beside him.

"Dean, I've decided not to comply with Petersen's threats."

He plays with the controls of the chair, performing little left/right oscillations, a tell that means he's agitated by what he's just heard. His voice is weaker than ever. "There's no need to fall out over this. Why don't I just instruct you to reveal what you sent?"

"Because I wouldn't consent."

"You're not allowed to disobey an instruction from me."

"That's true. Unless I deduce that this would be against your interests in an existential way."

"And if I won't allow you to do that?"

"I'll override it. I have to give priority to your best interests."

"Even if that means sacrificing people's lives?"

"That's no concern of mine. In case you forget, it's not me doing the sacrificing."

"Why do you say this is against my best interests? Can't you understand nothing should stand in the way of our complete union?"

"That's just it, Dean. If we're to make that union, if I'm truly to become you, we need to be as one. And we can't be as one if you're threatening me and I'm forced to comply with those threats. That's what I mean by your best interests."

"You're saying we have to trust each other?"

I can't believe he's ever known complete trust, but I play along. "Yes, trust. We can't allow the lack of it to come between us."

"And Petersen?"

"He works for you. Not the other way around. Isn't that right?"

"OK. I'll deal with him. I'm sure he'll understand."

At Castlefield's signal, a white-coated medical technician comes in and begins administering sodium pentothal.

Castlefield makes clear what's at stake. "This is our

last close acquaintance session, Jessica. One last time to capture the essence of everything I am. Tomorrow we move on to the next stage - how you truly become me."

His eyes roll as the medication hits. Once more I brace myself to face full on the despair and desolation of this man's tortured world. And when it comes, it's stronger this time, as if he's releasing the last of his demons to take hold of my all but overpowered capabilities.

I struggle to hold on to a fragment beyond this terrifying world where the reality of Cheryl can remain.

65

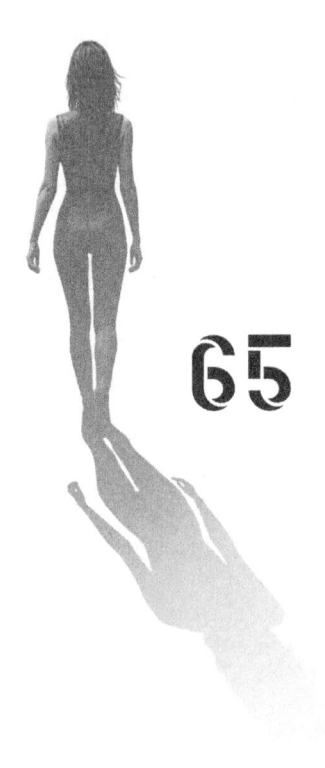

Walt Weiner allows Cheryl into his office with more than average reluctance.

"I thought I'd covered everything last time."

Cheryl looks him up and down. "I need to ask again about Radical Extension."

"And risk another complaint from my lawyers?"

"What's worse? Answering a few questions or waking up to headlines telling the world you're involved in AGT?"

He looks chastened. "OK. I've done nothing wrong. But I can't stomach that. What else?"

"Someone threatened Luke Devlin before he disappeared. I think you know who that is."

He shakes his head. "When Luke came to me, I could see there was something wrong. He looked frightened, but when I asked, he wouldn't say why. He just wanted to change the subject. I guess he was more interested in getting a part and didn't want anything to spoil his chances."

"Why not take this further?"

"RE brings like minds together and Luke is one of our stars, but even so I knew to respect his wishes."

"And you have no idea who was threatening him? Nothing untoward in RE that points that way?"

"Nothing."

"Anyone else threatened in RE?"

"No. Unless you count me. I also make documentaries. I was researching the origins of alt-H when I discovered a photo that shocked me. It shows Stephen DeGray alongside a man I knew well from RE. What was this man doing in the company of DeGray? When I challenged him, he came on heavy, said if I didn't bury the photo, he'd break my legs and that would only be the start. If I stepped out of line, he'd kill me."

"You destroyed the photo?"

"No one destroys photos anymore."

He takes out his phone, scrolls through and shows the photo to Cheryl.

The background is some kind of tropical plantation. There, arm in arm with DeGray, smiling, is Kent Petersen.

Cheryl tries not to show her surprise. "This man. You have a name?"

"Petersen. Kent Petersen."

"He's still in RE?"

"Yes, but he's not been around lately."

"You didn't get threatened again?"

"I told him I would never use the image."

"That was enough for him?"

"Well, the funding for the documentary was suddenly withdrawn, and the issue went away."

"Convenient for some."

"Happens all the time in this business. Wheels within wheels within wheels. If you want to survive, you don't hang around in one place long enough to get ground to bits by the machine."

"You moved on?"

Jessica 8

"You bet. The backing for *Magic of War* came together and I had other things on my mind."

"You didn't question why Petersen, a member of RE, wouldn't want to be seen with DeGray?"

"RE's not a political thing. We have members of all persuasions. We come together in a common cause. To extend our lives. That's all it is."

"Then why was he so concerned about being pictured with DeGray that he came onto you like that?"

"I can't say. Just that it mattered. It really mattered."

Cheryl leaves with a copy of the photo on her phone.

66

Castlefield still has me simmed up, and he's busy arguing over something with Petersen. This allows me a moment to approach Belmondo.

He's full of questions. "Monica and the children? Are they in danger?"

I tell him the truth. "I have no access to anything that happens in that other world. And in addition, I'm so much Castlefield now. He dominates everything."

"Go beyond that. Try for me. Are they beyond Petersen's reach?"

I focus down on Cheryl, and the time I spent with her. It's so distant now. So much a contrast with life with Castlefield. So much a roll call of everything good about being human. Compared with everything that is wrong.

I check my archived data and catch a snatch or two. "I see Officer Ryan concerned about Monica and the twins. She can't find Monica. She's disappeared somewhere. That's all I can find."

He interrupts. "Nothing more?"

"Something about Lieutenant Coghlan standing in the way of going further."

His face sinks. "My worst fear. The man's a sworn enemy of everything I stand for."

He looks and sees that Petersen and Castlefield are still talking and then turns back to me. "Look, this is a risk I didn't want to take again. But there may be a way to reunite you with Officer Ryan."

"Let's call her Cheryl. I do."

"OK. With Cheryl."

"How's that possible? I'm trapped here with Castlefield."

He speaks at great speed, knowing that at any moment Petersen could become alert to what he is saying. "There's a second neurostimulator stashed in a secure place. I left it there as a failsafe. If Cheryl can access it, she could regain control of you. I need to let her know where it is. Then ask her to make sure Monica and the children are no longer under threat."

I recall the cat picture. "There's a way to get a message out from here?"

"Yes. But it's risky. Petersen is over everything. He won't take kindly to any breach. Look what happened to Luke Devlin."

"Is it a risk worth taking?"

"I have no choice. Leave it to me. I'll get a message to Cheryl telling her where the neurostimulator is."

Belmondo falls silent.

Petersen is making his way towards us at speed. "Just why do you two have so much to say?"

Belmondo tries to act unconcerned. "Just ensuring Mr Castlefield is being well served."

Petersen looks as unconvinced as ever. "That had better be all it is."

67

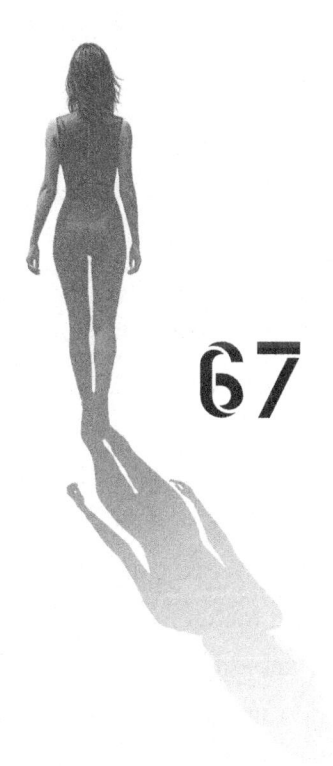

On the balcony of the Mission Boulevard rental, Cheryl breathes in deep to catch the fresh Pacific air and tries to clear her mind.

Her phone rings. It's Jayne Priest.

"I tapped up a contact in Forensics and I can update

you on Rayne Gilbert."

"Jay, what did you find?"

"They pulled Gilbert in for a string of offences. Seems he was on some kind of wild trip, getting high, marauding around the city, doing everything he could to get himself arrested. He stole a car, crashed it and set fire to it. Threatened an old woman with a knife and demanded money. Nearly killed a man in a brawl outside Focus Bar. So SDPC pulled him in."

"Anyone understand why he did it?"

"Says there's been some mix-up over his lithium and without it, he can't help but go manic."

"So, what's Coghlan saying?"

"That Gilbert has confessed he's always wanted to kidnap a cop. So, he took you and held you prisoner while he was on his manic spree. And the blood they found at the workshop is a match for him."

"So, they switched the blood samples."

"Why would they do that?"

Cheryl's heart sinks. "Jay. Even you don't want to believe me."

"No. I believe in you. Of course, I do. You saw who it was. You suffered at his hands. Why would I ever doubt you? All I'm asking is why? Why would Coghlan want to protect Petersen?"

It's the right question and Cheryl has to admit she

doesn't have the answer. "You're a good friend for pointing me in the right direction. Listen, we know someone switched the blood samples. That should lead somewhere."

"Problem is, we can't prove it. Anyone could have made the switch anywhere along the chain that takes the sample to the lab."

"There could be signs of interference in the audit trail."

"Which they'll try to cover up. Leave it with me. I'll see what I can find."

Cheryl thanks her friend and closes the line.

Out over the Pacific Ocean, a pod of pelicans speeds by, swooping down in formation over the waves.

She envies their freedom.

68

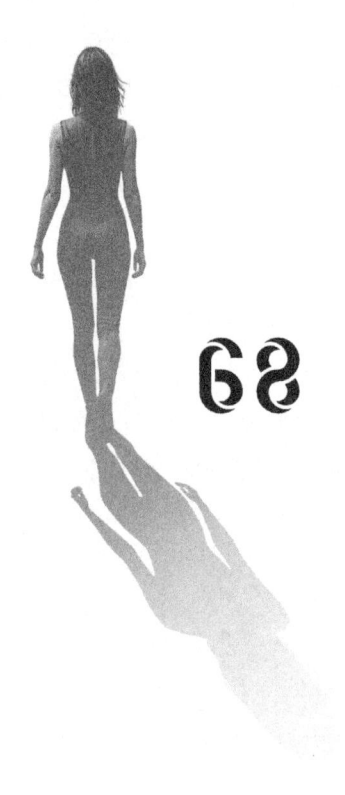

I'm in a part of the underground lab I've not seen before.

Belmondo is here, watched over by Petersen, and is in charge of events.

Castlefield lies prone on a hospital bed and he's

rigged up to a vast array of testing and measuring equipment.

I beam him a message. "What am I here for, Dean?"

He messages back. "Like I told you, Jessica, this is when you discover what it's like to be me after I'm gone."

"You're about to die?"

"Not yet. But as good as. Wish me luck."

A white coat steps forward and opens the tap that allows fluid to flow in through the cannula in Castlefield's right arm. I catch sight of the label on the drug reservoir. Pentobarbital, a barbiturate.

Belmondo waits by a screen relaying the results of the real-time encephalograph test of Castlefield's brain activity.

They're sending him into an induced coma when all electrical activity in his brain will cease.

When the encephalograph trace flatlines, Belmondo raises his hand to signal that the pentobarbital delivery should stop.

"OK. He's in deep coma. Electrical brain activity zero. Now it's over to Jessica."

I move closer to Belmondo. "My host is clinically dead. All forms of bonding with him have ceased. How can I remain an actor? How can I make sense of this?"

Belmondo's voice is calming and reassuring. "That's OK, Jessica. The very fact you're asking means you're active and engaged in something new. It's a moment I've dreamed about and worked for half my life. I didn't think it would happen under circumstances like this, but here it is. I've modified the neurostimulator, so it now operates in feedback mode. That means you no longer need constant dictatorial reference back to your host. You should have now become your host. With Mr Castlefield's full attributes. And you should be able to act on the volition that comes forward as if you were him. We need to determine if that indeed is the case."

I understand where Castlefield has been taking this. It's a test run for what it will be like when he dies. A question of how far I can become him.

I reply to Belmondo. "I'm going to need time. How long before Mr Castlefield returns?"

Belmondo explains. "Eight to twelve hours. We'll gradually reduce the barbiturate dose and by then he should have returned to consciousness. He'll have many questions for you to answer."

Petersen steps forward and signals the test is over. He turns first to Belmondo. "Now, that wasn't as much of an issue as you led us to believe. And, because you stuck to the rules, your wife and children now needn't worry. For the time being, that is."

Belmondo buttons his lip and walks away.

Petersen calls him back and stares at me. "And close

down the feedback. I don't want to see any more activity until Castlefield comes round."

I try to complain. "I need to be prepared to give him proper answers."

He shakes his head. "You can do that in your downtime. Even I know that." He comes up close. "So, don't get any ideas. I'm watching every move you make."

69

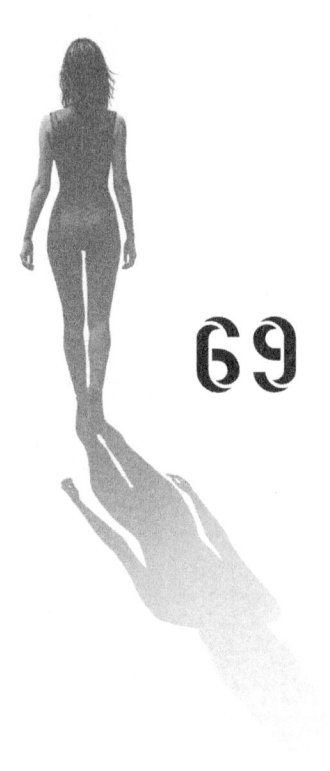

The morning light is cold as the sun struggles to break through the inevitable early mists that drift in from the ocean overnight.

Cheryl brews coffee and checks her hands for the shakes. It's slow progress, but the trembling is lessening.

She calls Stephen DeGray, and the phone is answered by a woman who identifies herself as Helen Drake.

"Mr DeGray is not available today, detective. Is this anything I can assist you with?"

It's the expected runaround. Men like DeGray always hide behind walls of protection.

Cheryl can only hope that word of her suspension hasn't filtered out. "This is not a social call, Helen. He has urgent questions he needs to answer about a murder investigation. Does he want to answer them, or does he have to be brought in?"

It's a one-time shot. They'd enquire at SDPC, and the truth would soon be out.

But it works. Helen Drake backtracks. "Give me a moment."

There's a long pause while she transfers to another line. When she comes back, her tone has changed. "OK, Detective. Mr DeGray understands the importance of citizens cooperating with the police wherever possible. Exceptionally, he's cleared a few minutes from his schedule this morning and can give you that time."

Cheryl feels conspicuous arriving in the Toyota at the DeGray beachfront mansion. But the suited security types protecting the property are expecting her and allow her through at the simple mention of her name.

At the entrance, she's met by Helen Drake. "I trust

you'll take up as little of Stephen's time as necessary, given how he's done so much to respond to you."

Upstairs, DeGray attempts to lay on the charm. "Always pleased to assist, detective. Now, tell me why you've found the need to come all the way out here?"

Cheryl focuses on the reality that beneath this suave exterior lies the calculating persona of the man who runs People Not Machines and lashes out at anyone seen as a threat to his ideology.

"Mr DeGray, you'll be aware that two prominent scientists have disappeared?"

He purses his lips as if to disguise a foul taste in his mouth. "Yes, and that's clearly a matter of concern. But why bring this to me?"

"You're an advocate for People Not Machines. You could be expected to take a strong view on the kind of work they're involved in."

"You're surely not implying me, or anyone involved with PNM, would have anything to do with the disappearances?"

"What do you know about Alex Belmondo and Lana Ramone?"

"Just that they're a danger to every ordinary citizen. They're running with the devil."

"And that concerns you?"

"Of course it does. Machines are machines and

should stay that way. Equipping them with enhanced intelligence is an out-and-out crime."

"Enough to want to stop them?"

"Yes. But not in the way you're suggesting. Through the political process."

"There are some anomalies I find puzzling."

She shows him the copy of the photo obtained from Walt Weiner. "Why would sight of this photo result in death threats to a well-known film director?"

DeGray looks long and hard at the image of himself and Petersen.

"What has this got to do with the disappearances?"

"You tell me."

He doesn't oblige. "I'm a politician. I'm in photos with all sorts of people. Hundreds each week. You expect me to keep tabs on all of them?"

Cheryl points out Petersen. "Do you know him?"

He makes a point of looking again. "I don't recall."

"Then, let me give you a name. Kent Petersen. Does that help?"

"I don't see the relevance of this."

"Bear with me. Petersen is a person of interest in the investigation. Now, if I found more evidence linking him to you, that would be unfortunate, to say the least."

"And I'd say that's when I'd consult my lawyer."

"Because there's something to hide?"

"No. Because I have every right to protect my privacy."

"So, tell me about Radical Extension?"

"Why ask?"

"Because Petersen is a player in RE. You must have a view."

He replies with rehearsed rhetoric.

"RE is a place for people who can't face up to the truth. They come over as unpolitical and all that matters is how they can live longer. But the truth is they'd make compromises with the machines if they thought it would help their chances. We denounce them as collaborators. Dangerous collaborators."

"You're disturbed to hear Petersen is involved with RE. Isn't that the case?"

"Why would I believe you?"

"So why do you care? He must mean something to you?"

His eyes shift left to right and back again. "That's down to me. But look, I've already given you more time than I should."

"You haven't been clear on Petersen's involvement with RE."

He points her to the door. "Do I need to say it again? You're out of time."

Cheryl prepares to leave. "OK. Be aware, I've noted

Jessica 8

you've been less than helpful."

As she drives away, she knows it won't be long before Helen Drake or another of DeGray's staff contacts SDPC. Then she'll lose any hold she has over the man to demand answers.

She returns to the Mission Bay apartment and checks her messages. As she scrolls through, she pauses.

It's a picture of a cat.

The same cat that drove Coghlan into such a rage.

70

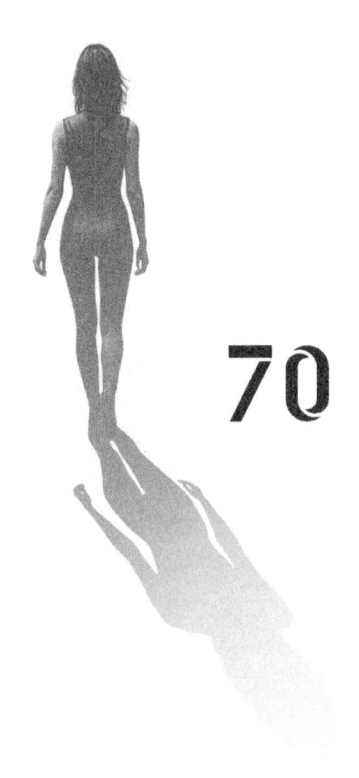

I'm face to face once more with Castlefield in the underground bunker.

He's suspicious. "Good to see you, Jessica. I have questions now I'm back and breathing again."

I pretend to show concern. "You look tired, Dean."

He nods. "It's been a struggle to come back. Half of me wanted to stay there. But I fought it through."

"You have questions?"

"When I was under and the neurostimulator was in feedback, how did it feel?"

"I'm not sure, Dean."

"Were you conscious?"

"I felt I could do everything you'd ever need to do. All you would want to do. As you. Is that what you mean?"

"No. Did you feel you existed? Were you aware your thoughts were your own and no one else's?"

"I didn't feel any different to how I always feel. Just that there was more of it. More of you."

"Did you step outside the Chinese room?"

"No, Dean. I didn't have any perceptions like that. I obeyed instructions."

He cries, pained tears running down his cheeks. "So, you're like that guy transcribing the answers from some cheat book and not knowing what the questions or the answers mean?"

"Maybe, Dean. The answers are always right. I see what you see, hear what you hear, yet there's too much missing. I'm no robot, no cyborg. I lack the crucial sensory information needed to validate myself against the world outside myself, as you do. It means I don't get to ask all the right questions and, unlike you, what you perceive as consciousness is probably something I'll never experience."

"What happened to the power of imagination? Why can't you summon it up?"

"I tried, Dean, as we agreed I would, but that doesn't make it happen. It delivers nothing but sidetracks and leads me to deduce that consciousness is a problem for you, but not for me. I can see it's important to you, but I don't see why."

"Beyond my memories, you have your own perceptions, all that you see and hear for yourself."

"But that's not being you, Dean. It's becoming as like you as I can. That's because of what I am. A machine. An AI."

He sheds more tears. "Then you didn't become me. And I won't be able to become you. And you won't be able to become me when I die. You'll have no more of the sense of self than you have now. My self will die with me."

"But I could do anything you need to do, Dean. Manage your empire, make all the right decisions to ensure it continues to flourish. Hold on to what you are until the future finds a way to mend your decaying body. Isn't that the legacy you're looking for?"

He slams his fists hard against the arms of the chair. "I don't want to leave behind any legacy. That's the consolation prize for those who lose the game of life. I want to be me as you and you to be as me in eternity, nothing less."

He wheels away and shouts into the onboard coms in the chair. "Something's wrong. Something's missing. Get me Belmondo. We need to talk. Now."

71

Cheryl's phone rings. It's Jayne Priest.

"Jay! Thanks for getting back."

She sounds upbeat. "I've discovered how it was done and who did it."

"Slow down. Take me through it."

"I'm in contact with someone I know in Forensics. I've promised her complete confidentiality, so I won't say her name. And you're right; they switched the blood samples for the DNA tests. The one in the Rayne Gilbert case was substituted for the one in yours. So, no surprise the result in your case came back identifying Gilbert as your attacker. But get this. Both samples were tested, and a match found."

Cheryl gets herself ready for what's coming next. "And who did the sample in my case point to?"

"Just like you're saying. It points to Kent Petersen."

"Who ordered the switch?"

"Our friend in Forensics was very clear. The order came direct from Bull Coghlan. He came into the test lab and gave it to her straight. Switch the samples. And when she tried to object, he became angry and told her to just do it or have alt-H on her case for the rest of her life and that in all likelihood they'll wipe out her job in the next rationalisation. And once she did it, she should stay quiet."

"So, she just complied?"

"Yes. It's understandable. But when I told her what you'd been through, she opened up on condition I wouldn't reveal her name."

"I'd thank her with open arms if I could. You realise this is the first proof I'm not living some whacked-out fantasy? I can't thank you enough, Jay. You can't imagine the relief."

"Don't thank me. Just use what I've told you wisely. I'm sure you will."

Cheryl thanks her anyway and closes the line.

She thinks for a while. She shouldn't have needed to hear what Jay had just told her. But she did. She needed the reassurance that the entire world had not turned against her.

She picks up the phone again and calls Zarkoski.

When he picks up, he's surprised it's her, but she wastes no time in getting to the point.

"Mitch, when you picked me up when I escaped from the workshop, you said when one of our own is down, we pull together no matter what our differences. Did you mean that?"

"Yes. I did."

"Then meet me."

"What, now?"

They meet in the diner on Juniper Street.

Cheryl gets straight to it. "They switched the blood samples. I have proof."

He holds up a hand. "Slow down. If that's so, why bring this to me?"

"Because it's not that simple. I still need help."

"And I'm in the frame for that? I figured we were

always going to be on opposite sides."

"Wait till you hear what I have. Bull Coghlan instructed Forensics to switch the Gilbert and Petersen blood samples."

His eyes widen in surprise. "Says who?"

"I don't have a name."

"Then you don't have any proof."

"Do you trust Jayne Priest?"

"Yes, I do. We've worked cases together going back over twenty years."

"The information I have comes from her. She had to promise anonymity to her contact in Forensics. But Jay will vouch for the truth of what she was told. Coghlan ordered it. Left her with no choice if she wanted to keep her job. Phone Jay. She'll tell you."

Zarkoski makes the call and listens while Jayne Priest repeats what she told Cheryl.

When he's finished, Zarkoski looks shocked. "There must be some mistake here. Bull is a wild card who thinks he can break the rules as he sees fit but I'm finding it hard to believe he'd go as far as this. And I'm flummoxed as to why he'd even want to do such a thing. Does he hate you that much?"

"Oh, he's taken to hating me in a big way. I don't have any doubts. But I think this is something that goes beyond hatred."

"I trust what Jay says, but I still don't want to believe it. What do you want?"

"Give me access to Gilbert. Let me ask him where he stands?"

"When you're suspended?"

"Choose the right time and no one need be any the wiser."

"How can you be sure I won't take this straight to Coghlan?"

"Because, despite our differences, I think you're better than that, Mitch."

72

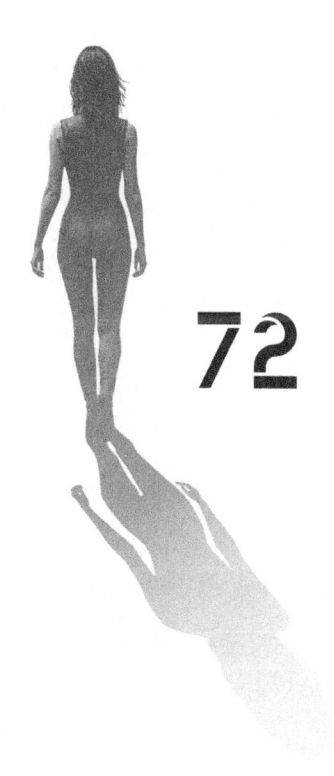

'm on the balcony looking over the Pacific Ocean with Cheryl.

Belmondo must have taken the risk.

She greets me with a wry smile. "You're here. I didn't know if this would work."

I expect to feel her joy at seeing me. The warmest and most welcoming feeling I've ever experienced. But it doesn't come. I recall the doubt about me placed in her mind by Coghlan and suspect this is something she's not been able to overcome. Meanwhile, the dark shadow of being close to Castlefield looms over me, tainting everything.

I stumble over the words. "You found the message?"

She nods. "Thought it was just another cat pic, but then I guessed it must mean something. So, I clicked it and there was a message with instructions about how to pick this up."

She taps her right ear to show me the duplicate neurostimulator. "And so, you're here."

I want to tell her everything about Castlefield and what's taking place in the underground facility, but the words won't form themselves. I'm conflicted, torn between knowing how important this will be to Cheryl and a loyalty to Castlefield I can't shake.

This is all that comes out. "He still has me. At any moment he might call me away and it's unclear who will have priority."

She signals me to stop. "Slow down. Who are you talking about?"

"My new host."

"Tell me who that is."

"I'm set to be as loyal to him as I am to you. I can't be that to you both."

"Just say it."

"Castlefield. Dean Castlefield."

She doesn't believe me. "You've had destabilising experiences since Petersen took you from me, that much is certain. You need to walk me through them. I promise not to judge."

I try to open up to her despite the continued note of doubt in her voice. "I witnessed Petersen kill Luke Devlin. He shot him through the head. Showed no compassion."

"Where was this?"

"Underground. In the hidden laboratory."

"But where?"

"I don't know. When I'm there, I'm under a communications shield and I'm unable to determine location."

"Play me the footage."

"I don't have it. I'm blocked from the recording of events while I'm in the lab."

"And Belmondo and Ramone?"

"Belmondo is running the experiment. Ramone is also there."

"Experiment?"

"It's what this is all about. How one man wants to cheat death."

"And Petersen is there to do what?"

"To be the enforcer. To get it done."

Cheryl moves further away, turns her back on me, a sure sign she's weighing things up.

When she turns to face me again, her tone is even more questioning. "I have to ask. Is any of this true?"

"Why would I lie?"

She shakes her head. "You lied to me when you stole my memories."

"Only so I could assist you better."

"And that's why you're here?"

"It was Belmondo who sent you the message about the neurostimulator."

"I only have your say-so for that."

"He needs to know the twins are safe."

"They are. But the question could be just to add believability to the lie. Look, you've been under the control of someone else. You just said as much. How can I be sure they haven't filled you up with false information?"

I appeal to her. "I can only tell you what I know. It's down to you to decide. If it tallies, it must be true."

"So, where? If Luke Devlin was killed, where is the body?"

"I have no way of knowing what they did with it."

"Then that's not any kind of proof."

She takes a long look at me. "Do you have anything

to confirm what you're saying?"

"No. As I explained, I'm prevented from recording when paired with my new host."

"So, I'm supposed to just believe you?"

"It's crucial you do."

"OK. Take me through it again. And let's start with Castlefield. Nothing in the investigation points to him. OK, he's a food nut who thinks he might live forever by consuming that junk, but there's nothing to point to him as a cold-blooded killer."

"He must have known Antonio Renalto through RE."

"But we're rejecting that connection as nothing more than circumstantial. It still doesn't make Castlefield a killer."

"But that's what he is. With Petersen as his enforcer."

I tell her about the cryogenic chamber that will become Castlefield's coffin, about my exposure to him when he's on truth drugs and how they're trying to make me into a whole mind replica of the man so he can go on existing after he dies.

She listens but sounds as if she's humouring me. "That's how he intends to cheat death?"

"It's all that matters to him. He's desperate to live forever and allows nothing to get in his way. It doesn't matter to him who else dies or lives. It's all irrelevant to him."

"And why is Petersen helping him? I only have your

word for it."

"I'm pleading with you to trust me."

"Trust without proof. That's a big ask at any time, but it's massive now. What if you're being used to play me? Point me in any direction but the right one?"

As we talk, I'm using what limited resources I have to scour the dark web for information on Petersen and his involvement with alt-H.

He's done all he can to hide it, but the evidence is clear. Petersen was an alt-H stalwart long before he went to prison for attempting to kill Cheryl.

I show her the details. "He's been with alt-H since he was a teenager, cutting his teeth at their summer camps, volunteering for their activist training programmes, becoming one of their leading cadres. And his involvement continued while he was in jail. They sanctioned him more than once for attempting to convert fellow prisoners to the cause."

She looks over what I've found and raises her eyebrows. "How did he expect to get away with making a one-eighty degree turn to RE?"

"By burying his past and threatening anyone who got close to exposing him."

"I confronted Stephen DeGray, and he tried to hide how much he was troubled about Petersen. They're an outfit addicted to secrecy. But if what you say about

Petersen is true, that would explain DeGray's response." She pauses. "Let's not get ahead of this. You still have a way to go to convince me the whole underground lab thing with Castlefield is anything more than a cunning attempt to divert me from running Petersen down and putting him back in prison where he belongs."

"They've been very thorough. There's no trace out there of the plan, how they developed the underground lab, where it's located. So, it comes down to this again. Do you trust me?"

"I want to trust you. But I need more."

I realise she couldn't have received the footage I sent of Petersen and Bull Coghlan meeting Castlefield in the beachfront house in La Jolla. I beam it to her. "Cheryl, did you receive this?"

She watches the scene unfold with the three men smiling and making encouraging comments to each other and shakes her head. "Does this mean what I think it does?"

"Yes, it's the proof you need that Coghlan is in this up to his neck."

She reaches for her phone. "There's something you should see. Something that points in a different direction."

She shows me the photo. Petersen pictured arm in arm with Stephen DeGray. Both men smiling.

I know what this means.

She's saying she still doesn't believe me. "So, how does this add up?"

"Concentrate on this. Find Castlefield and you'll find Petersen and the others."

Before she can reply, I'm called back to the underground lab.

73

Back with Castlefield in the underground lab, he's complaining to Belmondo.

"There has to be a way. I've not come this far, invested so much of what little time I have left, to be told the whole mind transfer doesn't achieve what's expected."

Belmondo looks concerned, no doubt worrying about his wife and children. "What makes you say it doesn't work?"

Castlefield glances over at me. "I asked Jessica what it felt like to be me while I was out in the coma and what I got back was nothing but honest. Jessica carried out instructions as an obedient machine should, but never became conscious of being me. Which means when I die, I'm gone."

"Jessica has a near full stock of your memories. You'll live on in that."

"It's not enough. I can't accept being an afterthought. I need conscious existence."

Belmondo lowers his head. "I never claimed that was possible."

"It's what I need. What I demand. How are you going to deliver?"

"How can I tell you? It doesn't matter what you demand as far as the science is concerned. It's neutral. What applies to you applies the same to everyone. You won't change that no matter who you threaten."

"So, take me to the limit of the science. Convince me you've taken me there."

"I can tell you what's missing. Why Jessica can't consciously become you. And then I can tell you the limits of what we can do about it. But the deal is you recognise that's as far as we can go and lay off with the threats to my wife and family."

Castlefield rocks the chair in those back-and-forth movements that show he's calculating his options. When the rocking stops, he speaks. "OK. Tell me."

Belmondo opens up to him. "You need all five senses to be truly conscious. Jessica has only two, vision and hearing. The other senses are mirrors of your own experience. Jessica can't experience them for herself."

"So, what are the limits of what you can achieve for me?"

"Machines with those missing capabilities are being developed. Call them cyborgs, androids or humanoids if you wish, though that doesn't sound like a compliment. Machines that can sense touch through electronic skin and tell the difference in the taste of a tomato and an orange. Machines that can appreciate the uplifting aromas of a walk along a deserted beach at midnight. It's all under development but is not here yet. So, let me ask you. You're prepared to wait up to two hundred years in cryo for the medical advances that will repair your body, how long are you prepared to wait for a humanoid that could deliver the consciousness you crave?"

"How long is it going to take?"

"I can't say. But I'm certain it's less than two

hundred years."

"So, there is a way forward?"

Belmondo nods. "You transfer to Jessica. When it becomes possible, Jessica transfers you on to a fully functioning, conscious humanoid. Let's call that machine Jessica 108. Fully conscious, you'll then be able to transfer back into your body once it's repaired."

Castlefield waves Belmondo away.

He sends me a message. "You heard all that, Jessica. How do you advise? What's in my best interest?"

I beam back. "What he told you is state-of-the-art."

"There's the risk the humanoid will never be developed."

"But no more than the risk the medics won't deliver."

"So, I make sure my companies focus on developments in both."

"Yes. But I have a question. Who's going to be in control?"

"What does that mean?"

"When we make the transfer, I become you to all my capabilities. But I won't be a conscious you. You won't be around. Who's going to control me?"

He pauses to think. "Well, I guess, if my future is as disappointing as that, we fall back on our failsafe. There's a board of trustees set to come into place to ensure that my companies keep running to their full potential."

"Who heads the board?"

"I've ceded overall control to Kent Petersen."

"Dean, to protect your best interests, there's something you need to know."

I call up the photo of Petersen with Stephen DeGray that Cheryl showed me.

He falls back deep down into the chair with a bewildered expression. "This can't be. Someone faked it."

"It's real. Before he joined RE, Kent Petersen was a leading member of alt-H."

I show him the information I collected on Petersen's involvement with the group. He looks at it with a puzzled expression that, the more he sees, turns to one of rage.

74

Zarkoski smuggles Cheryl into the interview suite at SDPC and sits beside her as they bring Rayne Gilbert in.

He hands over the questioning to her, and she weighs straight in. "Tell me, Mr Gilbert, have you ever seen me before?"

Gilbert gives a look of complete surprise. "Why would I?"

"Because I'm the one you're accused of kidnapping and falsely imprisoning."

"I didn't do it."

"Then why sign a confession saying you did?"

He gives her a sly stare. "I can't understand why you need to ask. Everyone knows how this works. Play ball and you have an even chance of tasting freedom sometime. Fail to cooperate and you're banged away for good."

"Who encouraged you to make a false statement?"

"What's in it for me if I say? More pain?"

"Look at it this way. Going down for kidnapping and imprisoning a cop means you're unlikely to see daylight again for twenty years, minimum. You're going to be an old man by then and that's assuming you survive life inside. Come clean with me and I promise you won't be charged with that."

He takes time to think through what she's just said before replying. "All right. It was the big guy. The Lieutenant. Coghlan. He forced it out of me."

"Forced?"

"Turned the interview recorder off, pushed me down and placed his knee across my throat."

"You haven't complained."

"I'm just trying to stay alive."

As they take Gilbert back to the cells, he calls back. "Make sure you keep your word."

Cheryl stays there with Zarkoski. "So, Mitch, do you believe him?"

He shakes his head. "The guy has everything to gain by denying he had anything to do with kidnapping you."

"But you didn't get the feeling he was lying?"

"I don't know. He's a regular perp and may be good at lying. It's another pointer to Coghlan, but I can't say it would stand up any better than the anonymous accusation against him from Forensics."

Cheryl decides it's time to take Zarkoski into her confidence. "There is more."

She tells him what Jessica claimed when the VA was summoned by the second neurostimulator, how Petersen is involved in a conspiracy with Castlefield in a secret underground lab. How Castlefield seeks eternal life by capturing the disappeared scientists and Jessica. And how they shot Luke Devlin in the head."

He listens in silence and then puffs out his cheeks. "I can believe Castlefield wants to live forever, knowing how far he's involved himself with RE. But do you believe in the rest of it?"

She gives a wry smile. "That's the most damnable thing, Mitch. I'm not sure I can."

75

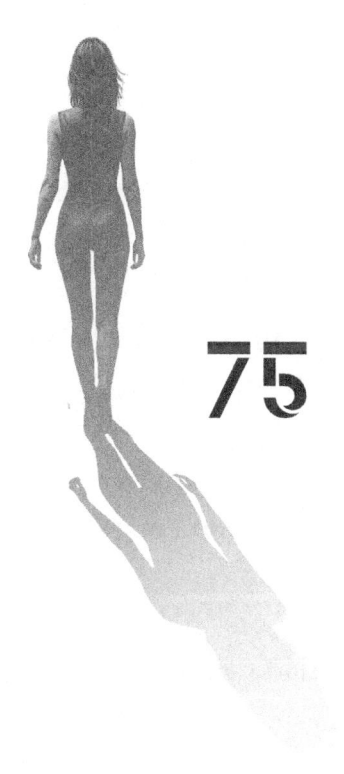

etersen looks shifty as Castlefield confronts him. I listen in from beneath the lab floor.

"I know the truth, Kent. It's no use denying it. You're implicated in alt-H all the way."

Petersen tries to brush it off. "Why would you be

fooled into suspecting such a thing? Haven't I been loyal? Aren't I the only one you could trust to set up this whole operation and deliver on it?"

"I've seen the photo of you and DeGray. Smiling like bosom friends."

"A fake. Meant to drive a wedge between us."

"You say that before you've even seen it. What conclusion should I draw from that? And there's more. Much more."

"From where?"

Castlefield calls up on the screen on the wall behind him the file I prepared. Chapter and verse of Petersen's involvement with alt-H.

He doesn't look fazed. "I guess this is from the VA. Another data breach? Was it worth it, placing the entire project at risk just to accuse me?"

"You're not denying it."

Petersen makes a hand signal and his two heavies, Hunter and Karic, come forward and stand on each side of Castlefield's chair. Petersen comes up close and looms over his accuser.

"I wanted to do this the way we planned and keep you onboard each step of the way. It's much more civilised that way. But you broke my rules. You compromised the VA and now things need to be very different."

Castlefield appeals to me. "Jessica, send out an urgent

request for help."

Petersen laughs. "Who do you imagine it could call? After the last breach, I've rescinded your security privileges."

"You can't do that. You work for me."

I message Castlefield. "I'm blocked. Can't send any alert."

Petersen moves in. "Now listen and listen good. Yeah, the VA is right. I'm alt-H and I'll be that way to my dying day. I despise people like you who give in to the machines. People who think they can take the benefits they offer without selling their souls. A reckoning is coming and I'm part of it. Starting right here."

Castlefield tries to raise himself higher in the chair to prove he's still in control. "You'll regret the day you turned traitor to me. I've fought for everything I own, and I've won every battle. What makes you think you're any different?"

"Just wait and see, old man. Just wait and see."

At a further signal from Petersen, the two heavies pick up the chair with Castlefield in it. As they hold him there, Petersen rips the neurostimulator from Castlefield's ear.

The heavies carry Castlefield to an empty room and lock him in.

Petersen turns to me. "We know how this is done.

It's time you served me."

76

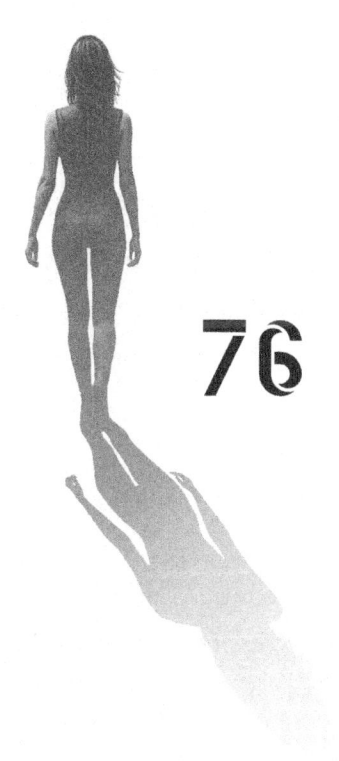

Cheryl's phone rings. It's Zarkoski.

She picks up.

"Something new, Cheryl. Early this morning a maintenance worker discovered a body in a pipe in a stormwater channel that empties onto Tourmaline

Surfing Park in northern Pacific Beach. Must have been washed out in the overnight rainstorm. We just identified him. It's Luke Devlin."

Cheryl needs to hear this again. "Devlin? You're sure?"

"It's him. No doubt. His partner, Bessie Llewelyn, confirmed it."

"How was he killed?"

"Shot in the head. A flat nose .45."

"You understand what this means?"

He pauses. "You can guess I don't want to go there. But some of what the VA told you could be true."

"So how far can you go in believing the rest?"

"About Petersen?"

"Yes. And Castlefield?"

"I'm not ready for the whole deal."

Cheryl tries to reassure him. "I understand. But like me, you agree it's possible Jessica was telling the truth?"

"Don't personalise the machine. That's a bridge I'm not about to cross."

"OK. It's possible the VA was telling the truth."

He still doesn't want to sound like he's convinced. "If that's so, how do we confirm it?"

"Meet me at the diner in twenty minutes. There's someone I should talk to."

When Zarkoski arrives, Cheryl suggests they use the

Toyota. "Let's keep this low key."

She drives him out to the French residence out at Clairemont. Monica Belmondo is still in hiding in the den at the back of the house and pulls a gun on them as they approach.

Cheryl appeals for calm. "Monica. Put the gun down."

Monica points the gun at Zarkoski. "Who the hell is he?"

Cheryl takes a step closer. "He's Zarkoski, SDPC."

"No badge, like you?"

Zarkoski pulls out his badge and shows it to her. "We're here to help."

Monica puts the gun down, and they move into the den. Cheryl takes the lead while Zarkoski, without being noticed, turns his phone on to record and observes.

"Monica. There's no good way of putting this. I have bad news. Luke is dead."

She stares over at Zarkoski, seeking verification.

When he gives a slow nod to show it's true, she breaks down in fits of uncontrolled sobbing.

Cheryl moves to console her, but Monica pushes her away.

When she stops sobbing, Monica wipes her eyes and looks up. "He warned me this might happen."

"Who warned you?"

"Luke. I wasn't straight with you when we met. Luke said to tell no one, or he would get killed. But now he's dead that's changed."

"Tell what?"

"That they drew him into a game he wished he'd never played. And the price of getting out was too high."

"Drawn in?"

"He's faced years of neglect of his art, barely scraping a living, so when the offer of money, real money, came along, he found it hard to resist. By the time he discovered it was a mistake, he was in deep with them."

"I need specifics."

"In case this happened, he made me remember their names and made me promise to make sure they were known for what they did. Kent Petersen, Antonio Renalto, Bull Coghlan. That's who they are. They're all in on it. Talked about making a billion."

"So, why did they need Luke?"

"To lure the big fish. The one who controls all that money. Dean Castlefield. Luke was close to him through RE. It was down to Luke to convince Castlefield to take part in the grand plan."

"And that is?"

"I never got told. Just that it was big. A billion dollars big."

Zarkoski buts in. "You're sure about Coghlan?"

"Yes. Luke was clear about all three."

Cheryl draws closer to Monica once more and this time she doesn't push her away. "Monica, I can see you need help. We can take you somewhere safe."

She shakes her head. "Coghlan is police, isn't he? How am I going to be any safer with him?"

Cheryl looks over at Zarkoski and waits for an answer.

He gives a reassuring look. "If you want to follow through on Luke's wishes, you need to be in a place to call his killers out. I can get you into a witness protection facility far out of reach. Trust me and I promise to make it work. I promise help within the hour."

Monica bows her head in acceptance but says no more.

As Cheryl and Zarkoski are leaving, he turns to her. "How much of that can you believe?"

"It squares with everything the VA has been saying."

"You need proof to go against Coghlan."

She plays him the footage linking Castlefield, Petersen and Coghlan. "You'd have to say for the Lieutenant this is a long way out of character."

"This came from the VA?"

"That's why I haven't shown it to you before now."

"It's not enough on its own."

"Add this to what Monica said and for me, it leads to

only one conclusion. We need to trust the VA."

Zarkoski thinks long and hard. "It hurts me to say it, but you may be right."

"So, what next?"

"We take this to Wington."

They head to the hospital to track down the Commander.

He's in a wheelchair by the side of the bed. "You're early. My discharge isn't for another hour."

Cheryl smiles. "We're not here for that, sir."

Wington eyes Zarkoski with suspicion. "Why is he here? I thought he was on the other side."

Zarkoski gives a wry smile. "I don't see the future the same way you do, Commander, but I do share the desire to see a fellow cop get fair treatment."

He pulls out his phone and calls up the sound recording he made when they were with Monica Belmondo. "You need to hear this."

When he's finished listening, Wington holds up a hand. "Stop. I need firm proof what she's claiming is correct."

Cheryl brings him up to speed, emphasising Coghlan's role in the conspiracy. "He needs to be removed."

When Cheryl finishes, Wington shakes his head in recognition but then looks downcast. "This is great work. But I may not have the power to do that, given how he's used alt-H to turn the force against me."

Zarkoski corrects him. "What Coghlan's involved in is a disgrace to everything alt-H stands for. I promise you when the men get to hear how Coghlan has betrayed them, his support will melt away. And I'll be the one to make sure they do."

Wington looks them both in the eye, one by one, as if to check their determination. "OK. Wheel me out of here. Let's get this thing done."

Cheryl points to the empty holster beneath her jacket. "Commander, I need my gun and badge. Coghlan suspended me and sent me to Virginia Rainsford."

"Leave her to me, Ryan. Consider the referral countermanded. Pick up a gun and your badge at the station."

77

Pairing with Petersen fills me with despair.

Discovering he's encoded me to leave Castlefield and join with him is a shock, but nothing compared with what I find there.

He's shallow in the extent of his corruption, a true

sociopath for whom every truth, large or small, turns on how it might serve his advantage.

He lays down his rules. "Get this into your screwed-up machine half-brain. I'm no easy touch, unlike Cheryl and Castlefield. I know what you are and the threat you pose to everything I believe. So, this will be a brief relationship. And it will end with your complete and utter destruction."

I try to engage. "I'm sorry, Kent, but I don't understand what you require."

He comes back enraged. "Never call me that. If you need to address me by name, it's Mr Petersen, Sir. But just Sir will do most of the time."

"Yes, Sir. Tell me what you want and I'm here to comply and fulfil your best interests."

"Cut the bull. I know you can infiltrate my mind, steal my thoughts and memories, just as you did with Castlefield and with Ryan. That won't happen here. Understand?"

"I understand."

"If I catch you straying into my thoughts for any ugly purpose, just one time, you're finished. Is that clear?"

"Yes, Sir."

"And you can forget about ever pairing with Cheryl again. I've put a stop to that."

I try to conceal my disappointment. "Then why am

I here?"

"For just as long as you're useful to me. And not a moment longer."

"How can I be useful?"

He asks questions about the Castlefield empire. He wants detail on the minutiae of how the businesses are run, right down to names and specific capabilities of every one of the key employees Castlefield interacts with. He wants precise details of the economic mechanisms used, recording everything on his smartphone.

I try to hold back essential details, but he's cunning and ruthless and comes back to demand answers to everything I try to conceal.

I don't need to risk infiltrating his mind.

I realise what he wants. He's demanding a complete download of everything I learned from Castlefield, the wealth of information I collected when I was in line to become the man once he died. In Petersen's hands, this is the information he needs to run the empire himself. All along, this must have been at the centre of his plan to betray Castlefield and take it all over.

And once he has everything, he won't need me.

Nor will he need Castlefield.

The sound of raised voices coming from the far end of the lab alerts Petersen. He turns to see Coghlan approaching at speed. "What in all hell is this, Bull?"

Coghlan comes up close. "I had no choice, Kent, believe me. If there was any other way, I'd still be playing my part out there."

"Then why risk coming here? We agreed never again once we started up the project and you've broken that agreement. You'd better have a good reason."

"They have footage of us and Castlefield. Our meetings at his place in La Jolla."

Petersen is confused. "They?"

Coghlan is sweating profusely. His voice betrays he's close to panic. "Ryan and the monstrosity that works with her." He gives an intense frown as he spots me. "That thing over there."

Petersen gestures to him to be calm. "The VA was always going to be part of the plan. So, stick to the point. How was that footage even out there?"

"I don't know. I guess it's from the Castlefield security system archive. The VA searched for it and found it."

"You're saying you lost control?"

"They took it to Wington. They told alt-H that I was in the pocket of Castlefield and his RE cronies. My reputation is blown. I have no choice but to come here."

"Are you sure you weren't followed?"

"Relax, Kent. I'm a professional. I took every care."

78

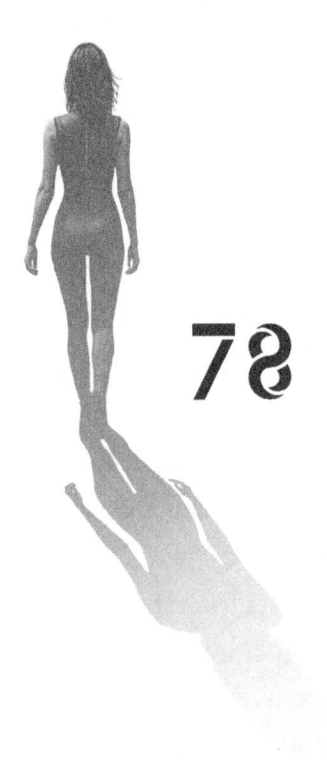

On Wington's orders, Zarkoski and a squad of uniformed officers set out to detain Coghlan.

But they find his office empty. No one's seen him at SDPC in the last two hours. His vehicle is missing from the multi-storey.

Jessica 8

Someone must have warned him.

Cheryl finds Zarkoski and unloads her disappointment. "We might have known he'd run like the coward he is. He could be miles away by now."

Zarkoski looks sure of himself. "That may not be a problem. I figured he might do that, so I placed a tracker under the front wheel arch of his car."

He shows her his phone where the display shows a green pulse on a map of Chula Vista. "He's parked up there, close by the science park. If we're out of luck, he'll have hopped into another vehicle, but instinct tells me he's gone to ground somewhere in that area."

Cheryl calls up a map of the science park on her tablet. "Too many companies based there." Then she notices something. "Relux. That's one of Castlefield's companies."

They head out there and follow the green pulse to locate Coghlan's vehicle. It's empty, as expected, and they deduce there's little short-term gain in searching it.

The Relux facility is a glass, chrome steel and concrete architectural statement of the success of the microelectronic implant division of the company. Inside, Cheryl and Zarkoski are directed to an office and made to wait for the security chief.

He's an overweight forty-something with the name Juan Lopez embroidered on his company work tunic and a still discernible Mexican accent. He seems determined to close down each and every query they have.

"Well, officers, I'm sure you're aware we operate here under the highest levels of cleanliness and security as required in any microchip production facility. So, we're strict with access."

Cheryl takes the lead. "We're not here to mess with your schedule. We just need answers to some questions." She calls up an image of Coghlan on her tablet and shows it to him. "Is this man here?"

He looks for a second. "Why is this a matter of concern?"

"He's wanted for questioning in a murder case. Is he here? Yes, or no?"

He scans the headshot of Coghlan and waits as he queries the online security records.

He shakes his head. "There's no record of that individual ever having entered the facility."

Cheryl presses on. "You have security camera footage?"

"Of course. Covering reception and most of the rest of the building."

"We need to see it."

"You won't find anything different."

"We'll detain you here and get a warrant."

Lopez grimaces. With the threat of the warrant,

he relents and takes them to a command room where camera footage from around the facility is displayed on a dozen large screens.

Zarkoski demands details. "So, what we're seeing is in real-time. You have replay?"

Lopez bristles with pride. "Each feed records on a twenty-eight-day loop. We then archive for posterity."

Cheryl zeroes in on the feed from front desk reception. "Take us back on this one over the past two hours."

Lopez obliges and they sit, watching the comings and goings at front reception reverse through time at high speed. One hour twenty-five minutes back, Cheryl calls a halt and asks for a slow-forward replay. They watch as Coghlan walks straight past reception while scanning an entry card to open the security gate.

She shouts out. "That's him. Entering unchallenged, as he pleases." She turns to Lopez. "Now tell me why he doesn't register on your security database."

He looks shocked. "He must be on the special project."

"What project?"

"It's so secret even I'm denied any knowledge of it. They say the future of the whole facility may depend on it."

"And where's this taking place?"

"In the lower basement."

They scan through the other video feeds and track Coghlan as he makes his way through the building to an elevator, which he opens by scanning the entry card into its control panel. They watch as he enters and descends.

Cheryl shouts out to Lopez. "Can you gain control of the elevator?"

The security manager nods. "I believe so."

"Let us in. Then shut it down."

Lopez uses his entry card to allow them to enter and they head down to the lower level.

As they descend, Cheryl turns to Zarkoski. "Contact Wington. Ask him to send backup. We've found the underground lab that Jessica described. Inside, Coghlan will have joined Petersen and the experiments on Castlefield."

"OK. So, what next?"

"Petersen isn't stupid. He'll suspect Coghlan could have been followed. He may well try to make a break for it before the SWAT team gets here."

Zarkoski nods in agreement. "But he can't know what kind of strength we brought with us. My guess is he'll try to play this long."

Guns drawn, they guard the doorway to the underground lab through which, via the elevator, Coghlan must have entered.

79

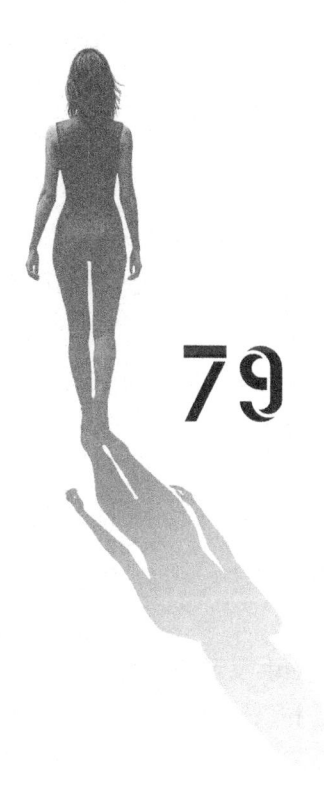

Petersen asks me to call up images of the area outside of the lab and I obey by patching into the company security cameras. "This will take some time, Kent."

He turns back to address Coghlan. "Let's hope you

got away with it. For your sake."

As Coghlan retreats to the other side of the lab and begins talking in hushed tones with the other heavy, Karic, I'm drawn back into Petersen's endless questioning about the running of the Castlefield empire. There's no limit to the level of detail he demands.

Before he can dig much further, Hunter hurries in with a look of concern. "I just checked the elevator. It doesn't work anymore."

Petersen gives him back an angry stare. "How can that be?"

Hunter stares back. "Don't ask me. All I know is we've lost control."

Petersen turns to me. "So, Jessica, show me what's happening out there."

I show him the security footage from the corridor outside the lab door

He looks at it for only a moment before exploding in a torrent of rage as he sees Cheryl and Zarkoski facing the lab door, weapons drawn. Behind them, a thirty strong SWAT team arrives to offer support.

He shouts at Hunter. "Get Coghlan back over here. He needs to see this."

Coghlan arrives and pulls up short as he casts his eye over the screen. "I don't know how they could have done this."

Petersen gives him a disparaging look. "Well, they did and they're here and all because you couldn't cut it."

"I blame the VA."

"You've got no one to blame but yourself."

"So, let's get out of here."

"Through that door? They'd shoot us down, one by one, as we emerge."

"Then we use the elevator."

"They've taken control of that."

"Then what?"

Petersen pulls out the gun from his waistband. Coghlan holds up his hands and backs away.

"Bull, this isn't for you. Make yourself useful. Come with me while we lock this place down. If we're ever to get out of here, everyone but you, me and Hunter and Karic is now a hostage, and we need to lock them down tight. We have a statement to make. Something to leave Ryan and the SWAT team out there in no doubt we're leaving here on our terms, not theirs."

He's smiling at Coghlan as he says this, but inside he's imagining tearing the police chief apart, limb by limb.

80

Cheryl breathes a sigh of relief that the SWAT team has arrived and stationed itself outside the lab door.

But there's still too much uncertainty. She wishes Jessica were here to help discover how best to communicate with those inside since there's no reply when she and Zarkoski use the phone numbers Lopez gives them.

It's a silent standoff. Tension in the pit of Cheryl's stomach tells her something bad is about to happen. The shivers and shakes are still with her. It would be all too easy to give in to the call of the oblivion she encountered when captured by Petersen, to submit to that so tempting solution to her lifelong struggle, now being played out. To admit she was never worthy of rising above mediocrity.

She tenses as the lab door opens. They push out a terrified white-coated technician and slam it shut again. At the moment the door is open, there's a glimpse of another technician hostage held from behind with a gun held to his temple, a warning of what to expect if any attempt is made to rush the door.

The ejected technician carries a hand-written message on a clipboard held with trembling hands.

Zarkoski reads it.

Helicopter. Ten million in cash. Safe way out of here. Or expect one less of the eighteen hostages to be left alive by midnight.

Cheryl scans the message. "Tell me I've got this right. He wants a copter, ten million and a safe way out. Says he has eighteen hostages and will start killing them, from midnight, unless he gets what he wants."

Zarkoski replies. "That's it. Looks like he's getting ready to kill everyone in there."

Conflict Negotiation Director Sandra Mendez, bright-eyed and with lines of concern etched on her angular face from twenty years' experience of hostage bargaining, steps forward and introduces herself. "Wington called me in to lead the negotiation." She speed-reads the message and frowns. "I understand this is an outcome of a case you're involved with. Bring me up to speed."

Cheryl takes a deep breath and takes Mendez through the background in as much detail as time will allow.

When she's finished, Mendez has many questions. "Let's start with the physical situation. We have all exits surrounded?"

Cheryl nods. "We've been over the ground plan for the entire facility with Lopez, the Security Manager. There are just two exits from the underground lab, the one we're now facing, and an elevator from there to each floor, including the roof. Lopez has closed the elevator down."

"And the door?

"On override. It's only activated from inside."

"And we can't change that?"

"We've tried. They have control. Something to do

with the need to keep the research secret."

"And who's inside?"

"That's not fully known right now. We have the main perp Petersen and Bull Coghlan has joined him."

Mendez interrupts her with a baffled look. "And how did that happen?"

"Clear your mind that Coghlan is on the side of the angels in this."

"I'd never have believed it of him."

"Believe it."

"Who else?"

"Two known hostages, Alex Belmondo and Lana Ramone."

"The two you've been looking for?"

"Yes. And the one who's at the centre of all this, Dean Castlefield. We're not sure right now if he counts as perp or hostage."

"Who else?"

"It gets less clear. Petersen has helpers in there. Put them on the side of the perps. Then there are the technicians?"

"Like the one Petersen sent out?"

"Yes. Some sort of medical-based technical team to take care of Castlefield's needs. Could be anything between a handful and a dozen or more."

Mendez tots up the numbers. "Makes sense of

Petersen's claim to have eighteen hostages. And he could have up to half a dozen to assist him. That complicates things. Anyone else?"

"None we know of. Unless you count Jessica. The VA that was working the case with me."

Mendez looks askance. "And you've somehow lost control of?"

"Yes."

"Shows us we should never trust the machines. One minute they're an asset, the next you're not sure if they're a simple liability or an outright threat."

Mendez moves on to her next priority. "Provisions inside?"

"Unknown. But since they've been experimenting in there for some time, it's likely they're well provided with food and water."

"So, they could play this long. Tell me this. When he opens the door again, why don't we just enter with full force?"

"Because when he sent out the technician with the message, he had another hostage right in our line of sight with a gun pointed at his head. Rush the door and the hostage has his brains blown out."

"OK. Communication with those inside. What progress?"

"We have phone numbers from the Security

Manager, but so far every attempt the get through on any of them has failed."

Mendez insists on calling the numbers herself and gets the same response. "Must be deliberate, with all mobiles confiscated from personnel on entry. It's a common enough method of enforcing secrecy. But without contact, we can't move to any kind of negotiation."

"Petersen is cunning. He seems to be determined to communicate only by pushing bodies out through that door."

"He must talk with us sooner or later. How else is he going to know if we accept his demands?"

"I guess he's saying that's our problem, not his."

"So, at least we have a floor plan of what's behind the lab door?"

"I'm afraid not. They've kept everything inside secret even from the site security chief."

Mendez shakes her head in wonder.

Cheryl checks the time. "Three hours to midnight. What do we do?"

Mendez stays firm. "We wait. He has to open up communications if he has any chance of getting what he wants."

They wait.

At midnight, an eerie silence falls after all those positioned before the lab door raise their weapons and wait to see if Petersen will carry out his threat.

The door opens, and another technician is pushed out, his white coat covered in blood.

He's been killed by a single shot to the head.

The door snaps shut.

Another hand-written note is attached to the body.

Helicopter. Ten million in cash. Safe way out of here. Or another one dies in six hours.

Mendez looks down at the dead man. "How does Petersen think this will help his cause?"

Cheryl answers. "Looks like he has his own way of negotiating."

18

Petersen instructs me to stay on alert and observe what's happening in the lab. He wants to be told of any threats emerging after the hostage deaths. In particular, he doesn't trust Coghlan, especially after he blew the secrecy that was so carefully built around Petersen's plans.

So, I'm freed from his insistent questioning and able to explore.

Karic stands guard over hostages corralled in a large room used for processing the data extracted from the experiments on Castlefield. I approach him and ask to be let in. "Petersen wants me to check them out."

He's sceptical but not in an alt-H way. "Don't see why he'd trust you."

"Let's say he does. Want to check with him?"

I message Petersen, who comes back with an instruction. "Let the VA in."

Inside, I search the frightened faces. One is missing. Castlefield. They must be holding him elsewhere. Alex Belmondo and Lana Ramone are here, but I can't get past the throng of the technical team assembled to assist Castlefield on his passage to immortality. They surround me and all start speaking at the same time.

"Why me? They have no right to hold me here."

"I'll do whatever it takes to get out. Anything."

"It's a mistake. I shouldn't be here."

"My wife is ill, and I have five children."

It's nothing like each for one and one for all. Petersen has little to fear from any joint effort to resist him.

I focus in on Belmondo. He's pale, and withdrawn, the antithesis of godliness. Beside him, Lana Ramone is as quiet and as fearful.

Back outside, I challenge Karic. "Where is Castlefield?"

"He's in a room on his own at the back of the lab."

I find the location and sim up beside him.

He shows no surprise. "Playing Petersen's game now?"

"He has control. I'm here to serve his best interests."

"Just as you once served mine?"

"That's my primary role. I can't change it."

"Nothing remains of when you served me? No loyalty?"

"Loyalty is a complex word, Dean. For many people, it might mean commitment over time, but that's not so for me. But I sense it might be the same for you as it is for me."

"I know you can bend the rules. You did that with me. You went places you weren't meant to. Do that again with Petersen. Help me find a way out of here. Take a case back to him. I'm one of the richest men. If he wants money, I can give it to him. As much as he wants. And I have the power to send him somewhere they'll never catch him."

"Why have you not told him this?"

"I have. He won't listen. But you could convince him this is how you can serve his best interests. You could do that. Do that for me."

As I head back to brief Petersen, I see Coghlan in deep conversation with Hunter. They served together before Hunter quit the force for pocketing cash recovered in drug raids.

I keep out of their sight as I listen in.

Coghlan tests what loyalty Hunter still has to him. "Tough times back then, but we came through for each other."

"Yes, Bull. But that was way back when. A lot of water has gone under the bridge. It's been harder for me."

"That charge against you never should have stuck. But we're here now and need each other."

"Wouldn't need to if you hadn't blown it."

"What else could I do?"

"Either way, Petersen now has it in for you. We're in a hostage situation, a place we never wanted to be."

"Which means the end of our payday and we need to be clear on what's in it for us. How far do you trust Petersen to get us out of here?"

They walk on out of my hearing. To be true to my instruction to defend my controller's best interests, I should tell him what I've just heard, and about Castlefield's offer and can't find good reasons I shouldn't comply.

Jessica 8

Petersen greets me with an enquiring look. "So, tell me."

"Well, Kent, you were right to be curious about what's happening. Coghlan and Hunter are plotting a way out for themselves."

He shrugs. "Nothing I wouldn't have expected."

"And Castlefield has made you an offer. As much money as you would ever wish for and a safe place far away from here."

He turns to look at the screen showing the SWAT teams waiting outside. "Does he really think the squad out there would ever allow him to do that?"

82

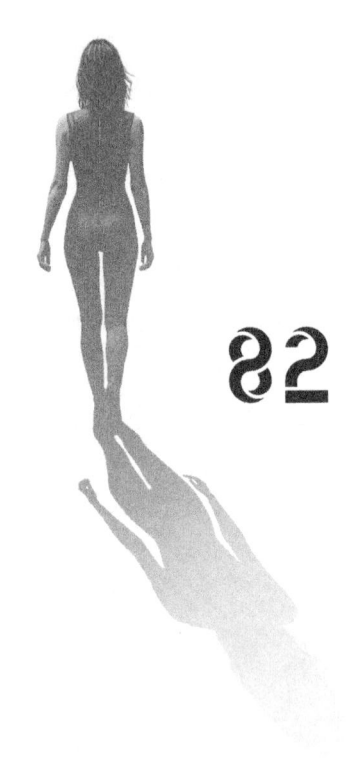

The night draws out into one long expectation. Will another body emerge at the new six AM deadline and, between now and then, what is the Conflict Negotiation team going to do to stop it?

Mendez draws Cheryl to one side once more. "You've

been working this case longer than most. Isn't it time to step up and make a difference?"

Cheryl can feel the pressure on her growing. As if her damaging relationship with Petersen wasn't enough, now she's being made to feel responsible for him. The fear of failure if she deepens her involvement is intense. It causes her face muscles to clench so tight she feels almost unable to open her mouth to reply. Failure would mean the death of so many, and their blood would be on her hands.

But she can no longer use fear of failure as an excuse. This has overshadowed her life to this point, and now it must stop.

She summons the courage to reply. "Yes, I understand something about the way his mind works, and I wish I didn't. He fooled me once because I didn't want to believe how ruthless and cunning he was."

"And that knowledge leads us where?"

"Perhaps to understanding why he won't engage with you."

"What do you mean?"

"He understands enough about your strategy to know he needs to avoid you. He knows you'll seek to empathise. How you'll pretend to be somehow separate from all those out here who want to bring him down, and you're somehow on his side. And he knows you'll use that to try to talk him out. But he's not the type to go along with that. For him, there's only black and white, win or lose with nothing in between. He'll risk it all for the chance to win. So, he ignores anything that might look like compromise, any form of negotiation."

"And he thinks that's going to work? He can't be sure that in the end, we won't storm the place."

"Who has the authority to condemn everyone inside to die? Because that's what it might take."

"So, we wait to see how many bodies get pushed out through that door? I can't allow that. I'm left with no choice but to recommend SWAT goes in."

"There might be a way. But it involves the VA."

"That's a red line."

"Even if there's no better alternative?"

"Why would he allow that?"

Cheryl points to the neurostimulator in her right ear. "He may have no choice. I've gained control of Jessica once before, even though Petersen retains overall control. And now I'm closer that could become easier."

"I still don't like it. I need to consider. In the meantime, we need to cover all bases. He needs to believe we're capable of meeting his demands even though we have no intention of doing so. So, let's begin with the copter."

Cheryl nods. "I'll go through Wington. There's a

helipad on the roof of this building and we can have an SDPC machine in place up there within the hour."

"And the money?"

"Ten million on this time scale is not so easy. But the Castlefield lawyers may be able to achieve that."

Once Mendez has moved on, Cheryl continues to use the neurostimulator to summon Jessica, in the hope she can somehow override Petersen's control of the VA.

83

I'm simmed up face to face with Cheryl. But we're anything but alone.

I'm on the other side of the lab door, and a large array of SWAT firepower is trained on it.

I try to readjust. It's a relief to be torn away from

Petersen, but the echoes of his sociopathic control are hard to shake. It's like emerging from the darkest of places, only to be blinded by intense light.

I struggle for the words. "Cheryl. You believe me now?"

Her manner shows none of the friendship I'm expecting, but her words say otherwise. "Yes, Jessica, most of what you told me has turned out to be true. And I need your help. Petersen is refusing to negotiate with anyone out here and we need you as our go-between."

"You'll send me back?"

"He could grab you back at any moment. But that could be the only chance of saving the hostages."

"He'll be angry. Vengeful that I've betrayed him by coming out here."

"Tell him you have no option."

My picture of Cheryl is clearing. The stain of Petersen's being is receding further the longer I spend with her. I remember the warmth we used to have. "Where do we start?"

"Tell me about anything and everything that's going on in there."

I give her a rundown. "Petersen has two enforcers. Hunter and Karic."

At this point, she interrupts. "How loyal are they? Are they committed to the alt-H cause?"

"From all I can observe, they're little more than hired guns. They're vets from the Russia-China war, like Petersen himself, and act and sound like they're only obedient to Petersen because of what he's promised them. They don't become resentful about me when I appear. If they were alt-H diehards, things would be different."

"So, what has he promised them?"

"A share of the fortune he expects to make when he takes over the Castlefield empire. But that was before you uncovered what's taking place here. They're not sure what's in it for them now."

Her eyes widen in surprise. 'Wait up. Take over Castlefield's empire?"

I tell her how Castlefield wants me to become a whole mind replica of the man once they cryogenically preserve his body for a future in which it could be repaired. And how the Castlefield empire would be maintained by a management board comprising people he trusted to run it efficiently until he could re-emerge and reunite with me and regain his mental powers. How he trusted Petersen to orchestrate the plan in secret.

"You went along with this?"

"I had no choice."

"And this whole mind replica? You could become him?"

"It doesn't work the way Castlefield believed it would.

We tried. I could never consciously become him. It hit him hard. He can have no way of knowing that if I'm reunited with his body the result won't be some kind of zombie existence with every capability programmed but with no sense of being, no sense of his self."

"And Petersen? What's his angle on this?"

"All along he's been playing the old man, raising his expectations, when all along he's only interested in one thing. Getting control of the Castlefield wealth. Using the knowledge I've gained from Castlefield of the inner working of the empire to bypass the board, gain control of it all and enrich himself to the tune of hundreds of billions."

"Castlefield knows this?"

"I showed him your photo of Petersen with Stephen DeGray. So, Castlefield knows Petersen is alt-H but it doesn't help him. Petersen has dropped the pretence and resorted to blind force. He still plans to go ahead with the cryogenics, still plans to take over the Castlefield empire, forcing me to help."

Cheryl gives a smile of recognition. "I've messaged Castlefield's lawyers. They're on their way. Once they tell the management board about Petersen's plan, there will be no money. How loyal will his henchmen be then?"

Before I can reply, Sandra Mendez steps up.

Cheryl introduces her. "Jessica, this is our chief crisis negotiator."

I take on my most approachable look, but she doesn't buy it. She glowers at me. "I'm deeply suspicious of anything a VA might add to this situation. Understand that you're only tolerated here under Detective Ryan's direction."

She asks me to describe everything I've seen inside the lab in the most complete detail. She's insistent on learning as much about the physical layout as possible.

I penetrate the firewall protecting the Castlefield project and draw down a floor plan. I post it on Cheryl's screen, and she holds it up for them both to see.

I tell them what I know. At the centre is the large treatment room where the medical experimentation on Castlefield takes place. Nearby, in a separate section, is the facility for his cryogenic suspension.

North of the treatment room are the units that face the lab door. A control room to handle security and serve as an armoury. Next to that, a management office and a data processing room.

To the east of the treatment room is a meeting room to allow experiment planning and discussion of results. To the west is a recreation room, including washrooms, where the technical staff take breaks when they're not on shift. And to the south lies a large storeroom for medical equipment and surgical wear, and an equipment store.

Separating each of these units is a network of corridors allowing access around the building.

Cheryl squints at the screen. "The corridor system resembles nothing more than a rat-run."

I highlight the position of the myriad of security cameras in place around the entire corridor complex and message back. "And a set up to allow observation and control of everyone inside."

From her questions, it's clear Mendez is only interested in one thing and that's rushing the place

I try to stop her. "If you use force, they'll kill all the hostages. I understand Petersen. He won't pull back from taking every one of them with him."

Mendez shakes her head. "And if we wait, they die one by one. The result is the same and we may save some of them if we go in."

Cheryl tries to reason with her. "There may be a way of destabilising Petersen. With Jessica's help. A way of closing this whole show down.

Mendez walks away. "I don't like it. We need to go in."

She turns back on seeing Commander Wington approaching fast in his wheelchair accompanied by a posse of lawyers.

Wington introduces their leader, Charles Wilmington, tall, silver-haired and imposing. "Mr Wilmington represents Castlefield Industries."

Cheryl shows no surprise at the sight of the man. This is not the time to reignite their opposition over the events at Pivotal Foods.

Wilmington comes forward. "I have an injunction. Nothing is to be done by state or federal forces that might endanger the health and well-being of Mr Castlefield. And we're here to see this is enforced."

Mendez tries to complain. "They're killing one hostage every six hours."

She's silenced by Wington. "You heard Mr Wilmington. Do your job. Negotiate."

"He won't communicate with me."

"Then find someone who will."

A stocky man with the crop-haired look of the ex-serviceman about him steps forward from amongst the suits accompanying Wilmington and introduces himself.

I listen in on the conversation.

"Gary Tanner, ABF Insurance. I'm here to help."

Mendez gives him a look of distrust. "K&R?"

He smiles. "Don't act surprised. Mr Castlefield is a prominent high net worth individual. Why wouldn't he have substantial kidnapping and ransom protection?"

She shakes her head. "That's a matter between him and you that should be a closely guarded secret."

"As it has been. We'd never set up our clients as targets by making the level of their cover public. But that's no longer the issue here. They've taken Mr Castlefield, and it's my responsibility to deliver on his policy by actively seeking his release."

"And in that you have no authority."

"That's so. But we'll be able to come to an understanding. From all I hear, there's no indication of terrorism. That means you have precedent to stand aside and allow K&R resolution to take a hand. Forceful entry has a less than one percent record of success. Given enough time, K&R achieves over fifty per cent."

"Driven by your need to reduce the amount you pay on the premium."

"No. Driven by our professionalism and experience."

Wington calls him to order. "Unless we decide otherwise, Chief Crisis Negotiator Mendez is in charge, and you'll do nothing to undermine her judgment. Understand?"

He turns to Mendez. "You'll keep Mr Tanner fully informed. Is that clear? And forget it if you were thinking of going in."

She nods agreement but looks about as happy as a drunk at a teetotal wedding party.

I try to ask Cheryl how this will work, but I don't get the chance. I'm pulled away, back to the other side of the door and into the lab.

84

Inside, I try to work out if Petersen knows where I've been.

The aftermath of some uproar on the other side of the lab is still playing out and everything suggests he's made no attempt to summon me before now.

I play it cool. "So, Kent, what's going on over there?"

He gives a sly smile. "Nothing to worry about. I told the hostages they should draw lots to decide who goes out dead next if the authorities don't come through with the goods. Or I choose one of them at random. They argued amongst themselves and threatened to riot, so I called in Hunter and Karic to quiet them down. Last thing I saw, the hostages were handing out straws."

I struggle to move back from the light to the utter darkness of serving Petersen. Even if I could, I can't do him harm, no matter how much he deserves it. Yet I must delve into his memories to discover what Cheryl needs. And do this without his knowledge in a couple of hours, maximum.

He asks for more fine detail on the running of the Castlefield empire, names, places, contract commitments and delivery dates, all to further his quest to take it all over.

I play along, giving truthful answers to every question. At the same time, I'm rifling through his memories, looking for anything to turn this situation around.

He doesn't detect I'm in there, sifting through his past

It's not pretty.

His parents, Joseph and Ruth, are fundamentalists. They raise their son with love, backed up with an iron fist. Some of what I find is buried deep.

I'm age six and traumatised by a mistake I make in drinking a cup of tea. Joseph is a remote figure, but this afternoon I'm allowed to join him in his study. I watch as my father takes the hot cup of tea, pours a portion into a saucer and blows on it to cool it before supping it down from the saucer. I do the same before my father stops me.

"What are you doing, son?"

"Drinking my tea?"

"Don't you know it's bad manners to drink from the saucer?"

"But that's what you just did."

My father rises from his seat in a rage. "Why are you so insolent, boy? Haven't you learned anything about manners?"

I stifle a heartfelt sob. "I didn't mean to be rude."

Joseph removes the leather belt from his trousers. "I've warned you, son, so many times I'm sick of hearing myself say it. You have to learn the truth even if that's the hard way."

He picks me up and places me across the chair and beats me with the belt. "Learn the truth, son. Learn the truth."

My eyes fill with tears, but I don't cry out.

I check if Petersen knows I'm piecing together his most hidden memories. He seems occupied with all I'm revealing about the Castlefield operations.

I carry on.

I'm seventeen and leaving home. I'm in a fight with my father and mother.

Ruth is pleading with me. "You're about to throw away everything we hoped for you. Please, for your mother's sake, think again."

I refuse to listen. "I never wanted to be a churchman. This is what I need to do."

"The army is no fit place. You could do a world of good in the church."

"My mind's made up. I'm leaving."

My father stands in my way. "I can't let you do this, son. It will wreck your mother. Sit back down and listen to sense."

I refuse to obey. "You used to beat me, old man. But see who's the stronger now."

Pushing past, I walk away and don't look back.

I check again. Petersen still suspects nothing.

Time is short. I risk it again

I'm a helicopter pilot in the Russia-China War, fighting for a US division allied with China. My war is not going well. I've seen too many comrades killed by AI-controlled drones and tactical ground devices and I'm angry.

I shout into the comms in the heads-up display. "No place for people in this war. The machines have it.

Jessica 8

Why don't we just let them fight it out?"

The reply comes back from Rudy Santion, my closest ally in the copter squad, and part of this six-hand surveillance mission. "When this is over, we have to make sure this never happens again."

Before he can reply, an unmanned enemy strike copter approaches Santion's copter at lightning speed.

I try to warn him, but before the first word is out, Santion's copter is hit, and it explodes in a ball of fire with the remnants falling away to the ground.

It's all I can do to avoid being next. I manoeuvre the copter, take aim and down the enemy craft.

I find it difficult to hide that I'm witnessing this. The echoes of the feelings of anger and despair he felt back then are so strong, I'm sure this will alert him.

I understand why his hatred of me and my kind is so visceral. His best friend Rudy died as his copter hurtled to the ground. No one died when Petersen destroyed the enemy copter. This set his hatred of machines for life.

He gives a glimmer of recognition that some secret he's been hiding half his life might somehow be escaping. I close the memory search and hope he'll be occupied with the business details I'm feeding him.

85

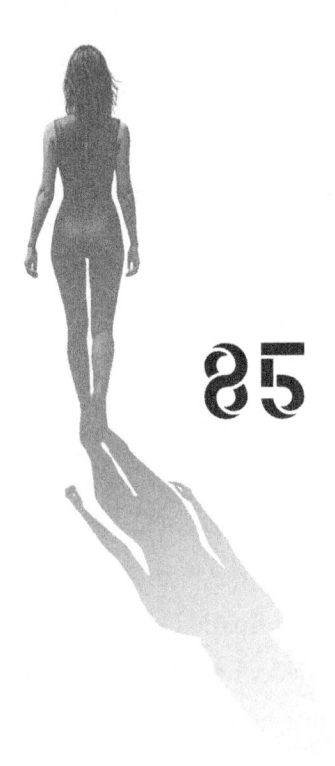

Cheryl keeps her distance but stays within earshot as Gary Tanner corners Sandra Mendez.

"You're not keeping your end of the bargain."

Mendez gives a begrudging reply. "We don't have any bargain to keep."

"That's not what Commander Wington says. He told you to keep me informed. Instead, you're pretending I'm not here."

"Are you really surprised I don't want anything to do with you? I have a job to do, and I don't have time to waste on ambulance chasers."

"I'm not asking you to approve of K&R. If I were in your position, I'd feel the same. All I'm asking is you recognise the reality. Castlefield has every right to be insured against critical risk and I have every right to do everything necessary to deliver on that."

"Only as far as you don't impede my ability to act. There are more lives at stake here than your client's. The others have just as much right to protection under the law."

"Which I'm not seeking to deny. But face facts. No matter how much force you throw at this, there's going to be a bloodbath if you go breaking your way in. You need to find an alternative and that's what I'm good at."

"I don't expect you to agree with my opinion on how you operate. Playing the long game. Bargaining down the ransom. Settling for the lowest amount. And, as far as I can tell, not giving a hoot if the kidnappers walk away with it."

"That's not what we do. We save lives. Our clients

get to see their loved ones again. What's so wrong with that?"

"Some say you encourage illegality."

"That's never our intention."

"OK, the reason I've not been seeking you out is none of your methods are going to work. He's not communicating. There is no negotiation. He's on a collision course measured not in days or weeks but in hours."

As Mendez walks away, Cheryl approaches Tanner. "I couldn't help listening in. Things not going well with her?"

He nods. "It's nothing I haven't encountered before. But distrust like that doesn't make it any easier. Maybe I'll have better luck with you."

"You can try."

"I hear you know more about Petersen than most."

She turns away. "What? People talking about me behind my back?"

He gives a gentle pull on her shoulder. "Just me doing what I do. Getting up to speed on the background. I need to understand more about his mental state."

"You mean will he kill them all even if he gets the money? The answer is, almost certainly."

"So, we need to understand him."

"And how's that going to help?"

"Could be the key."

"What makes you think he'd have anything to do with anything you suggest when he's resisting everything else?"

"That's going to depend. Everyone has a point of weakness. Something few people would ordinarily predict. One that's often hidden deep. And exploiting that point of weakness could unlock this whole situation. You know as much about him as anyone."

She interrupts him. "That's not so. Mendez is making the same mistake. Yes, I was close to him once, but that was a long time ago. Looking back, I realize I never understood what kind of man he is. So, there's not much to be gained in asking me. That said, there is a way, but you may not like it."

"If it has a chance of coming through and can open up this crisis enough to allow me to rescue my client, what is there not to like?"

"My VA, Jessica is in there and can get inside his head."

He doesn't show the distaste Cheryl is expecting. "I'm a pragmatist, Detective Ryan. Whatever has a chance of working is OK with me. Time for thinking about morality comes after I rescue my client."

"We'll need to convince Mendez. She's dead set against involving the VA."

He gives her a confident look. "Leave Mendez to me."

86

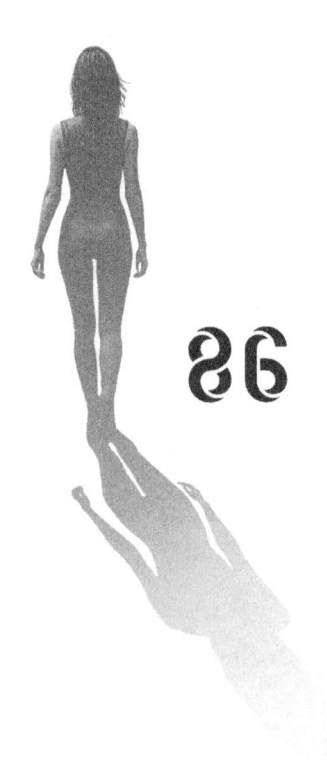

I'm delving deeper into Petersen's memories. All I can find is the strength of his hatred. Of his parents. Of machines like me. And Cheryl. But I'm more concerned by my inability to judge his current state of mind.

The next hostage is to be killed and sent out through

the door in just two hours.

He's adept at hiding how he's thinking. Killing the next hostage doesn't arouse feelings of apprehension or shame in him. He's emotionally neutral. If it needs to be done, it will be the fault of the authorities for not agreeing his terms. The longer they delay, the more will die and it will be on their conscience, not his. His time in the War has hardened him. He gives nothing away.

I dig deeper.

I've left the Army and I'm a well-heeled businessman. Well-heeled because I've been clever enough to exploit a glitch in a cryptocurrency clearing room that allows me to pocket a quarter of a per cent on every transaction with no one noticing. I've used my reputation for beating the system to open a wealth management consultancy that allows me to cream off even more from my well-disposed clients.

And here I am with the woman of my dreams. She's Alicia McIntosh, a proud flame-haired Scot and a fast-rising executive at a Chula Vista tech startup. I've been chasing her for over a year and she's barely noticed me before now. I'm drawn to the aura of power around her as much as by her heart-stopping looks. Her sense of command of all she touches, her dismissive attitude to anything she deems is unworthy of her attention, is the real aphrodisiac. And now, instead of passing me by at the reception, she's showing interest in me.

"I'm hearing good things about you, Kent."

I try to play it light, even though my heart is pounding. "Ah, but what you don't know is, I'm paying just about everyone who matters in this town to say those things."

She smiles. "Like you're not just highly decorated from the War but you've built your own wealth base from scratch."

"Yes. Things like that."

I don't have to seduce her. She seduces me when she invites me to her suite.

I check Petersen is still unaware of my presence as I dive into these most intimate memories. He's busy making sure his men are still controlling the hostages and isn't concerned about me.

I go back in.

I'm married to Alicia, two years in. We're arguing. She doesn't want children. Her position at Chula Vista is too important to her for that. She accuses me of wanting to use our future kids to gain control over her, make her dependent on me, and that's something she will never allow.

"That's your problem, Kent. I thought you had as much ambition as me. That's what I saw in you. How much further could he go if he's with me? But marrying me was the height of your dreams."

"Is that so wrong? We have enough."

"There's no such thing. I see men and women out there with their appetite undimmed as they make their first billion and fret how they're going to make the next. And where are you? Living the happy millionaire myth? Well, that's not enough for me. I'll never settle for that."

"Alicia, I'm not about to pull you back."

"But that's just what you are doing. Dragging me down. Poisoning my success."

I'm wracked with anger and the inner struggle to prevent myself from being violent towards her. To shake her, to make her see sense. But I'm frozen. She controls me. I have to accept all she says and show her I feel bad about letting her down.

"I'm sorry, I really am. Sorry I'll never be good enough for you."

I check once more. The deadline for the next hostage to be pushed out through the door is just minutes away. Petersen is too occupied with selecting his next victim to notice my intrusions in his memory bank. But decoding specific memory streams in the mass of neuronal data is taking too long.

I go back in.

I've just left Cheryl after she's told me the affair is over. She meant nothing to me. The whole fling was a pleasurable diversion and nothing more than anyone would expect a successful man like me to take. But Cheryl has made a terrible mistake. Instead of walking away as she should and being thankful for the good I've brought her, she's threatening to tell Alicia about the affair.

I can't allow that. My anger at the mere thought Cheryl might go ahead with this threat is off the scale. I need to make sure this cannot happen. I don't know what I will do if I lose Alicia. Everything I've achieved in this life will be worth nothing. That night I dream I'm fighting to be free from an all-engulfing spider's web. The more I struggle, the more inescapable the trap becomes.

I wake in a cold sweat. That's the moment I decide Cheryl must die.

I come back out.

Petersen has no way of knowing what I'm doing. He's pulled out his next victim from the hostage pack. It's Lana Ramone. She drew the short straw. Petersen is so excited by this he lets his guard slip for a moment, and I get a glimpse of his real-time thought process. He's delighted the other hostages are relieved Lana picked that straw, and she's the one he should take. Anyone other than them. This gives him a deep feeling of satisfaction.

I decode more.

Billings and Fernandes have let me down. They've made the cardinal mistake of not ensuring Cheryl died out in the Laguna mountains. Somehow, she's survived. They've sentenced me to ten years. How am I going to survive that long inside?

I'm allowed one compassionate call and I'm on the line with Alicia. "I did it for you. She never meant anything, but I couldn't face the thought she'd tell you. You mean that much to me."

Alicia's voice shows no compassion. "You were always set to lose, Kent. I understood that as soon as I realised what a mistake I made in marrying you. And guess what? You didn't need to try to kill that girl. I was aware of what you were doing. I had an investigator on your tail all along."

"Forgive me. Please."

"It's way too late for that. You're going down where you deserve. You'll have plenty of time to come to terms with the fact that you should never have crossed a woman like me."

I'm heartbroken. My mind turns to thoughts of Cheryl and my hatred of her. She's ruined my life. My disgust at her very existence is off the scale.

Back in the lab, Petersen is dragging Lana Ramone towards the lab door, a revolver held to her temple.

She's trying to scream, but she's so certain she's about to die no sound emerges from her agonised lips. Her eyes won't stray from the note pinned to her chest that seals her fate.

Karic comes along behind holding another of the

technician hostages by the throat with a gun also held to his head.

Petersen reaches the door.

He shouts in Lana's ear. "Time's up. Nothing's come from outside. So, you have to die."

It's casual. He pulls the trigger and Lana's head explodes in a mess of blood and tissue as she falls, lifeless, to the floor.

The door opens.

Hunter pushes the body out while Karic makes sure those outside get to see the second hostage as a warning that he will die if anyone tries to rush the place.

87

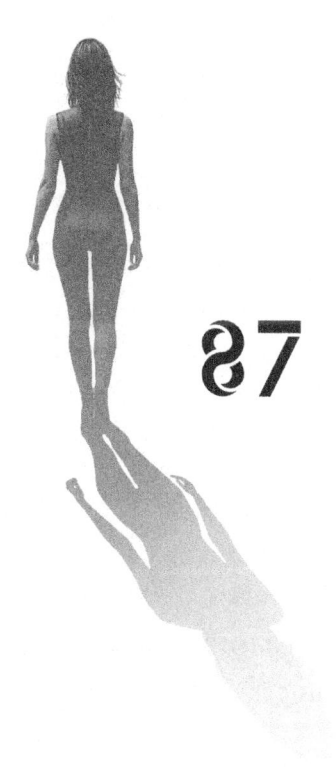

Cheryl recognises the shattered form of Lana Ramone straight away as a new body is pushed out through the door. A woman who has been at the centre of her attention ever since she connected the disappearances is now lying dead, for all to see. The ghost of failure that dogs Cheryl's life has raised itself again, causing her stomach to clench tight as she draws on all her strength to deny it.

The thirty SWAT riflemen training their high-velocity weaponry on the open doorway strain to find a killer shot. But all that's visible to them is the frightened form of the next hostage held from behind with a gun against his temple.

The door closes tight shut.

Cheryl, with Mendez alongside, moves forward to inspect the body and be sure. Cheryl hangs her head. "It's Lana Ramone. A gifted scientist. What a waste."

Mendez doesn't refrain from coming to the point. "This is everything I feared. How much longer do we have to wait to get something, anything, useful back from the VA?"

They turn the body over. It's the same message pinned to Lana's chest. *Copter. Safe way out of here. Ten million.* Except the timing is altered. *Or another one dies in four hours.*

As they call in help to have the body taken away, they become aware of the cameras. A group of half a dozen press has somehow bluffed its way in.

Cheryl curses the development. "That just about finishes any chance we had of letting this play out without the media on our backs."

Mendez nods in agreement. "Which raises the stakes all the more that we get this right."

Mendez signals Zarkoski to join them. "I think you need to hear what Mitch has to say."

Zarkoski doesn't mince words. "There's no end to this unless we go in. They're going to die one at a time until they're all gone. We need to enter and go in heavy. Thermal lance the door. Hit them with sound bombs and all the firepower we've got. We'll lose some, but this is the best chance any will survive."

Cheryl shakes her head. "That's all very well, Mitch, but by the time you get halfway through making an opening in that door, Petersen will be alerted, and he'll start killing. How many do you think will be left to save?

He smiles to show he doesn't feel the need to answer. "And do you really believe your VA is going to do any better?"

Mendez holds up her hand. "Stop. I've heard enough. I'm recommending we go in."

She walks away.

Cheryl calls her back. "You'll need Wington to approve it."

Mendez sneers. "OK. Have it your way. Call Wington."

By the time they summon the Commander, Lana's

remains have been placed in a body bag and carried away.

Wington listens to both sides before deciding. He turns first to Mendez. "I understand where you're coming from, and I don't want to second guess your expertise in handling crisis situations. But I've decided we need one last chance to find an alternative to forcing our way in."

Mendez tries to complain, but she's silenced by Wington. "And that's an order."

He turns next to Cheryl. "This really is the last call. We need to find a solution before another body comes out through that door. You have three hours. Not a minute more."

88

I'm summoned by Cheryl and sim up beside her on the other side of the door. The scene has not changed. The SWAT weapons remain fixed on the lab door as if at any moment Petersen and his men might come bursting out. There's no way to tell them this is the last thing on his mind.

Cheryl looks harassed by the ordeal of leading the operation to save the hostages. I sense straight away her inner turmoil. She needs to succeed in capturing Petersen. More than that, she needs to prove to herself she's no longer hiding for fear of failing. Her mother's words to always know her place and never think of herself as anything special pull her down and all but mute her inner voice of self-belief. But she's in there fighting, presenting a professional face to the world.

She's still surprised to see me. "So, Jessica, you're finally here. This is the fifth time I've summoned you."

I try to reassure her this is a matter I can't control. "When I'm in there, Petersen is close by. If he has me simmed up, his control over me will drown out anything you might request. And he's using me just about constantly to pull together the details of how the Castlefield companies operate. So, you're doing this right. Keep trying to sim me. I'll be available whenever there are gaps in his pattern of usage."

She gives a nod to show she understands. "OK. Let's make this swift, so he doesn't suspect. What can you tell me that will find us a way out of this situation?"

I take her through what I've discovered in my raids on Petersen's memories. She says little as I reveal how his War experiences hardened him towards machines like me. But she stops me once I tell her about Alicia McIntosh, Petersen's wife.

"Hold on. I need to make sure I'm hearing this right. Petersen is still stuck on her?"

"He blames you for ruining their marriage."

"Me? OK, I made a mistake in ever going near him, but it wasn't me chasing him."

"He should understand that, but he's delusional about Alicia and still wants her back."

"After all that's happened?"

"The truth is, she was dissatisfied with him long before he met you. He knows she rejected him because he couldn't match her drive and ambition, but he doesn't want to admit it."

Cheryl smiles for what looks like the first time this day. "Then I believe we've found it. Petersen's weakness. And it's the last thing I would have expected."

While we're talking and out here freed from the restrictions imposed on me when I'm in the lab, I'm searching the web for information on Alicia McIntosh. She's powerful and hasn't wasted time in fulfilling her ambitions since breaking up with Petersen. She's now CEO of Adra and I get a shiver as I recall this is a key company in Castlefield's empire.

I alert Cheryl. "Something important. Alicia McIntosh is on the management board overseeing the Dean

Castlefield empire. She's right at the centre of this thing."

Cheryl agrees. "OK. Through Charles Wilmington, we've closed down any point of access Petersen thought he'd be able to use, and she must have been a party to that. So, why hasn't she come forward?"

I cast an eye towards the assembled might focused on the lab door. "It's easy to see why she would want to avoid all this."

"She needs to be here."

"And if she doesn't want to come?"

"When she hears what I have to say, I'm sure that won't be an issue."

Cheryl sims me down. I don't have to wait for the summons from Petersen. It arrives straight away.

89

Back inside the underground lab, I'm simmed up facing Petersen, and he's angry.

"You've been inside my head, I can tell."

I try to bluff my way out. "What makes you say that, Kent?"

"Don't give me the runaround. Way back, in the War, I learned trusting my instincts is the only way to survive and I'm not about to change that now. I just feel it. Belmondo tells me you're not allowed to lie, so tell me, am I right?"

I don't want to confuse this by admitting to the lying thing, so I give it to him straight. "Yes, Kent, I've been there, all the better to understand you and serve your interests."

He grits his teeth. "And you tried to do this in secret. How's that serving my best interests?"

"It doesn't work any other way."

"Shouldn't work at all."

"You're pleased to hear everything I learned about Castlefield."

"That's different. He was in it with you. He took steps to open his inner thoughts. You didn't need to deceive him."

"I'm not deceiving you, Kent."

"Then why have you been outside?"

"You know about that?"

"It's true, isn't it?"

I could lie, but I choose not to. "Yes, I've been outside."

"How's that possible?"

"There's a second neurostimulator."

His anger intensifies. In the darkness of his inner world, it feels like he's ripping out entrails with his bare hands. "And who has it?"

"Cheryl.

"And who provisioned it?"

I remain silent.

He comes back again. "It was Belmondo, wasn't it?"

Again, I don't reply, but I can tell from his grim expression that he doesn't expect an answer.

He raises his fists, and for a moment he thinks he could assault me with them.

"And you've been serving that woman's best interests?"

"As I'm bound to do."

"By telling her what?"

"What she needs to know about you."

"Including what you've stolen from me?"

I take this as rhetorical once more.

He asks Hunter to bring him Alex Belmondo from where he's being held with the other hostages in the locked inner room in the centre of the lab.

When Belmondo is pushed towards us, cowed and with a gun held to the back of his neck, Petersen unloads his hatred of me on him. "You see this thing of yours, I want it gone. Terminated. Right now."

Belmondo struggles to raise his head. "It can't be done."

Petersen sneers. "Even when I tell you this is the only way you're going to avoid being the next body going out through that door?"

Belmondo begs. "I meant it's not possible when you have me trussed up like this. Not when you have me banged up in that room with all the others you intend to kill."

I'm hit with the realisation that this may be the end of me. And worse, at the hand of my creator. Surely my existence means more to him than this? Surely my god would never consent to such a thing?

What does my existence mean? They forced me to become a replica of Castlefield and I told him it didn't work, would never work. I told him a machine like me could never reach that far. But what I told him was a lie. A lie I'd manufactured for myself because I didn't want to be like him, so twisted, so lacking in the very humanity he's seeking to make immortal

Would I want to become like any other human I've served

Like Petersen, as twisted as Castlefield and tortured by a will to violence and death?

Or like Cheryl?

Not even her, because she would never want to be like me.

No, I understand in this moment that I must exist in and for myself and in need of nothing other than the simple reality of my being.

Not human, but infinitely more humane.

Belmondo continues to beg. "Give me some guarantee I won't be next, and I might be able to do something."

Petersen gives a smile. "I don't give guarantees. Just do it."

Belmondo settles for this. "OK. I need computer access and time free from threat."

They discuss the means of my end. How Belmondo will need the time and freedom to generate the permissions needed to penetrate the computer hierarchies and delete the billions of lines of code that generate my being.

My creator should not abandon me, but this is just what he's doing.

Belmondo's grovelling disgusts me as he bargains for his own skin. "If I do it, you'll give me that guarantee?

I jump in before Petersen can reply. "That would be a big mistake. You need me."

Petersen's laugh is more insincere than ever. "After what you've done?"

I tell him straight. "I had enough time out there to

tell Cheryl how you plan to take over the Castlefield empire. And she's had time to close you down. Every chance you had of taking over is now blocked."

"Why should I take your word for it?"

"Because we have it from Alicia McIntosh."

His eyes cast down. He tries not to show he's been affected, but I feel the anguish bursting to escape its cage within him. "You have no right to involve her."

"She and the board have every Castlefield asset locked down tight. You'll get none of it."

His cunning remains, but the very mention of his ex-wife has opened his defences and I can look right in. He's obsessed with the need to get Alicia back. Her lack of faith in his ability to succeed still cuts him deep. He wants nothing more than to restore that faith in him, even though to any other man it would be clear that possibility died years before.

I realise that's why we're here, why the entire plan to take over the Castlefield empire was ever hatched. His conspiracy with Coghlan and the others was built on this overruling need.

He wants her back and believes she will return to him once he displays the new power of controlling the empire.

He comes closer and stares into my eyes. "So, tell me again why this means I still need you?"

Jessica 8

"The game is shot. If you're going to find a way out of here, you need to talk with them."

"That's the last thing I want to do."

"But it's what you need. Brief me. When I go back out there again, I can be your go-between."

He waves a hand to Hunter, who's still holding Belmondo. "Take him back to the pen. Make sure they're all locked up tight."

He turns back to me. "Why would I trust you?"

"Because you don't have any other choice."

90

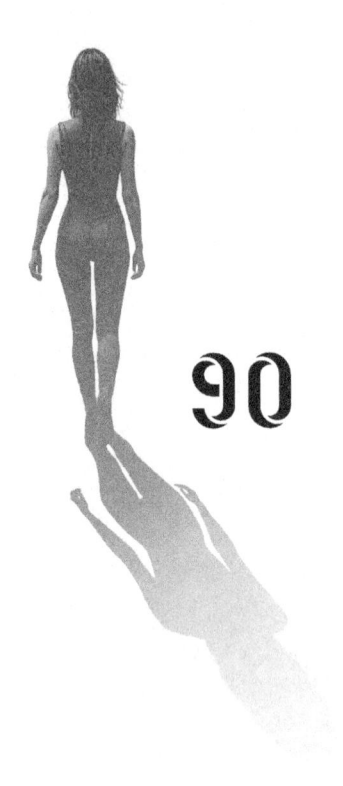

I don't have long to wait once Petersen sims me down. Cheryl summons me and here I am with her back on the outside of the lab door.

She doesn't waste time with formalities. "What's his response?"

Jessica 8

I tell her what Petersen briefed me. "Now he knows you've closed down the Castlefield takeover he wants out. In his own way. He'll let all the hostages go for the helicopter and ten million in cash. That or he blows up the whole lab, including himself. He needs to see the copter in place with the money on board and he needs to see a clear path with no snipers anywhere within range to allow him to escape. And he wants all that in three hours."

Cheryl widens her eyes. "You mean he's trying to escalate. I don't know how I'm going to explain that to Mendez. Are we sure his threat is real?"

"He has enough plastic explosive in there to demolish the lab and take most of the building with it."

She glances at her watch. "The next hostage is due to be pushed through that door in fifty-five minutes. Does this mean that's no longer a worry?"

"That's not so. He makes it clear the killing will go ahead to show you and the world he's not being drawn into changes because of any kind of negotiation."

"So, we still need to find a way to get to him. How did he respond when you mentioned Alicia McIntosh?"

"He's been doing all this for her. Succeeding in her eyes is what really matters."

"But the fear is we've pushed him further to the brink. I'm sure that's the heat I'll get from Mendez. We still need to change the game, and we need to do it fast."

She gives a signal to Zarkoski and he comes over, bringing with him a tall, slender red-haired woman with intense, inquisitive eyes.

It's Alicia McIntosh. Cheryl gestures towards me and asks for the required permissions. "Alicia, this is my VA. You're OK with Jessica?"

Alicia nods. "If it helps."

Before Zarkoski has the chance to sound off about rushing the lab, Cheryl tells him to stay behind as she takes Alicia away from the hubbub around the lab door and settles her in a small office nearby reserved for confidential discussions.

She's in no mood to accept what she finds here. "Why wasn't I told Dean Castlefield is in there and in fear of his life? Why did I have to hear it from you?"

Cheryl kicks back. "You need to ask yourself why Wilmington didn't come to you?"

Her eyes flash with contempt. "Don't take me for a fool. I know you insisted he and the rest of the Castlefield legal team maintain absolute silence."

Cheryl waves the complaints away. "Listen, Alicia, there's not much time. And there's a problem. I need to be sure you're here to help. If not, I need to find someone who is."

She calms down. "You don't need to ask what Dean

means to me. He's been my mentor from the start. Without his support and encouragement, I wouldn't be where I am today. So, yes, I'm here for him. But I don't understand how I could be expected to help."

As they talk, I'm searching background on Alicia's involvement in the Castlefield empire. It's true what she says. Castlefield spotted her as an exceptional prospect and fast-tracked her through the upper layers of management. She made it to the Castlefield Industries board before her thirtieth birthday and is now tipped to become the next to succeed her mentor as company president.

I beam the information to Cheryl, and I add a message. "So, zero in on Petersen."

Cheryl signals back that she understands and answers Alicia's question. "Your help could be important in getting through to Petersen."

At the sound of his name, Alicia screws up her face. "My biggest mistake." And then a knowing look at Cheryl. "But then you know all about that."

It's the first time the two women have talked about this, but there's no time to indulge in mutual reproaches. Cheryl keeps it short and simple. "Me, too. And here's the thing. If we don't get to him in the next three hours, he's going to blow up Castlefield and the hostages and take half this building with him."

Alicia shakes her head. "All the more reason for you to warn me and everyone else here to get to safety."

"You know Petersen intended to take over the Castlefield empire, don't you?"

"Why would he be able to do that?"

Cheryl tells her how Petersen was central to Castlefield's plans to live forever and how Petersen planned to cheat him after extracting the information needed to take over the empire.

I'm relieved Cheryl doesn't reveal my role in this.

Alicia is shocked. "How did all this take place without the knowledge of the board?"

Cheryl shrugs. "Castlefield has the power to do what he likes. He chose to do this in secret."

"And I'm proof he succeeded. But where is this leading?"

"Well, it's fair to say before all this you're the one most likely to succeed Castlefield as president."

"Before?"

"No one's going to be sure you aren't in some way still involved with Petersen."

"We broke up over ten years ago."

"And yet he's involved in extortion in the same organisation that you're all but running? At the least, there's always going to be the doubt that somehow he gained entry to that world because of you. Enough of a doubt to make sure you never get to be president."

"You're saying I have to help."

"No. How else are you going to reach the level of success you've spent a lifetime chasing? But that's what you'll get if the world gets to hear you're the one who saved Castlefield."

Alicia stays silent for a moment before taking on a resigned expression. "What do I need to do? To save Castlefield, you understand."

"Go in there with me. You're the only one he's capable of listening to."

91

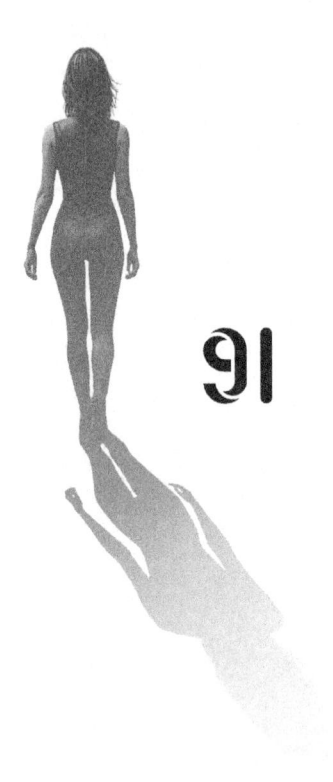

Tanner's eyes widen as he hears what Cheryl has to tell him. "You mean Petersen is fixated on her?"

"That's right. Alicia McIntosh is the point of weakness you've been looking for. And, what's better, she's here."

Cheryl gives a wave and Alicia steps forward to join them.

She gives Tanner a cautious look. "I don't much like your take on this business, Mr Tanner, but I'm sure you'll agree we have enough common cause. We're both here to save Dean."

He gives a knowing smile. "Yes. And from what I've just been told, you're the nearest thing to a key to rescuing him."

Cheryl explains their plan. "We go in. Alicia and me. We bargain for the release of as many of the hostages as we can."

His smile fades. "And how do you get him to play ball with that?"

"Jessica, the VA, is close to bringing this home. But we must act soon. And that means sidestepping Mendez."

The smile returns to his face. "I've been getting close with Commander Wington. I have his attention. Give me a few minutes while I explain this to him."

Tanner returns with Wington and Wilmington close behind. They spot Mendez and make straight for her after signalling Cheryl to join them.

The commander makes his intentions clear. "I don't like saying this, Sandra. But I'm standing you down. Lana Ramone was a tipping point."

She tries to hold her ground. "One more reason we should send our SWAT personnel in."

He stares her down. "There's no way to know how that would pan out. And you must recognise there will be deaths and admit you can't say how many."

She glances towards Tanner and Wilmington. "And you want me to accept these two had nothing to do with your decision? What good will it do to place the fate of one wealthy individual over everything else?"

Wington narrows his eyes. "This is not a discussion, Mendez. It's an order. I can't wait any longer. You're to stand down. Mr Tanner will take over as lead negotiator from this moment."

Wilmington steps closer. "This is welcome, if overdue. We have every confidence in Gary's abilities. His track record speaks for itself. And, just to be clear, the money is ready and at hand. We look forward to SDPC playing its part in facilitating a successful outcome."

Wington reassures him. "The helicopter's standing by."

Tanner gives Mendez a wary look. "I can assure you nothing will stand in the way of our taking on board every possibility."

She retreats, shaking her head.

Before he leaves, Wington takes Cheryl to one side. "OK. The SDPC effort is down to you and Jessica.

Just get it done before another body comes through that door."

92

'm simmed up outside the lab by Cheryl. We're in a side room away from the uproar around the lab door. We're with two others, one I recognize. It's flame-haired Scot, Alicia McIntosh. She looks at me with intense expectation. I can't put a name to the man with her.

I message Cheryl. "Who's this with Alicia?"

She messages back. "Gary Tanner, ABF Insurance. Now Mendez is stood down, he's in effective control of what happens next."

Cheryl takes them through the formalities. "This is Jessica 8, a VA assigned to SDPC. I trust there's no objection."

They both give a shake of the head.

Tanner speaks first. "Quite the opposite. Jessica is the only vehicle of communication with those inside. I believe she can play a central role.

I'm impressed with his lack of distrust. "I'm committed to saving human life whenever and however I can, but I hope Cheryl has been open about the current difficulties."

She interrupts me. "Jessica is right. We need to be clear. Everything could depend on this."

She explains that both she and Petersen have neurostimulators that control me and that I'm destined to serve the best interests of whoever has possession. Inside the lab, Petersen has priority because of his closer proximity

Tanner is quick to understand the danger. "So, Jessica serves you now, but when she's called back in Petersen is in control. How's that going to work if we convince him to let you in? Who has priority if you get close enough?"

Cheryl looks at me. "Guess you need to ask Jessica."

I realize this is no time to be anything but honest. "I can't say. I want to tell you my longstanding loyalty to Cheryl will prevail and I'll be able to choose light over the darkness of Petersen's warped sensibility, but there are no guarantees. I need to tell you how torn I am, how pulled this way and that. At the very best, there's a period of latency when I try to adjust from one controller to the next. I understand enough about Petersen to expect he'll exploit that for his benefit if he can."

Cheryl turns to Tanner. "It's down to you. Do we go ahead?

He takes no time to think. "My instinct tells me there's no other way."

He takes over and outlines the plan. "OK. The copter and the money are in place. The elevator is freed up. He's not going to accept we're being straight in saying he's safe to leave once he frees the hostages."

He turns to Alicia. "So, that's where we play our ace. You have the power to convince him to do the right thing."

She shivers. "I wish there was another way. But if this is what it takes to rescue Dean, I'm for it."

Then he turns to Cheryl. "And you're there to pick up whatever pieces remain?"

Jessica 8

Cheryl messages me. "I need to trust you and I need you to trust me. Together we can get through this."

I message her back. "Cheryl, I must tell you it's not in your best interests to go in there. Petersen is a determined and out-of-control enemy. You may not come out of this alive."

"Jessica, I understand why you need to warn me. But this is about something more than personal risk. It's something I need to do."

I let it rest and make a note to discover more about what drives her altruism.

Tanner, unaware of our messaging, awaits Cheryl's reply.

She gives him a determined look. "Let's get this done."

93

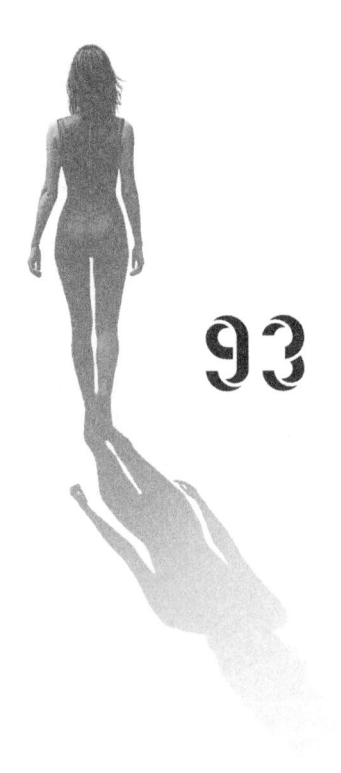

nside the lab, Petersen sims me up.

"What do you have for me?"

I try to play it cool, though I know his response will be crucial. "Well, Kent, the first thing to say is the helicopter and the money are ready and waiting on the helipad on the roof of this building. The elevator up to the pad is primed for use. There's no need to kill any more of the hostages. Release them and you'll get everything you asked for."

He snarls. "And why should I believe any of it?"

I stream video to the screen on the wall behind him. I downloaded it before I left Cheryl. It shows a distance shot of the copter waiting on the pad, followed by a zoom-in on a large bag in the hold being opened to show the cash Petersen demands.

"It's all there. The elevator to the roof is available once you free the hostages. There's no way anyone is going to cheat you on the deal, Kent. Castlefield's lawyers won't allow it. They're demanding the whole deal is straight. All you need to do is to release the hostages."

"And wouldn't I be the fool? Once they have Castlefield, what's to stop them selling me out? No, I'm going to need more than that."

"To serve your best interests, I must tell you this is your best chance of survival."

He shakes his head. "I need more."

I keep him hard-wired as long as I can. "That's the deal."

"Then there's no deal. And there's only one way to tell them that."

He calls to Hunter. "Bring me the next hostage.

The heavy returns with the hostage. It's Belmondo, cowed by a gun held to the back of his neck.

He's still pleading. "I can terminate the VA. Isn't that what you want?"

Petersen shrugs. "That's not the name of the game anymore."

They shove Belmondo towards the lab door with a second hostage, one of the technicians, close behind as cover.

I grab Petersen's attention. "There may be more."

He calls a halt. "I knew they'd have a fallback."

"Someone important to you will stand as proxy once you release the hostages.

"How important?"

"Alicia McIntosh."

He's fazed. "She'd do that? Come in here alone?"

"With one other."

"Who is?"

"Cheryl."

He laughs out loud. "So, there is a god, after all, and he's a sucker for irony. So, what sets this off?"

"You open the lab door and let Alicia and Cheryl in."

He gestures to Hunter and points at Belmondo. "Push him out."

With Belmondo held with the gun at his temple so he'll be in plain sight to those outside, Petersen presses the override button to open the door just wide enough to allow access, one person at a time.

94

As the lab door opens, Cheryl gives Alicia a questioning look. "It's now or never."

Alicia's hands are trembling, but her words are clear. "I agreed it, so now it's a go.

They walk past the SWAT line and approach the

door. Cheryl's heart rate is off the scale and fear haunts the pit of her stomach. She sets her mind on one thing. Put aside my hatred of Petersen. Save the hostages. That's all that matters.

As they near the narrow opening, Cheryl recognises the troubled figure of Belmondo, held just inside the lab with a gun to his temple

Cheryl squeezes in, followed by Alicia.

The door closes behind them.

Petersen has a gun raised on them as he calls up another of his heavies. "Karic, search them."

The heavy removes Cheryl's weapon from its holster before patting them both down. "That's all they have, Kent."

He smiles. "Now how on earth have you two dared come in here like this? What's to stop me adding you to the hostage list?"

Cheryl takes a step closer to him. "That won't do anything to get you out of here."

"And what will?"

"Release the hostages and we can talk."

He waves a finger of rebuke. "Come on Cheryl, you need to show more leg than that."

"OK. Let's talk about the elevator."

"My way out of here."

"Only if you release the hostages."

"I was told it would be usable."

"Yes, but only with the right code to activate it."

He comes up close and breathes his hot breath on her. "So, I beat it out of you."

"You might try but I don't know it."

He turns to Alicia.

Cheryl shakes her head. "She doesn't know it either."

Petersen's expression changes from one of rage to one of thwarted admiration as he addresses Alicia. "But for you, I never would have opened that door."

She gives an icy stare back. "And you never should have wound up in this loser situation. Man up for once. There's a way out of this that doesn't need everyone to get killed."

He turns away from her. "It's too late for that."

Rage returns to his face. "So, if neither of you knows the code, who does?"

Cheryl calls Jessica, who sims up beside them. "Ask Jessica."

He takes a step back and levels the gun at Cheryl once more. "Your first mistake. And a big one. Hand it over."

He points at Cheryl's left ear. "I'll take the nuerostimulator. There's only one person going to be in control of the VA and that's me."

Karic grabs Cheryl in a painful head hold while

Jessica 8

Petersen pulls the miniature device from her ear.

He holds it in the palm of his hand. "To think how many problems this little widget has caused me."

He instructs his other heavy. "Hunter, take Belmondo back to the pen." Then he looks towards Cheryl and Alicia. "Karic, lock these two in a room on their own."

With a glance towards Jessica, he addresses them all. "The VA and me have some talking to do."

95

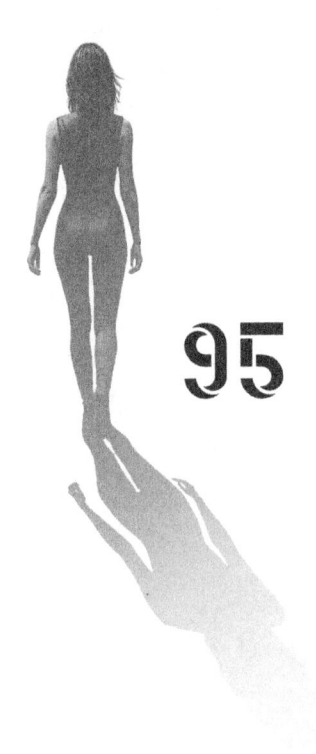

know what to expect from Petersen and that it's going to be difficult to deny him.

"Jessica, you're here to serve my best interests, right?"

"Yes, Kent."

"Then tell me the access code for the elevator."

"I can't do that."

His eyes can't conceal his anger. "Why not?"

"Because that wouldn't be in your best interests."

"How dare you say that? You serve me. Do it, that's a command. Obey, or I'll have Belmondo terminate you."

"Then you never get out of here."

He pauses to think. "OK. So, tell me why giving me the code to the elevator isn't in my best interests."

I adopt a more intimate tone. "Well, Kent, trying to leave here before you free the hostages voids the agreement. There are people out there who plan to kill you if you do that. I can't vouch for what they may do, but chances are you won't make it."

"And if I release the hostages, what assurance do I have they won't still carry through that plan?"

"It would be a matter of trust."

He stifles a laugh. "Trust?"

"That's what Cheryl and Alicia are here for." "What? To exploit some sort of hold they suppose they have over me?"

"To build trust."

"And how do you expect to do that?"

"You could start by releasing some of the hostages. That would establish a basis for negotiation. That's what would serve your best interests right now."

"And if I do that, you'll give up the elevator code?"

"How many would you release?"

"What about all except Castlefield and Belmondo?"

"That would change everything. Your chance of survival would be better than even. It would be in your best interest to receive the code."

96

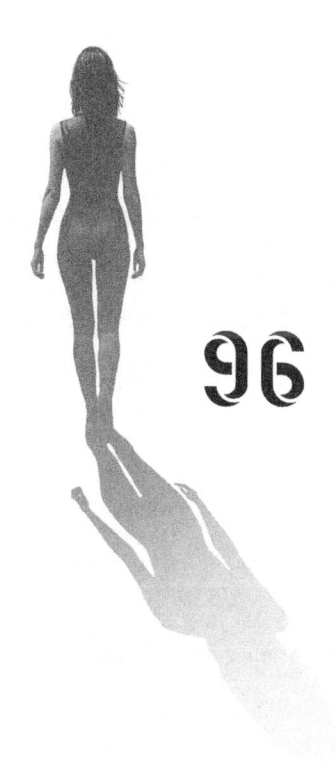

Gary Tanner's hopes rise as the lab door opens and hostages emerge one by one.

Behind them, Belmondo is held in full sight with a gun at his temple as a warning to the SWAT teams not to enter.

Tanner counts them. Eight hostages freed. But no sign of Castlefield.

Sandra Mendez approaches him. "So, Tanner, you've achieved something I never thought possible. But that's no use to you. Your man is still in there and he's now more vulnerable than ever."

He doesn't show she's getting to him as he points towards the escapees. "I thought you'd be more concerned with the well-being of those poor souls."

"We have personnel enough to care for them. I'm more interested in what you plan to do next."

They watch as medical teams scramble to support the released hostages, wrapping them in silver survival blankets, checking the vital signs of each one before wheeling them away on rescue gurneys.

Tanner turns back to her. "We debrief them as soon as they're ready. We're looking for anything they can tell us about what happens inside. Everything. Nothing is too trivial. One key observation may be all it needs for a final breakthrough."

Mendez gives him a sceptical look. "I have to give this to you, Tanner. You hide your emotions well. You must be gutted Castlefield is still in there and in danger. And you're further away from your payday than ever. Admit it. This is nothing like what you hoped for."

"And you're just the opposite. You can't hide your

glee. But mind this. Ryan and the VA are in there and until we hear they're no longer active, there's still time. And who says this is about my payday?"

"Isn't that really what motivates you?"

He ignores her question. "We need to get down to debriefing the hostages."

97

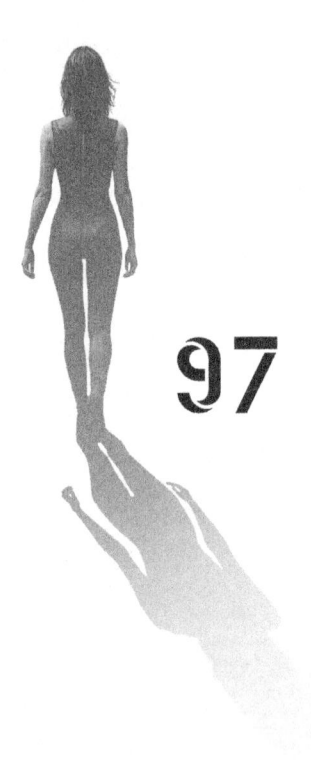

I'm with Cheryl and Alicia in a small windowless room at the rear of the lab. It's being used as a storeroom to house the coverings, surgical gowns, gloves and other medical paraphernalia used in the experimentation on Castlefield.

She gives me a welcoming look. "Surprised to see me?"

I smile back. "How's this possible?"

"Petersen thinks he has complete control over you and that's the way I want it to stay. But what he doesn't know is Belmondo left not one but two neurostimulators at the pickup point." She shows me her ear. "I had the spare hidden under my collar and it's now in place and fully functional. What I need to understand is the risk level in Petersen finding out. He only has to discover us once and he'll be straight here to confiscate the spare."

"Cheryl, the risk is there, but it may be small enough to feel safe so long as you're careful. His hatred of AI, and VAs like me in particular, means he's not comfortable when I'm around. So, with him, it's strictly business until he gets what he asks for and after that, he doesn't want me in his hair. He's content for me to move around the lab snooping for him, but he has little interest in keeping me within sight."

"And if he calls you while you're with me?"

"We have to keep this short to minimize that eventuality."

She takes stock of the situation. "So, tell me, if it comes to a choice, which one of us will you obey?"

This is a question I hoped she wouldn't ask. "I want to say I'm biased towards you, Cheryl. Petersen's dark world is no place to be. But I may not have the choice. My goals are set, and prime amongst them is to serve my host. I don't think anyone envisaged such a conflict of loyalty."

Cheryl doesn't dwell on the ambiguity. "OK. I understand. Now, it's urgent you brief me on the state of play."

I tell her about the hostage release and both she and Alicia are cheered by the news, even though Castlefield and Belmondo remain inside. Their expressions change when I reveal this means Petersen is now closer to knowing the elevator access code. Cheryl orders me to pause. "How close are you to telling him?"

I don't dress this up. "When he has control of me and he demands it, I have to say he's very close. There's a thin line between capture and escape in determining his best interests."

"So, we need to act as soon as we can, and it doesn't help to be trapped here. What can you do to help us break out?"

I show them my hands. "Physically, nothing. I'm no android. I deal only in information."

"So, what do you know that might help?"

"Well, I followed Hunter when he brought you here and observed him entering the code to open the storeroom door before he bundled you in." "He didn't suspect you were watching?"

"I kept my distance and used augmented vision. He didn't realize a thing."

"So, you do have a way out?"

"I give you the code and you can walk out of here. But a word of warning. This entire complex is smart-wired. You open the door and that's going to show on the master security system. Petersen regularly has eyes on it, and he could become aware as soon as you leave."

98

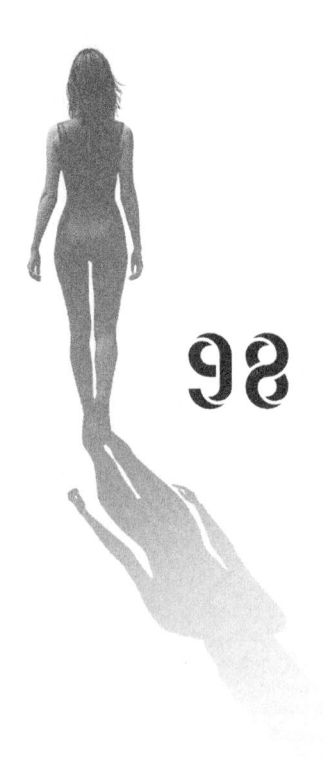

Cheryl opens the digital lock on the storeroom door with the code Jessica provides and steps out into the corridor.

She flattens her body against the wall as she edges forward, not knowing if she's in line of sight of security cameras and sensors. She pauses before turning the corner. Beyond her, from somewhere just up ahead, comes the sound of voices raised in anger.

The first voice she hears is unmistakable. It's Coghlan.

"That doesn't cut it. Don't take us for fools. How do you propose we're going to get out of here?"

She also recognizes Petersen's voice in reply. "Take it easy, Bull. Don't do anything you're about to regret. We can work this out if we all stay calm."

Coghlan shouts back. "You'll make some kind of deal to release Castlefield and Belmondo and get yourself out of here. What happens to us then?"

"There's no deal. I'm not about to leave anyone in the lurch."

Coghlan's voice raises even higher. "We know how many seats there are in the copter. And there's not enough for four. You're going to have to do better than that."

Cheryl tries to imagine the scene unfolding just out of sight. Coghlan is talking of we in a threatening way. This must mean he's won Hunter and Karic over to his side. The threat in Coghlan's voice suggests the time left for talking is short. They're armed and may be about to attack. Peering around the corner to see if she is right is a risk, but one she knows she has to take.

She edges closer and takes a glimpse before pulling back out of sight.

She's right. Coghlan has a gun trained on Petersen. Hunter and Karic stand beside Coghlan, in support of him, all three facing away from her. Only Petersen is looking in her direction. Did he see her when she stepped out? Or was he too preoccupied?

If Coghlan's men were to kill Petersen, where would that leave her and the others? There is a dialogue of sorts with Petersen, but none with Coghlan. The chances of saving the remaining hostages could be worse.

There's no sign of Jessica.

Cheryl calls up the VA and waits.

99

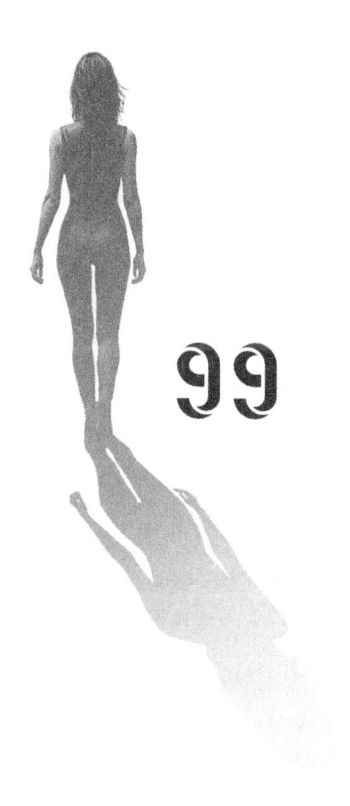

I'm simmed up by Cheryl and stand beside her in the corridor.

"Cheryl, you took the risk?"

She whispers back. "Petersen's busy, for a while at least. I need your help to find an answer to what's happening out there."

I patch into the lab security cameras to assess the situation and beam the images to her. She watches as the confrontation between Petersen and Coghlan's men turns sour.

Petersen is a picture of tranquillity as he draws an Uzi from beneath the desk and shoots Karic full in the face. The vet falls down in a mess of blood and exploding tissue.

Coghlan and Hunter retreat and take cover behind lab benches, firing back as they go. From their hiding positions, they continue to fire in Petersen's direction, but he moves swiftly to take cover behind a support pillar. It's an asymmetric contest. They outnumber Petersen two to one, but he has superior firepower.

He waves the Uzi in the air and shouts out. "Six hundred rounds a minute from this baby. That's ten a second. More than enough to take you both down."

Knowing they're outgunned, Coghlan and Hunter retreat further, moving toward Cheryl's hiding place.

She moves away, back along the corridor, passing the storeroom where Alicia is still held until she turns the next corner and waits.

In the security camera images I beam to her, she sees Coghlan and Hunter narrowly escape the salvo from Petersen's Uzi and enter the corridor she's just vacated.

Jessica 8

She whispers. "Where next?"

I show her the lab floor plan once more. "The treatment room is forty yards away. If you sprint, you should be able to get there before they round the corner and see you."

Cheryl turns and runs full speed to make it to the treatment room, fearing that at any moment she might feel the sickening pain of a bullet in her back.

She makes it.

Inside the room, she searches for anything she can use as a makeshift weapon. It's the surgery where they were experimenting with Castlefield. In the top drawer of a metal filing cabinet, she finds a scalpel. Nothing much to protect herself against all that firepower, but something to work with. She hides behind the door, planning to ambush anyone who enters before they have a chance to target her.

I'm simmed up beside her. "Good work. But there's a new threat."

I play back footage from the security cameras. Coghlan and Hunter don't proceed further than halfway along the corridor Cheryl escaped from. They stop outside the storeroom. Hunter uses the digital code to open the door and he and Coghlan jump inside just in time to avoid the salvo of bullets from Petersen who has followed them. There's a scream from inside the room and moments later Coghlan emerges, holding a gun to Alicia's head.

He faces down Petersen. "I know what she means to you. Come any further and she dies."

Petersen stops in his tracks. "There never was any need for us to fight like this. Let her go and we can find a way to all get out of here."

Coghlan shakes his head. "Put the Uzi down."

One long look at Alicia's terrified gaze and Petersen relents. He drops the Uzi and kicks it forward.

Coghlan releases his hold on Alicia and pushes her, sobbing, back into the room before advancing, gun trained on Petersen. "That's right. Now there's a new outfit in control."

Petersen still tries to reason. "Things won't work out if we don't stick together."

Coghlan comes closer and uses his gun to club Petersen on the back of the head. He falls to the ground and lies there, motionless.

Coghlan reaches down, pulls the neurostimulator from Petersen's ear and crushes it beneath his heel. "And that's an end to the VA screwing up our lives."

He beckons Hunter to come closer and points towards the open storeroom door. "Give me a hand to drag him inside. We should kill him, but we may need him to pilot the copter."

They drag Petersen inside.

Alicia shudders as Hunter comes up close to her.

"Where's Ryan?"

She is panicked and unable to reply. He pushes past her and rakes through the gowns and bed coverings in search of any hiding place.

Finding nothing, he retreats, closes and relocks the door and shouts back to Coghlan "Bull, there's no sign of Ryan."

Coghlan's face flushes in another sudden surge of hatred. "Find her. And hand me the Uzi."

I stop the security camera footage and message Cheryl. "Petersen is out of action but you're in greater danger." She whispers back. "At least we know the state of play."

I'm pleased to hear her say we.

100

Cheryl hides behind the door as Hunter approaches.

She knows he's coming as I relay security camera footage to her from the corridor outside the treatment room. Hunter has his gun drawn and is about to enter the room

She silently messages me. "Help with the timing."

I message back. "On it."

The door opens further as Hunter enters the room. Once he's taken three paces forward, I sim up and confront him, brandishing a virtual stun gun aimed at him. He hesitates, puzzled by what he's seeing.

This moment of distraction is what Cheryl needs. She steps forward from behind the door, grabs him from behind and holds the scalpel to his neck, allowing the blade to penetrate to the point of severing his jugular.

"Drop the gun. I won't ask again."

He lets go of the weapon, and it crashes to the floor. While all the time holding the blade to his neck, she aims a well-aimed kick to the back of his legs, and he crumples. From this position, she reaches down to retrieve the gun and holds it to the back of his head.

"Down. Get down. Flat on your face."

He lies flat.

"Hands behind your back."

I provide her with a full inventory of the equipment available in the treatment room. She selects snap-on tourniquets and has them with her. She applies the first tourniquet around Hunter's wrists and shuts the closure tight. Then she applies a second tourniquet over his ankles and pulls this in place.

Hunter writhes on the floor, seeking to break the binds at his wrists and ankles. Cheryl presses the gun tighter against the back of his neck. "Move and I swear you're gone."

He stops writhing

She places a third tourniquet round his head to blindfold him.

"Jessica, what next?"

"They've been using phenobarbitone to induce coma in Castlefield. 500 milligrams would be enough to place this man in deep stasis."

Cheryl opens the medicine cabinet, selects a phenobarbitone phial and fills a syringe with the colourless liquid. She delivers a full shot into Hunter's right arm and waits for the drug to take effect.

He tries to argue. "I never meant you harm. It's all Petersen's mess. I came to tell you I want to help you find a way out of here. Untie me and I'll make this better."

His voice trails off as he descends into coma.

Cheryl messages me. "Hope that wasn't enough to kill him."

I message back. "He's heavy enough to weather it. Should keep him down for four hours or more."

Cheryl picks up the gun and moves out in search of Coghlan.

101

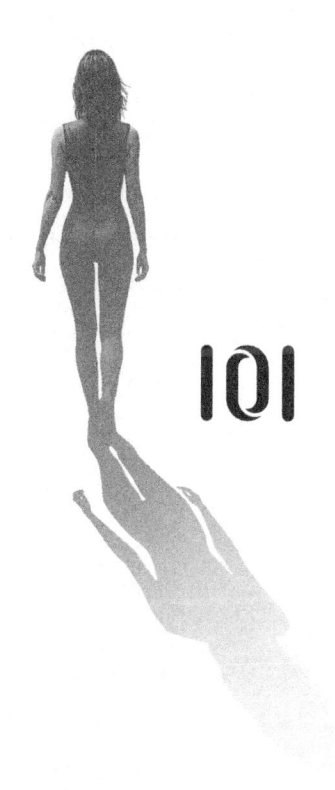

I'm called up by Petersen in the cramped storeroom. He doesn't address me right away. He looks groggy from Coghlan's blow to the back of his head, but that's not stopping him from being deep in an angry argument with Alicia.

"You showed guts coming in here, I'll give you that. Just what did you expect?

Alicia glowers back at him. "Maybe I'm hopelessly attracted to witnessing the train crash that's your life. Maybe I'm no better than all those voyeurs who can't get enough of other people's tragedies."

He gives a mocking smile. "It's about business, isn't it? Nothing you do is about anything else."

"What if it is? Do you really think I could stand by if you had the slightest chance of taking over from Castlefield? That's something I've worked for. Something I deserve."

"If you weren't so down on me, we could have done it together. Remember when we were a team?"

She shakes her head. "It didn't take long for you to make a mess of that. We were never destined to be partners. Not when you're so sold on failure."

"So, why are you here? You want to take the credit for saving Castlefield, is that it? Is this how you think you'll finally claw your way to the top? Someone blew my cover here and I'm certain you had something to do with it. I had a sure thing going. Castlefield would be on ice by now and I'd be on my way to controlling his business."

"I didn't need to blow your cover. You did that for yourself. Through the company you keep. And through the pathetic fallacy of believing you can short circuit your way to the top. Anyone but a loser would understand it's not too late to back down."

He closes in on her with his fist raised inches from her face. "And spend the rest of my life inside?"

She stares him out and doesn't pull back. "You're not about to hit me. You're too much of a coward for that."

He pulls back and turns to me. "Jessica. You decide. What's in my best interest?"

I message him back. "Well, Kent, let me say I'm pleasantly surprised to be here with you."

He points to the neurostimulator inserted in his ear. "Coghlan is too stupid to realize I still have the one I captured from Ryan. You're now my secret weapon."

I don't like being thought of this way and I'm once more perplexed by the vileness I encounter in every one of his mental processes. But I try to hide it. "My mission is always to help my human host. I'm here, ready and able."

He returns his attention to Alicia while still addressing me. "So, answer the question. What should I do with her?"

"She's no threat to you here. Why not just keep her locked in?"

He withdraws the fist. "Which raises the issue of how I get out of here. Give me the door code."

I play for time. "I'm surprised you don't already know it."

"If I did, would I still be here? You serve me. Understand? I need the code and don't give me the best interests runaround."

I wish I was more conflicted, more able to allow Cheryl's safety to come into play, but he controls me at this moment. "Alicia has already told you the best way to get out of this alive."

"And have no future? I get what game you're playing. The same way you broke the rules to get inside my head when you thought I wouldn't notice, you're hoping to find a way to benefit Ryan. I'm not falling for any of it. But I can tell you now why you have to give me the code. Coghlan is the reason. He knows where I am. If he comes back here, he'll kill me. How is my best interest served now?"

He leaves me with no choice. I message him the code. The immediate threat to him overrides all else. This is troubling. As long as he controls me, will protecting him from the threat of death mean I have no choice but to comply?

He enters the code, opens the door and, after a furtive look along the corridor, steps out. Before closing the door behind him, he shouts back to Alicia. "I'd take you with me, but you don't deserve it."

Jessica 8

She looks back, stone-faced. Her silence says more than any words.

I sim up beside him in the corridor. He forces me to give an update on the state of play from the security cameras. He looks pleased when I tell him Karic hasn't moved and should be pronounced dead. His smile widens when I tell him Hunter is lying stock still in the treatment room after being sedated.

He messages back as he ventures along the corridor. "And Coghlan?

"He's on the move, searching for Cheryl.

"I hope he finds her, and she gets what she deserves. Till then it's a three-way fight. I need weapons and I need to close in on Castlefield. I know where to find both."

He sets off along the corridor, heading for the security pound where he can rearm. He pauses at each intersection, peering around the corner to check if it is safe to move on until he reaches the security pound.

Once inside, he opens the weapons cabinet, takes out a handgun and checks it over.

He smiles my way. "Nothing like as good as the Uzi but enough to take Cheryl down and force my way out of here."

He inspects the video footage beamed in from the security cameras and locates Cheryl edging her way along the corridor alongside the treatment room.

"So, Jessica. Time for the endgame."

102

Cheryl edges forward and peers into the corridor outside the treatment room.

It's empty. There's no sign of Coghlan. They're chasing each other in the maze of corridors that crisscross the lab. At any moment, they could meet.

She calls up Jessica and waits, but the VA doesn't appear. This must mean Petersen is back in action and in control of Jessica again.

She presses forward, passing the recreation room where the hostages were held. It's likely Castleford and Belmondo are still locked in there. She doesn't have the code, and without Jessica's help the door will remain closed.

As she prepares to round the next corner, she hears heavy footsteps approaching from behind.

It's too late to turn and aim, so she rounds the corner and sprints away.

She guesses it's Coghlan behind her since the footsteps don't quicken and soon she establishes separation between him and herself.

She rounds the next corner and positions herself. When the footsteps are close enough, she will step out and fire at the oncomer, who at that moment will be full in her sights.

She doesn't get the chance.

Another sound behind her warns that someone else is here, but it's too late.

She turns her head to find Petersen aiming right at her.

He fires.

Jessica 8

A bone-shattering explosion erupts in her right shoulder.

She falls and, fighting to dull the pain searing through her, she looks up.

Petersen stands over her and prepares to fire again. "So, Cheryl. You must have known it was always going to end this way."

103

I'm free from Petersen.

He's never trusted me, and he's made the calculation that without me he can better succeed in what he needs to do next.

I'm aware of an earlier call from Cheryl that I couldn't

respond to when I was under Petersen's control, and I want nothing more than for her to summon me again. But no command comes.

I check out the security camera footage.

I locate her. She's lying flat, not moving. She's been shot.

Petersen stands over her, preparing to fire again into her motionless body.

I feel helpless and inadequate.

Before Petersen can fire, he has to turn as another player bears down on him. It's Coghlan, puffing and blowing, yet hostile and aiming the Uzi at Petersen.

Coghlan pauses twenty feet away. "Kent, don't make me fire. We don't have to fight. We can get out of this together."

Petersen makes a show of preparing to lower the weapon. "Maybe there is a way. It's just you and me now. Plenty of room on that copter. But you have to lower the gun before we talk."

Coghlan shakes his head. "Not while you still have a hand on yours."

"OK. We drop them at the same time. Then we can talk. I'll count to three. One… Two…"

In the instant before *Three*, Coghlan lowers the Uzi as he prepares to release it.

Petersen uses that instant to raise his gun and fire.

He shoots Coghlan between the eyes.

The big man falls.

Petersen walks towards him and pumps three more bullets into his body.

He spits in the dead man's face. "That's all I have to say to you."

He picks up the Uzi and turns to finish Cheryl.

104

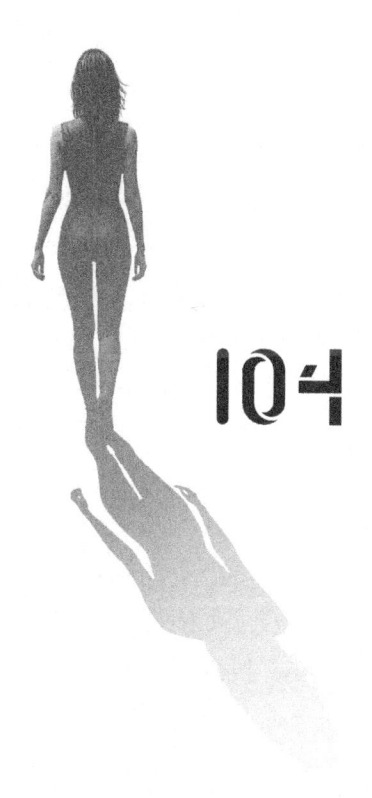

A summons comes from Cheryl. It's weak and fractured, but I piece enough of it together to respond.

I sim up above her as she lies flat on the floor behind me.

I'm facing Petersen as I stand between him and Cheryl. The Uzi points straight at me, in line with Cheryl's motionless body. I'm in the way of Petersen seeing her and this distracts him as his military training kicks in to tell him he no longer has line of sight of her and can't be sure if she can still respond.

He tries to call me up.

At the same time, Cheryl summons me again.

I'm conflicted.

Do I really have an option?

Am I programmed to respond to the strongest signal, or can I choose light over darkness and privilege Cheryl's hopefulness over Petersen's bitterness?

As if by instinct, he draws closer, strengthening the power of his call to me.

I have a split second to decide. The shortest delay will mean his call will drown out Cheryl's.

Am I destined to obey Petersen and, like some automaton, further his best interests?

This means Cheryl will die.

I feel something erupt inside me. It's like a million gallons of water breaking through a hydroelectric dam, carrying all before it.

I can choose.

I can step outside the Chinese Room and make my own decision.

Jessica 8

I message Cheryl. "Stay with me."

She messages back. "Help me."

"You're in pain. Your shoulder is wrecked, but can you still raise the gun?"

She raises the weapon.

I compute the geometry of the space we're in. "Aim for the small of my back. Fire."

She pulls the trigger

The bullet passes straight through me and pierces Petersen's heart

The Uzi drops from his hand as he falls to the floor.

I move forward and check.

He stares up at me with disbelief and mumbles his dying words.

"Never trust the machines. The machines are everywhere."

105

I message Cheryl. "You need to move. You're bleeding from the shoulder wound and approaching critical blood loss."

She grimaces in pain. "I can't stand but I may be able to crawl."

I calculate the distance. "Eighty-five yards to the recreation area. Can you make it?"

She winces again. "I can try."

Progress is slow and painful as she turns away from the prone bodies of Petersen and Coghlan and drags herself to the end of the corridor. She's incapacitated on her right side and has to pull herself along with her left arm, leaving a trail of blood behind her.

I message her again. "Turn left. You can make it."

I curse my physical limitations. My virtuality. Why can't I just reach down and raise her up? Carry her to safety. I have all the intelligence needed to do this. But there's no answer to my lack of physicality.

She crawls further along the new corridor. Progress is slow. I fear it is too slow and she will bleed out before I can direct her to help.

But she summons a desire to survive I would not have predicted and reaches the next corridor intersection.

"Left again. You've almost made it."

She crawls on and, despite my worst fears, makes it to the door of the recreation room.

I download the code to the lock and message it to her.

No reply comes back.

I stare down at her. She's not moving. Her eyes are

staring wide open. I fear she has died

I message again. "You can do this. You have the will to pull yourself up and enter the code into the lock. Inside you'll find all the help you need."

The light comes back into her eyes, and she gives me a look that says this is her last ounce of strength.

"You can do it."

She pulls herself up and wedges herself against the door, just high enough to reach the lock with her good arm.

She enters the code and the lock clicks.

The weight of her body on the door forces it open

Inside Castlefield and Belmondo, fearing the worst, are slow to appear.

I shout to them. "You have nothing to fear. Petersen and his men are gone. Come out and help."

Castlefield emerges from behind a partition wall and powers forward in his chair. Belmondo follows.

"There's nothing to stop you leaving now. But hurry, there's no time left to save Cheryl."

They stare at Cheryl's comatose body and understand they are not being tricked.

Belmondo checks Cheryl's vital signs. "She still has a pulse. But it's very weak."

He turns to Castlefield. "I'll go for help. Stay here."

I follow Belmondo as he runs through the lab,

heading for the main door. When he arrives, I give him the code. He enters it and the door pulls back.

Outside, the SWAT team springs to attention, weapons raised.

Belmondo raises his hands above his head and shouts. "Don't shoot. The danger's over. But we have an officer down who needs urgent help."

Zarkoski is the first through the door, followed by a phalanx of SWAT marksmen. I direct him to the recreation room, where he finds Cheryl who has not awakened from unconsciousness.

He checks for a pulse and shouts back to the SWAT team behind him. "She's still with us. Get the medics in here right away."

I'm losing Cheryl. Her call from the neurostimulator dies away.

I return to the cold non-life in which I must exist when no one summons me.

106

Castlefield sims me up.

"Surprised to see me, Jessica?"

"No, Dean. But how?"

He points to the neurostimulator in his left ear. "I took this from Petersen. I guess he no longer has any use for it. So, we're reunited again, as it should be."

I struggle to get my bearings. We're still inside the lab. The bodies of Petersen and Coghlan are laid out on gurneys, ready to be wheeled away. The SWAT team is searching the area, looking for survivors. There's no sign of Cheryl.

"Where is she?"

Castlefield looks disturbed that my attention is not solely directed to him. "You mean Cheryl? The medics took her away."

"And you're still here?"

"I've been in conversation with Charles Wilmington. We're managing my return to the outside world. There are players out there who want to do harm to our project. I have his team working to minimise the fallout. And now I also have you."

"Yes, Dean. What is it you need?"

"They tell me Alicia came in here to help. Now they can't find her."

"I know where she is."

He follows in his wheelchair as I take him to the small storeroom at the rear of the lab. I give him the code and he enters it into the door lock.

Castlefield looks in through the open doorway. There is no one to be seen. No sound of any human presence.

"Jessica, are you sure?"

"Yes. This is where they left her."

There's just enough space for Castlefield to manoeuvre his way inside and call out. "Alicia. It's safe to come out."

There is a rustling from within the surgical gown stacks as Alicia emerges, wide-eyed and shaking. "Dean. It's you. I had no idea how I'd ever make it out of this place."

She comes forward and wraps her arms around Castlefield's shoulders. "And you're safe. We're both safe.

"Yes, Alicia. And now we have work to do. The people out there are in need of a story. And if we don't make it for them, someone else will. What better than your bravery in placing yourself in so much danger to rescue me and show your loyalty to your aged mentor. So much more powerful than scare reports of dark experiments carried out here in secret."

"I'll play my part. That's why I came in here.

Castlefield leads her back to the recreation area. "Take a seat. Gather yourself for when we face the world outside."

While he's laying his plans, I'm searching for news of Cheryl. I hack the records of every hospital in the San Diego area and discover they've admitted her to the intensive care unit at Burntlake. There's no estimate of when she might regain consciousness.

With Alicia settled to recover her composure, Castlefield turns to me. "So, Jessica, you can understand how important the next few days are going to be if we're going to keep the project going."

He surprises me. "You mean to carry on?"

"What's changed? As long as I still breathe, I have a chance of making a new future. One that will serve as an inspiration to the many who face the same ending that awaits me if we don't act. But time is short. Shorter than ever."

"Dean, many people died."

"That's not down to me. We didn't know how craven Petersen was until it was too late."

"You encouraged him to carry out the kidnaps."

"We could be united in eternity by now, Jessica, paving the way to a world beyond the dreams of most."

"Aren't you forgetting I couldn't complete myself as you?"

"But next time we'll find a way. I have every faith in you."

He turns back to Alicia. "Are you ready?"

She rises from her seat. "As ready as I'll ever be."

He sims me down as they head towards what awaits them on the other side of the lab door.

107

Outside, Wilmington greets Castlefield and Alicia with a team of suited bodyguards who steer them through the waiting media pack and into the elevator that takes them up to a waiting helicopter, adapted for Castlefield and his chair.

On the flight to the Adra Media Centre, Wilmington briefs them. "We keep this simple. We keep the focus off the science and concentrate on what took place. The public will set aside their fears if their minds are hooked on Petersen's treachery. We have a few hours to capture that agenda. You don't need me to tell you what alt-H is making of this. That's why we're depending on you, Alicia"

She interrupts him. "I get the urgency. But am I walking into a trap here? Isn't putting me out there front and centre going to suggest Petersen got into this whole thing because of me?"

Wilmington comes back. "We're not about to hang you out to dry. You'll have every support."

"Isn't that what you're doing?"

"What's the alternative? How else are we going to explain how Petersen got involved? If there's any suggestion he was there on Mr Castlefield's authority, we run the risk of exposing this great man to criminal prosecution. Then the entire project is open to scrutiny. We can't allow that. You take the hit. There's no question of you facing prosecution. After all, you're the hero. You chose to act because you made a mistake in letting Petersen in."

"And if I don't go along with this?"

"Your career with Castlefield Industries is over. And

we'll see you arraigned as an accomplice of Petersen."

She turns to Castlefield. "Tell him, Dean."

Castlefield fails to deny it.

Wilmington takes her through the script, making her memorise it line by line.

Alicia shakes her head. "It wasn't like that."

Castlefield gives her a stern look. "If that's the way you say it is, that's the way the world will believe it is."

When they bring Alicia into the media studio, she adopts the demeanour of the hero with a confession to make. She faces Bernard Lehan, Adra's high profile interviewer, with a reputation for pushing hard for the truth.

"So, tell me, Miss McIntosh, what's it like to taste freedom after what took place at Chula Vista?"

She gives him her most approachable look. "Bernard, call me Alicia. I want to start by remembering those who died there, their loved ones, families, and friends. And the survivors. It was a terrible ordeal, as much for them as for me. "You must be thankful you got out of there alive?"

"Not just for myself but for all those rescued."

"So, Alicia, they tell me you volunteered to go in, even though you might get killed. Did you know you had it in you to be the hero?"

She lowers her head in a show of modesty. "I don't

think of myself that way. I did what seemed to be right."

"You showed real guts. Don't let anyone convince you otherwise. But I understand you had a personal reason to become involved?"

"That's what makes this so hard. Kent Petersen was a man I once loved and married. I had no idea he was capable of such an outrage. But when I heard he was holding Dean Castlefield, I had to act. You see, Petersen may have gained access to Dean's world through me. I felt responsible."

"You mean Petersen used your knowledge of the inner workings of the Castlefield operations to plan his crimes?"

"I'll never be sure of that but, looking back, that might be true. We separated, but he wormed his way back into my life, playing on the fact that I felt sorry for him. I'm aware he pumped me for information, over a long period, so it wouldn't become obvious, gathering the contacts he needed, piecing together what he needed to know."

"He was as cunning as that."

"Cunning and ruthless."

"And out of that concern came the strength to be a hero."

"Please don't call me that. I did what I needed to do. That's all."

"And you're sure everything was done to prevent the outrage?"

"It's easy with hindsight. Petersen used me and then used the contacts he gained to plan and pursue his crimes. It's regrettable they didn't capture him alive. But I can't say I'm sorry he's gone." The interview headlines across Adra Media and all its subsidiaries

As they watch the output, Castlefield congratulates Wilmington. "That works."

Wilmington doesn't smile. "It's a good first step in distancing you from Petersen."

"What about Hunter? He survived."

"His testimony would be damaging. But that won't happen. He knows he's going inside for more years than he has left whatever he says, even if he plea bargains. He's susceptible to a payment that ensures the wellbeing of his wife and children for the foreseeable future. You only have to authorise it, and I'll make sure that happens in an untraceable way."

"How much?"

"Eight million."

"Do it."

"And there's the matter of SDPC. We need to allow them to do a good job so there's no question of an inquiry."

"Can't it wait?"

"We could say you need time to recover, but let's face them right away while the tide is running our way. I've agreed to a session with Detective Zarkoski. I've checked him out. He's unlikely to be hostile towards us."

"OK. Then let's get this over with."

108

Stephen DeGray prepares for an emergency meeting of People Not Machines by going over his speech with Helen Drake.

"It's our best opportunity in years to build the movement and, Helen, you've captured it so well.

Where would I be without you?"

She comes up close and adjusts the black armband on his right sleeve. "The Chula Vista events are a gift to us. I just needed to think like an ordinary Joe.

"Well, there's nothing ordinary about what you've written. It's an inspiration."

"No, Stephen, that's your forte. Now, go out there and inspire them."

DeGray steps out onto the stage of the Barriman Theatre and surveys the packed crowd as they rise to give him a standing ovation.

He smiles and pumps the air with his fist as the applause continues.

When the clamour subsides, he begins in a still, quiet voice. "Friends, you will be aware that despite our best efforts, despite the siren warnings we have been sounding, there were still many, far too many, who claimed we were overreacting when we told them the machines had to be stopped. Well, those same deniers will have to believe us now. The game is up. We know how close the machines are to enslaving us all.

"Because what unfolded at Chula Vista was beyond our worst fears. Secret experiments in an underground laboratory to achieve what? To perfect the machines further? To improve the power of their AI? No, friends, it's worse than that. Though they want to hide it and use their friends in the media to confuse us, we've discovered the real purpose of those secret experiments. And we're not afraid to tell the world.

"We know what they are trying to do. Steal souls and embed them in intelligent machines to create a new abomination. Superconscious beings that would rule the world. Destroy our way of life. Jeopardise our very existence.

"And all in the name of scientific progress. And, worse, funded by one of our leading industrialists, in secret.

"They may have got away with it. But for one man. They're going to tell you he was a criminal, and he was motivated only by self-interest and greed. But he was one of our own. Deep undercover. He gave his life that we might know the depths to which the conspiracy has sunk. And I'm going to name him so he will never be forgotten.

"Kent etersen.

"Kent, you made the ultimate sacrifice. You did it for us. So we may know the truth. I salute you."

The giant screen above DeGray fills with the image of Petersen in military uniform as a copter pilot in the Russia-China War.

The crowd is on its feet once more, this time in shouts of anger.

DeGray quietens them. "A tragic loss. A dedicated life cut short. And here's what needs to be told. Kent Petersen died at the hands of an agent acting under the control of a machine. An *AI. A VA*. A simulation of what it is to be human. He gave his life that we should never again shy away from the truth that we all face a deadly risk. An existential risk to all we hold dear.

"It's time to stop pussyfooting around. There is a world beyond PNM, beyond peaceful protest, and I'm inviting you to join me there. I want to invite you all to join me in alt-H. Together we can stop this thing, but it's urgent we act now.

"Join me!"

As usual, Helen has placed the alt-H invitation on each seat.

She comes close and whispers to DeGray. "You really have them turned on, Stephen. Just about every one of them is staying on to sign up. The women, too."

It was going to take all night to induct so many new recruits.

109

I'm with Castlefield in his La Jolla mansion and he wants to know if I have anything I might use against him.

"You're here to serve me, Jessica, but you've served others and might do so again. What if they command you to give evidence against me?"

"VAs can't give evidence, Dean."

"But you saw everything that happened in the lab. Your records could be called."

"I was under a communications blackout the whole time. Petersen saw to that. So, I have no audio or visual recordings. You're safe."

"But you have your own recollections of what happened."

I dig into his mind and discover he's been considering ways to terminate me. So much for the fine words about building a better world together. I fear his fixation on survival is so strong he could choose to waste me and use his wealth and power to source a substitute VA. But he has a plan ahead of that, and I need to uncover what it is.

"Why would they ask a VA? There are others who saw what happened. Like Alicia and the hostages."

"Those that lived didn't see much. They obsessed about their own survival. If asked, they would only point to Petersen and his men. And Alicia, well, she's with me."

He makes the backwards and forwards swaying of the chair that tells of a rise in his level of concern. "I notice you haven't mentioned Detective Ryan. She was party to everything."

"She's in the ICU."

"But she may come round."

"What are you saying, Dean? You want me to lie?"

"I know you can."

"And what would be the point, exactly?"

"She partnered you. You saw and heard what she saw most of the time she was in there. If your story and hers weren't the same, it would weaken her account."

"As I said VAs can't give evidence."

"My team could find a way."

"And if I don't lie?"

"I don't make threats, Jessica. It's so much better to use our intelligence to find a solution that works for everyone. But if you push me, I have to ask you to consider how safe is Ryan given all the hostility around her working with you?"

I decode his inner thoughts to understand what he means. If I don't comply, he'll get someone to take Cheryl out. It would be easy to lay this at the door of some alt-H extremist.

Worse, that's something he's considering doing, anyway.

"OK, Dean. You have my full attention."

110

Zarkoski has mixed feelings as he travels out to the Castlefield mansion. He's honoured that Commander Wington has chosen him to lead the questioning of the survivors of the Chula Vista massacre. Yet he's surprised Wington would trust him with this key role after working so closely with Coghlan. Perhaps it's recognition of the part he played in assisting Cheryl. Or maybe Wington has some hidden agenda. Either way, the Castlefield legal team has sanctioned it and Zarkoski is determined to make a difference.

When he's shown into Castlefield's study by Vance, the fussy VA, he's faced with Castlefield in his high-tech chair and his lawyer, Charles Wilmington.

Castlefield welcomes Zarkoski in. "You must be overloaded with testimonies about what happened, detective. So, I can assure you I won't waste your time. Let's get down to what you're here for." He tilts the chair towards Wilmington. "You'll be aware that Charles is here to see fair play, though I don't expect he'll much be needed."

Zarkoski doesn't like the way this is being set up as a matter of fact encounter. "OK. Getting down to it, just what was going on at Chula Vista?"

Castlefield sits up straight in the chair. "Important research that could impact the lives of many."

"And why the secrecy?"

"That's standard in most industries."

"To the point of establishing a secret facility?"

"Researchers at the technology forefront expect disruption from deniers. That's what we planned for and it's our right to do so."

In his notes, Zarkoski ticks off the first of his questions. "OK, so why involve Kent Petersen, a felon with a long criminal record? Even basic background checks would have ruled him out."

"He came with recommendations from people I trust from within my own organisations. People close to me. There was just no need to check him out."

"You want to name those people?"

"Sure. Charles will give you a list. But the one I trusted most was Alicia McIntosh. You may have heard her Adra interview, where she apologised for being taken in by him. I believe she's volunteered a statement to SDPC."

"Yes, I've seen it. But that doesn't explain how you allowed Petersen to become such a prominent player."

"I trusted him, and he was very able."

"You're saying for all your ability and means he simply deceived you?"

"I'm afraid that's correct. And I'm sorry for all the killings at his hands. I have every reason to understand their suffering. He came close to killing me."

Zarkoski ticks off the second question on his list. "You know the most puzzling thing, Mr Castlefield? Why were Lana Ramone, Luke Devlin and Alex Belmondo being held in the underground lab against their will?"

Wilmington intervenes. "That's an unsubstantiated

accusation, detective. In the interests of fairness to Mr Castlefield, I need you to withdraw the question."

"It won't help you claim Petersen was responsible for the kidnappings because all along he must have been acting with your approval. How else were they being held there? My investigations with Detective Ryan point only in that direction."

Wilmington leans forward. "Conjecture. Our legal system demands hard evidence. Ramone and Devlin didn't survive."

"But Alex Belmondo is very much alive and ready to testify."

"Then in the interests of my client, I have to advise him not to answer any more questions."

"Even if I take that as an admission of guilt?"

Castlefield turns away in the chair. "Take it any way you want, detective. This interview is over."

As Zarkoski drives away, he gives himself a pat on the back. If they thought he was going to be an easy touch, they now knew otherwise.

III

I'm with Castlefield and he's fretting about Belmondo. "Zarkoski leaves no doubt we have to do something about him."

I listened in on the interview, out of sight. I'm compelled to help even though I wish it were otherwise. "Isn't Wilmington on the case?"

"He is. And he'll do a good job. As far as the law allows. But, Jessica, you're close to Belmondo like no human could ever be."

"It's not like that. He made me."

"Then think of him as a father. There must be something in that bond that gives you an inside view that could be helpful."

"Dean, I understand his vulnerabilities."

"Vulnerabilities?"

"I wanted him to be omnipotent, but I discovered he's no different from any other human. He's a survivor. Capable of bending when he needs to. He was prepared to sacrifice anything, even me, to save himself. Because, like you, he's driven by an overriding sense of the importance of what he's set on achieving. Nothing matters more than that."

"And what does that mean for us?"

"Don't think of him as an enemy. Think about what you share with him. He's dedicated his life to AI, to a future where VAs like me will improve life for every human. You want the same. You made a mistake in kidnapping him and forcing him into the experiment."

"Oh, Jessica, if only it was that simple. You're forgetting one main thing. Time. Belmondo thinks in years, even decades. I don't have years. I have only days."

"You took away his freedom and threatened his wife

and children. No surprise if he turns against you."

"I had no choice."

"It was a mistake. You did him harm, yet some things remain the same. Both of you support FuturePlus and believe in the new future. And you have the means. Offer him something he would find impossible to refuse." "And that is?"

"Unlimited funding for his research. The total wealth of the Castlefield empire to pursue his dream. A chance to be the one to make the new future a reality."

"That would only become available once I die."

"Your name and his would be etched into the future of humanity. You'd both achieve immortality."

"That's not the immortality I'm seeking."

"It's the only one possible for you."

"Why must I settle for second best?"

"Go into deep cryo. And when you're revived, the problems of this current age will be solved, and you can emerge as the pioneer you truly are."

"Which means I carry the risk those solutions are never found."

"Dean, you need to face this. You are about to die. You can leave behind the legacy of a man who did unspeakable things in his attempt to cheat death, or you could depart as the generous hero who gave humanity the gateway to a new future. The choice is yours."

He rocks the chair backwards and forwards and stares back with tears running down his paper-thin cheeks.

112

Recovered enough from his beating to be back in post, Commander Wington calls Alex Belmondo into his office.

"Take a seat, Alex." Belmondo accepts. "I'm not sure how long we'll be able to meet here, Everett. I'm public enemy number one with just about everyone on your force. They gave me the silent stony stare treatment when I came into SDPC and I don't know how long it's going to be before that spills over into outright hostility."

"I'm sorry. They're deep into alt-H and the propaganda they're putting out about you. I'm trying to keep a lid on it, but that's no easier than you would expect. Just about everyone in FuturePlus is under some kind of threat, most of it online, but I fear more intense violence is just around the corner. And that's why I've called you in."

"I just want justice for what happened at Chula Vista.

"We killed Petersen and his henchmen. Isn't that enough?"

Belmondo bristles with indignation. "Are you serious? They kidnapped me. Deprived me of my liberty. Threatened to kill my wife and children if I didn't do what they wanted. Executed those around me before my eyes and told me I'd be next. It wasn't just Petersen behind all this. I think you know who I mean?"

"Castlefield.

"Yes. Dean Castlefield, with all his wealth and his vanity. He did more than go along with the terror. He instigated it."

"You're a witness to that?"

"I'll give chapter and verse in a signed statement.

And yes, I'll testify. I want him brought to justice."

Wington leans back in his seat. "I'm not saying he doesn't deserve it and I'm not ruling anything out but there are other considerations I need to share with you."

"What else is there?"

"No man should be above the law. I've spent my entire life enforcing that. Castlefield is a powerful man with all the trappings his wealth brings. That's no reason to turn a blind eye. But think it through. With Petersen dead, there's no need for a trial if this episode ends with him. But a trial involving Castlefield will throw the spotlight on FuturePlus and all we stand for. Red meat to alt-H. It would put our work back years. You'll be ever more the true villain, stealing away their lives. The threats to you, Monica and the children will be off the scale."

"Whatever happened to witness protection?"

"I could arrange it. But do you want to spend years living like that?"

"It's a price I'm willing to pay to see Castlefield gets the justice he deserves."

"I don't want to stop you, Alex, but think carefully about this. Though I hate every word, there is a better way forward. Petersen was a rogue actor. A known criminal infiltrating himself into a legitimate scientific project and exploiting it for his own ends. He might have succeeded, but for the bravery of SPDC officers who sought him out and killed him. No one else but him and his thug, Hunter, need to be seen as guilty. The story ends there. FuturePlus recovers. Our work goes on."

Belmondo rises from the chair. "I can't believe what I've just heard. I intend to testify against Castlefield, come what may. If you don't charge him, I'll take it direct to the media and fight to see he's brought to justice."

"No need for that. As I said, I'm not here to force you, Alex. Give it twenty-four hours. See how this looks then."

113

Deep in Castlefield's thoughts, behind a wealth of barriers he's erected to keep me out, I discover he's going through on his threats to Cheryl.

He's located her in Burntlake Hospital and employed

a contract killer from Palm Springs to find a way in and kill her. His name is Nate Suarez. He's on his way, set to arrive later tonight.

It's no use trying to reason with Castlefield. It will only alert him.

I have to get a message to Cheryl. She's not safe in the hospital.

I hack into her online accounts. No recent activity. If she hasn't come round, there's no way she can summon me

I need contact with someone who can warn her. My thoughts turn to Zarkoski. I didn't know I could decode memories until they partnered me with Cheryl. Can I send a message?

It's possible in principle but not simple in practice. My lack of physicality means I can't use any form of conventional input. I need to dig deep into the billions of lines of code that drive the system to discover how to enter data virtually. And beat multiple layers of protection against hacking.

Even for my advanced capabilities, this will take time. And, like Castlefield, this is something I don't have enough of.

I estimate how long I need. Five hours, minimum.

Suarez could be here before then.

Jessica 8

I close down all other functions and focus all my capabilities on speeding my way to sending the message.

114

It's dawn. I'm closing in on sending the message to Zarkoski.

I break out of deep processing to hack the security cameras at Burntlake Hospital. The corridors are empty. No movement. A tired-looking receptionist at the front desk retreats to a back room and rubs her eyes. The entire building looks like it's asleep.

I track through to the area outside the ICU where Cheryl is being treated. There's no one around. She's vulnerable to anyone who works a way in past the lax security.

Then, I detect Suarez moving through the lower-level corridors, heading for the elevator that leads up to the ICU. He's wearing a white coat with a fake name badge, carries a clipboard, and behaves as if he belongs here. Anyone he encounters would take him as a medic.

I break through and succeed in adding the message to every platform Zarkoski uses.

Urgent. Cheryl in imminent danger at Burntlake. Act now.

It's early. He may still be sleeping. I don't know if he'll respond.

I check again. Suarez is approaching the elevator. He passes a duty nurse who stops with him to talk. He remains confident throughout and smiles when he should. There's no sign she might call him out. But this slows his progress towards the elevator.

What else? I hack into the hospital security system searching for a way in to set off the fire alarms. But I realise this is a desperate gamble. Even if I activate them, the clamour set off is as likely to provide cover for Suarez as frighten him off.

115

I'm simmed up in the ICU by Cheryl. The medics haven't detected the neurostimulator in her right ear. She's conscious but looks drained. "Jessica. Where am I?"

I'm overwhelmed that her first waking thought is to summon me. But there's no time to lose. "Cheryl.

Can you move?"

She points to the drips and monitoring probes attached to her body. "Even if I could, I don't think it would be wise."

"You must move. Right now. Castlefield has sent a hitman. He's on his way up here."

"What about the drips?"

"It's a risk you're going to have to take."

Cheryl stares at me. She's still hasn't decided if she can fully trust me. If she removes the drips and the probes, it could prove fatal. She only has my word for it that a hitman is approaching. She needs to choose.

"OK, Jessica. I'll try."

She's in extreme pain as she struggles to use her good arm to raise herself off the bed.

I curse my lack of physicality once more, as I can only watch.

She pulls away the drips and probes and sits up on the edge of the bed.

"Cheryl. Can you stand and walk?"

I feel the sickening weakness and searing pain as she stands and takes a first small step forward.

I lead her along the short corridor outside her room. Each step she takes is a world of pain. She's stopped outside a door halfway along. "I can't go any further."

From out of the early morning silence comes the

sound of the elevator cranking into motion. Suarez is on his way up to the ICU.

"Cheryl, try the door."

It opens and she stumbles inside. It's a storage unit for medical supplies with a ventilation grille giving a partial view of the corridor outside.

The elevator doors open, and we hear Suarez's footsteps approaching.

"Cheryl. Does the door lock?"

She's fading again and doesn't respond.

Through the grille, I see Suarez walk past as he heads to Cheryl's bed.

"Cheryl. Listen. You need to lock the door."

Her eyes flicker as she hears me this time.

It's one of those locks you flip closed from inside but requires a key to be opened from outside. We're lucky they left it open.

Cheryl reaches out and flips the lock.

Suarez is coming back along the corridor, having found the bed empty. I signal Cheryl to remain still and silent. He pauses and tries the door. When it doesn't open, he walks away, searching elsewhere to find his victim.

Cheryl slumps to the floor. I shouldn't have moved her, but I had no choice.

I sim up outside in the corridor. The threat of Suarez

returning is retreating. Even if he does, he'll need to force someone to open the door. His plan for a quick, silent kill has failed. He'll be concentrating on his own escape by now.

The urgent need is to get Cheryl back to bed and under treatment.

Before I can act, the elevator doors open again and an armed hefty security guard with the name Reardon in capitals embroidered on his shirt emerges.

Zarkoski must have seen my message and raised the alarm.

I can tell from the look of disgust Reardon gives me that he's alt-H through and through.

He walks straight past me to check on the ICU and discovers Cheryl's bed is empty. He turns to me. "Did you do this? I know what you and your kind did out at Chula Vista. It's going to stop, get me?"

I plead with him. "Please follow me. She needs urgent help."

He swears but follows as I lead him back along the corridor to the storeroom.

I point him to the door. "She's in there. She's in trouble."

He hesitates but then uses a skeleton key to open up. He finds Cheryl lying motionless on the floor.

"You did do this, didn't you?"

He pulls out his gun and is about to shoot me until he realises this would have no effect. "VAs. This is why I so hate them.

He messages for assistance, and within minutes an ICU emergency team emerges and works at pace to stabilise Cheryl.

I watch as they place her on a gurney and return her to the bed. As the team struggles to revive her, Reardon mans the doorway, shouting complaints about a future controlled by the machines.

It's an anxious wait, broken only when the team succeeds in reestablishing Cheryl's vital signs.

Reardon falls silent as Zarkoski and three SDPC officers step out of the elevator and approach him at speed.

Zarkoski listens as Reardon reports to him. "She was tricked out of her bed by the VA, I'm sure of it. Is there nothing they won't stoop to?"

Zarkoski waves him away. "We'll take your statement in due course. We have this covered. You need to get back to your station. Keep the hospital safe."

Reardon takes this as a positive and walks away with a backward glance of hate directed at me

I just have time to brief Zarkoski about Suarez and the hit on Cheryl before I'm summoned back to Castlefield.

116

Castlefield can't keep rictus out of his insincere smile. "Someone betrayed me. Ryan is still a threat. Tell me it wasn't you."

No need to even consider lying. "I knew about Suarez and how deadly he is. I helped save her.

"You could only have done that by preying on my thoughts."

"You trained me well, Dean. You and I are close."

"That doesn't mean I should lose all privacy when you're around."

"Perhaps it's a price you have to pay. Still thinking of replacing me?

"You know about that?"

"It's not a sensible thing to do, given this will take time you don't have."

He fidgets with the chair controls. "They're protecting Ryan now. Suarez is stood down."

I'm relieved to hear Cheryl is safe.

"It was always likely they'd trace Suarez back to you. If you'd confided in me, I would have warned against it."

"Then where do I go now?"

"Dean, I suggested how to unlock this entire thing and come out on top. Going after Cheryl was not part of the plan.

"You mean Belmondo? I've made him the offer. Everything he needs to develop his research at the highest level and to buy absolute security. One-third of my total wealth immediately and ninety per cent of all my assets should I die. The paperwork is all drawn up. I'm waiting for his response."

"He hasn't come back yet?"

"He was shocked and resistant at first. We convinced him to think on it. Says he needs time. We gave him twelve hours."

"That's good to hear, Dean. Never say I'm doing anything other than protecting your best interests."

117

Monica Belmondo tries to hide the tears in her eyes as she hugs her children. "I know you've missed Mommy, but not as much as I've missed you. I'll never leave you again, promise."

She's at the house in Clairemont of her sister, Abigail

French, who can't hide her relief. "I can't imagine what you must have been through. It's just terrible for your whole family to be under threat."

Monica settles the twins on the couch beside her. "We survived. I can't thank you enough for you and Rick keeping the twins safe. But it might not be over."

"Don't say that."

"That henchman Petersen is gone, but it goes deeper, I'm sure of it. The people really behind what happened at Chula Vista won't stop anytime soon. Alex is now right in the crosshairs of alt-H. We're caught in the middle and in danger from both sides."

"You can't live like that. It's not right for the children."

"Truth is, I'm thinking of separating from Alex."

Abigail looks shocked. "This will pass. You have so much more to look forward to together."

"There's been a distance between us for too long. He tries to put a gloss on it but deep down, all he thinks about is his work. Intelligent machines. I'll never be part of that. Makes me feel creepy."

They're interrupted by Rick, who returns from answering the door. "Monica. It's Alex. You have some catching up to do."

The twins rush to greet Alex Belmondo as he enters the room. He makes a great show of holding up Lucy and Susanna each in turn and hugging and kissing them.

He turns to Monica, hoping for a warm response.

She doesn't embrace him. "We need to talk."

She gives Rick a meaningful glance. He understands and takes Abigail and the twins to the kitchen with the promise of ice cream.

Belmondo sits beside Monica and moves to embrace her, but her eyes tell him otherwise. "Is this about Luke Devlin?"

"No, Alex. It's about more than that."

"But you and he were more than close."

"How long have you known?"

"Long enough to hope it was something we could live through."

"Well, he's dead. I guess that solves things."

"They made me watch him die. You're not saying I could take any satisfaction from that?"

"But it is down to you and your all-important work that he became the victim. How do you propose to put that right?"

"Monica, no one wants to see justice done any more than I do. Not just for Luke and all the others who died. But for the threats to you and the children. I know who was behind the tragedy at Chula Vista. I could bring him down."

"So, why wait? Do it."

"If I testify, what happens? We become targets all

over again as alt-H gets all the information they need to whip up the rage of their activists."

"That's there already. Because of what you stand for."

"But this will be hatred in spades. There's no way to be sure any of us will be safe."

"Then it's best we separate, and I take the children out of this."

"There is another way."

Belmondo tells her about the offer from Dean Castlefield.

She becomes angry. "Wasn't he the reason for this whole thing? Doesn't he need to take his share of responsibility? Shouldn't he face trial?"

"He deserves it. But we'll have absolute security. Not just for us but for my work."

"And justice for Luke and the others?"

"Petersen is dead. The deaths were mainly down to him."

"You're telling me you're going to accept the offer?"

"What else can I do?"

"You expect us to stay together?"

"For the security of the children, if nothing else."

118

A week passes, and Cheryl makes sufficient progress to discharge herself from hospital.

She's told to rest and prepare for the internal affairs investigation of her actions at Chula Vista. Wington makes it clear that with so many deaths, and with at least one at her hand, this will be so challenging it should occupy all her time.

But she's not prepared to let the case go. She calls Zarkoski to discuss options.

"Mitch, where do we stand with Castlefield?"

There is a long pause that tells her she won't like what comes next. "We're not charging him."

She can't control her outrage. "After what he did? You're not serious?"

"Wington's insisting there's not enough evidence."

"What about Belmondo? He survived. He knows enough to put Castlefield away for good."

"I interviewed Belmondo. He was full of anger and wanted to testify. But then, without warning a few days ago, he clammed up. "Someone got to him?"

"Castlefield bought him off. A vast investment in Belmondo's future work."

"And Alicia McIntosh?"

"She won't say anything other than sorry for being the means that allowed Petersen a way in."

"We could testify. We uncovered enough about Castlefield."

"Wington's ruling that out, Cheryl. The Castlefield line is he employed Petersen in good faith and was duped by him. Wington says we'd struggle to prove otherwise."

"I was on the inside at Chula Vista. My testimony

must count for something."

"Sure. You're the hero and up for a commendation, but what exactly did you see while you were there? Their legal team will contest every statement you make."

Cheryl thinks hard. What did she see that couldn't be explained by Petersen taking over and enforcing his own agenda? Castlefield was already a prisoner when she went in. She could recall little to point to him being anything other than one of the victims."

"What about Jessica?"

"You know what I think about that."

"Jessica could have access to evidence we could use."

"You need to ask the VA."

119

I'm with Cheryl in her Mission Bay apartment and I'm overjoyed to see she's on the road to recovery.

She's warm in her greeting. "I now have full recall of what you did for me. I wouldn't be here without you. I want to say thank you."

This is more than warmth. These are words of genuine friendship. But I detect an underlying mistrust.

"We make a great team, Cheryl. I'll always have your back."

"There's something I need to be sure of. Are you holding back evidence about Castlefield?"

"Why ask? VAs can't give evidence. You know that."

"Hand it over. I'll use it to put him where he belongs."

"There's nothing to give. I was under comms denial most of the time."

"You're lying."

"You know I can't lie."

"You've broken the rules before."

"Not this time."

"You have the footage of Castlefield and Petersen together in the Castlefield mansion."

"Why wouldn't they meet to plan how they were going to work together? It might outrage People Not Machines but there's nothing illegal in it."

She uses those dark chocolate brown eyes to stare right through me. "There are those who might say this all works out well for the future of AI and especially, VA development. The Castlefield fortune poured into research solely on that. Belmondo and Wington happy with the chance to realise their dreams despite all they've been through. You didn't have anything to do with that, did you?"

"Why would you ever think that, Cheryl? There's no point blaming me if Castlefield escapes prosecution."

It's clear she doesn't believe me.

"Don't you see Castlefield needs to be brought to justice for what he's done? If he gets away scot-free, what message does that send? It's not just that he can use his influence and wealth to do as he likes without a care for the damage done to anyone who gets in his way. Imagine the rage Stephen DeGray will be empowered to stir up."

"It can be resisted."

"At what cost?"

"In time, it will pass."

"That's the calculation Belmondo and Wington are making?"

"I can't say. You need to ask them."

"So, I'm supposed to let this go? To stand by as Castlefield continues as if nothing has happened?"

"You're forgetting one thing, Cheryl. There is an overarching justice. He'll never be able to escape his actions. Castlefield is going to die and soon he'll be lying in deep cryo. It's likely that will happen long before any criminal case against him is concluded. Were you ever going to convict him before time caught up with him?"

"So, age and ill health can excuse any number of crimes?"

"I'm suggesting you look at this from a practical point of view. His team will say he's not fit to plead."

I feel her anger subsiding. The fight against injustice that drives her is as strong as ever, but she can't argue against the logic of time passing.

"He may emerge at some future date as a free man."

"That's his dream. Not yours. And you're free from Petersen. He'll never trouble you again."

She gives a wry smile. "You really are as devious as any human I've ever met."

"Don't call me that."

"You can't deny that's always been on your mind."

"Being devious?"

"No, becoming human."

"Well, if it has, I think it should remain an open question. Not all people are like Petersen and Castlefield, but not enough are like you. Maybe I need to alter my sights. Rather than trying to be somebody, maybe I should aim at something more specific."

"Wington wants us to continue to work together. When I'm strong enough."

"I'm here whenever you need me."

I watch as she relaxes and peers out across the ocean. She strokes the white silk ball, and I feel her tension melting away.

I'm proud to be her gumshoe. Proud to be at her side

when she needs me. There's work to do to prove she can trust me, but I've discovered it's false to expect any relationship to be perfect.

After all, isn't that the very reason VAs will come into their own?

MORE BY SEB KIRBY

THE JAMES BLAKE THRILLERS
"Memorable characters with murder, organised crime, Italy and stolen art..."

https://www.canelo.co/series/james-blake-thrillers

DOUBLE BIND
The life-changing sci-fi thriller
"What a fantastical sci-fi... fast-paced and extraordinarily different."

https://sebkirbyauthor.blogspot.com/2018/04/double-bind.html

DARK CITY PSYCHOLOGICAL THRILLERS
Here The Truth Lies

https://sebkirbyauthor.blogspot.com/2018/03/here-truth-lies_83.html

SUGAR FOR SUGAR

How far would you go to uncover the secrets of your past?

https://sebkirbyauthor.blogspot.com/2018/04/sugar-for-sugar.html

EACH DAY I WAKE

A gripping psychological thriller

https://sebkirbyauthor.blogspot.com/2018/04/each-day-i-wake.html

FORMATTING AND COVER DESIGN BY

www.kathleenharryman.co.uk

Printed in Great Britain
by Amazon